A SECRET BROTHER-SISTER THING

In any case, I'm starting to wonder if Peter really does still think of me as the little girl I was then, tagging along after my big brother and impressed by everything he did. I mean, we haven't really had much of a one-on-one relationship for the past few years. . . . It's almost like we don't know each other at all these days.

Anyway, I'm not sure how to respond to his letter. He's probably not really expecting me to write back. I could just ask Mom if I can add a note at the end of her next letter.

But every time I think of doing that, I remember the look on Peter's face when he first showed me how to shift the car out of neutral. "Don't tell anyone about this, okay?" he told me with a wink. "It's a secret brother-sister thing."

I can't help thinking this letter should be strictly a brother-sister thing, too. Maybe it's a chance for us to get to know each other again.

Other books you will enjoy

THE SADDLE CLUB

LISA: THE INSIDE STORY

BONNIE BRYANT

A SKYLARK BOOK

NEW YORK • TORONTO • LONDON • SYDNEY • AUCKLAND

Special thanks to Sir "B" Farms
and Laura and Vinny Marino

RL 5, 009–012

LISA: THE INSIDE STORY

A Bantam Skylark Book / July 1999

*I would like to express my special thanks
to Catherine Hapka for her help
in the writing of this book.*

LISA: THE INSIDE STORY

Diary of Lisa Atwood

Dear Diary,

Page one of a new diary . . . what a big event! Especially since I haven't written in months and months. I know I used to write almost every day, but somehow I've gotten so busy I almost forgot I ever had a diary. That's going to change. I really want to start writing regularly again, once a week at least. That's why I spent most of my allowance buying this new diary.

Actually, at first I was just going to start again in my last diary. But when I dug it out of my desk drawer, I remembered one of the reasons I put it away in the first place. My brother Peter sent it to me for my birthday last year, and Peter's so much older than I am that I guess he thinks I haven't changed at all since he left for college. I mean, the last time we saw each other every day, I was still wearing pigtails and playing with dolls and stuffed animals, so he must have thought that diary would be right up my alley. I would never want to hurt his feelings by saying so, but I don't think fluffy kittens with big blue eyes and bonnets on their heads were *ever* up my alley. I mean really!

Anyway, that's why I went out and bought this new diary yesterday. But the reason I got inspired to start writing again in the first place was a magazine article I read a couple of days ago. It was called "Life Journals" and it was about people who keep really good diaries. One of the people in the article was a middle-schooler like me, but most of the others were adults. The article was really interesting—a lot of the people have been keeping journals and diaries since they were kids, and they love looking back over the years and remembering their lives that way. Some keep journals all the time, while others like making scrapbooks for big vacation trips or other important events, like weddings and stuff.

The most interesting part, though, was that a lot of the people go beyond just writing down what happened to them that day. For instance, this one woman has a big, oversized diary, sort of like a photo album. She writes in it a couple of times a week, plus she pastes in things to help her remember all the interesting things she does from day to day—she's saved napkins from nice restaurants, movie ticket stubs, letters from friends, play programs, snapshots, even her dog's obedience-school diploma! She's really creative about finding ways to remember the little things that are pretty easy to forget.

I think I want to do something like that, too. I'll probably skip the snapshots (I have my photo album for that already), and I doubt Dolly will be getting a diploma anytime soon (though Mom keeps threatening to send her to doggy detention if she digs up the petunias one more time), but I'm going to try to paste in any other things that seem interesting and will help me remember. I can at least put in letters (not that I get that many) and maybe print out some e-mails from my friends (though I may have to edit some of the longer horse-related ones from Carole, unless I want to buy a new diary every week! Ha ha!).

Speaking of my friends, they're already giving me a hard time about this diary project. Naturally, as soon as I told them about it at the stable yesterday, Stevie started making jokes: "Only Lisa Atwood could come up with her own homework to do during the summer," and so on. I know she thinks it's crazy—the last thing Stevie would ever do is volunteer for more homework—but in a way she's right. I've been feeling like my brain is starting to rot from underuse this summer, and this should be a fun and interesting way to keep myself occupied.

As for Carole—she doesn't have anything against

3

diaries, since she's kept one herself from time to time. But of course she thinks mine should be all about horses. She couldn't believe I didn't get one with a picture of a horse on the cover!

Still, whoever said best friends always have to think alike? It's not like there's ever been much danger of that with the three of us. Since the first day we all met at Pine Hollow Stables, I've known that Carole Hanson is the horse-craziest person on the planet. I've also known that Stevie Lake can't be serious about anything for more than two seconds, especially if it's got anything to do with school. Despite all that, somehow we manage to work pretty well together as a team. I'm sure The Saddle Club has something to do with it. Ever since we started it, it's just seemed natural that we all have our own different, unique personalities and yet we fit together so perfectly. I used to think The Saddle Club should have more than two rules, but I've changed my mind. I think the two we have are just perfect—members have to be horse-crazy, and they have to be willing to help each other. That leaves a lot of room for us to include different people.

Anyway, I'm getting away from the point here, which is that I'm really excited about this diary/scrapbook idea, no matter how much my friends tease me about it. For one thing, it will be good practice in case I decide to become a newspaper reporter or some other kind of writer someday, like my English teacher kept saying I should. For another, it will give me something really nice to look back on in the future. I'm definitely going to try to write at least once a week for the whole summer . . . although this new diary is so nice and fat it will probably last me all the way through high school!

So here goes—my first weekly entry. Unfortunately it's been kind of a slow week. Not much is happening other than the usual stuff. Prancer, my favorite new horse at Pine Hollow, seems to be getting better every day. Max isn't letting anyone ride her, of course, because her injured leg is still weak, but her sweet personality is as healthy as ever. Carole is still working hard at training her horse, Starlight. They've been spending a lot of time jumping lately. Stevie has been trying to teach Topside to nod his head when she says yes, but it's not working so far. Max says it's because he's a sensible horse and not a circus performer, but naturally Stevie isn't giving up. In other words, things at Pine Hollow are pretty normal. My friends and I spend tons of time there, going to lessons and Pony Club meetings and taking trail rides together. And of course we've been spending plenty of time at TD's, our favorite ice cream place, as well. Yesterday Stevie ordered marshmallow topping and pineapple chunks on rum raisin, and I thought the waitress was going to dump it over her head when she brought it to the table. Boy, if that's the most interesting thing I can come up with to write about, I guess my life must be pretty boring!!!

Let's see, what else? Mom and Dad are the same as always. Peter called home the other day from England, but I was at the stable so I didn't get to talk to him. Mom told me his college in London just finished for the year and he's planning to spend the next couple of months traveling around Europe. Sounds like fun! Maybe if I could do something like that, I'd have more interesting things to write about . . .

FROM:	LAtwood
TO:	Steviethegreat
TO:	HorseGal
SUBJECT:	Where can it be?
MESSAGE:	

Well, Mrs. Reg still hasn't called. Maybe she hasn't noticed yet. Either way, I feel as guilty as can be! Are you sure we looked everywhere? Never mind—*I'm* sure. I just keep thinking a pin can't disappear into thin air!!! It's all my fault . . . *Aargh!*

Dear Diary,

I thought about not pasting in the above e-mail because I feel so terrible about what happened. But all those people in that article talk about how they like to record everything, good and bad. They claim that after a few years, they often look back on the bad stuff just as fondly as they do the good. I doubt that's going to be the case here, but I figure I might as well follow their lead and try to record everything. Besides, it's not like anyone but me will ever see this. And since it's almost eleven o'clock and I can't sleep, I might as well write. Right?

It's Monday night. Today started out nice and boring and fun, just like last week. I can't believe I ever complained about my life being like that! I miss it now, that's for sure.

Anyway, after jump class and our Pony Club trail ride, I had stable chores to do as usual. One of the things my friends and I were assigned to do was to check the hay in the loft for mold and mildew. Since that's such an important job—moldy hay can make horses really sick, and it can also start fires—I went to tell Max when we finished. I couldn't find him, but I found his mother, Mrs. Reg, which was just as good since she helps run the stable. She was on the phone when I got to her office, so I waited around for a couple of minutes until she finished her call.

One of the first things I noticed when she hung up was that she looked kind of serious. I guessed it had something to do with her phone call, and it made me feel a little embarrassed about almost eavesdropping (even though I hadn't actually heard anything). As I was thinking that, I suddenly noticed something shiny on the desk.

"What's that?" I asked Mrs. Reg.

"Pretty, isn't it?" she said with a smile. "Go ahead, pick it up."

I did, and I saw that it wasn't just pretty—it was beautiful. It was a gold pin of a galloping horse with a diamond for an eye. Mrs. Reg told me her husband had given it to her long ago.

"It would be our fortieth wedding anniversary this week," she explained as I admired the pin. "It was his wedding present for me."

That made the pin seem even more special. I was sure Carole and Stevie would love it just as much as I did, so I asked if I could borrow it for a minute to show them.

"Sure," Mrs. Reg said. "I have to talk with Max about something. If I'm not here when you bring it back, just put it in my center drawer, okay?"

"Okay," I promised. "Thanks." I really appreciated her trust in me.

Holding the pin carefully, I hurried to the locker area, where Stevie and Carole were already changing out of their riding clothes. They were probably wondering where I was—Stevie gets really impatient when she thinks we're late for a Saddle Club meeting at TD's—but they forgot everything else when they saw the pin.

"Oh, the diamond is so perfect!" Stevie exclaimed. "Wouldn't it be wonderful if we could have a pin like this for The Saddle Club?"

I didn't know about that. I loved Mrs. Reg's pin, but I also love our club pins. They're silver horse heads, and they're just right for us.

Before I could say so, Carole started raving about the conformation of the horse on the pin, pointing out that it looked like it was supposed to be an Arabian.

That made Veronica diAngelo, who was also in the locker area, look up and take notice. Normally Veronica doesn't bother to pay attention to us at all, unless she's saying something snobby like how expensive her new riding boots are or which upper-crust member of Willow Creek society her family had dinner with the night before. But her horse, Garnet, is a purebred Arabian, so she came over to see what we were doing.

We didn't have much choice but to show her the pin. While she was looking at it, the ruckus began.

At first there was just a sort of skittering sound, followed by an unmistakable squeak. Before we knew it, one of the stable cats came racing by in hot pursuit of a mouse.

Veronica jumped onto the bench, screaming bloody murder. The rest of us might have laughed—who could really be afraid of a tiny, furry creature like a mouse?—but a second or two after the cat chased the mouse out the door, we all heard a frightened whinny.

"Come on!" Carole said, racing for the door.

She didn't have to say it twice. I'd already realized what was happening. The chase had ended up in or near Prancer's stall. Prancer is a wonderful horse, but like all horses—especially high-strung Thorough-breds—she has her quirks. One of them is a fear of cats.

To make a long story short, we managed to oust the cat from the stall, calm Prancer, and shoo the mouse outside, safe and sound. After that bit of excellent teamwork, we decided it was past time to head to TD's and celebrate.

So we did. But we'd hardly taken our seats in our favorite booth when I realized I had no idea what had happened to Mrs. Reg's pin. We raced back to Pine Hollow and searched the locker area, but there was no sign of it. I even called Veronica at her house to see if she knew where it had gone.

"Pin . . . pin . . . ," Veronica said when I asked her about it. "I don't know. I think I threw the darn thing at the cat."

That wasn't much help. I hung up, a sinking feeling in my stomach, just in time to see Max coming toward me. At first I thought he might be mad because I'd used the office phone without permission. But he was in a good mood and let it slide.

"Isn't it time for you to get home now?" he asked me. "We want you rested for tomorrow's jump class. You're doing very well, you know."

"Thanks," I said, pleased in spite of my worry. Max is a fantastic riding teacher, and he does a terrific job running the whole stable. He's so busy he doesn't have much time to hand out compliments, so when he does, it really means something.

Still, part of me felt worse than ever at his nice words. If he only knew that I had just lost his mother's beloved pin . . .

Mademoiselle Lisa, what a wonderful essay on the Eiffel Tower! You have such a fine command of the French language already, after less than a year of study. Keep up the good work! Bien fait!

Dear Diary,

I just found that note from Madame Smith last week when I was cleaning out my last year's notebooks, and I thought I'd stick it in for moral support. I just hope I can remember everything I learned in her class when I meet the French ambassador tomorrow! Anyway, there's lots to write about—it's amazing how much can happen in two short days!—but I'm too exhausted to write another paragraph tonight. I'll have to describe this busy, busy week sometime when I can keep my eyes open.

Dear Diary,

I really wish I hadn't used such strong glue to stick in that note from Madame Smith! I feel so stupid about what happened—today is definitely *not* a day I'm going to want to look back on and remember.

I'm just as exhausted tonight as I've been this whole exhausting week. I can't believe it's only Thursday—it feels like months have passed since Mrs. Reg's pin disappeared! But tomorrow afternoon feels all too close. That's when she comes back and finds out it's lost. I guess that's why I'm too nervous to sleep. Even though my eyelids feel like they have lead weights attached to them, every time I let them close, I start worrying about where the pin could be and what Mrs. Reg is going to say, and then I'm wide awake again. So I might as well write down what's been happening . . .

All Monday evening I kept expecting Mrs. Reg to call and ask me where her pin was. I was a nervous wreck. But by the time I was getting ready to leave for Pine Hollow on Tuesday, I still hadn't heard a peep from her. I couldn't imagine why—unless she was waiting to yell at me in person.

Then I thought of something. Maybe the reason Mrs. Reg hadn't called was that she trusted me. Maybe she figured that if I hadn't put the pin in her drawer as promised, it was because I had a good reason. That idea made me feel worse than ever, since I'd obviously

12

proved myself totally *un*trustworthy by getting distracted and losing the pin.

Stevie and Carole were waiting for me when I got to the stable. Without a word, we headed straight inside to face the music. I really appreciated their being there for me. Even though it was my fault, they were willing to come along and support me. That's what friends are for.

When we reached Mrs. Reg's office, the only one there was Max. "What are you looking for?" he asked when he saw us, sounding a little tense.

"Where's Mrs. Reg?" I asked.

"She's gone for the week," he replied. "She had to go visit a sick friend who called yesterday. She won't be back until Friday, and there are a zillion and one things for me to do."

He went on to complain about some new horse he had to train and a new class beginning and some other things, but I wasn't really listening. I was still trying to figure out what this meant. Mrs. Reg was gone for the entire week. Could I wait until Friday to confess what I'd done, or would I go completely crazy before then?

A moment later Max dashed away, looking more harried than ever, and Stevie rubbed her hands together. "This is our chance," she said.

"Chance?" I said. "What do you mean? You think this gives me a four-day head start on leaving the country?"

Stevie shook her head. "It gives *us* a four-day head

start on finishing what we started last night," she said. "We're going to run Pine Hollow for Max this week while Mrs. Reg is gone. It will be the perfect opportunity for the three of us to be everywhere, look everywhere, do everything. If that pin is here, anywhere, we'll find it."

Carole looked as skeptical as I felt. "And if we don't?"

Stevie shrugged. "Then we'll have spent the week earning dozens and dozens of brownie points. How could Max and Mrs. Reg want to kill us when we're indispensable?"

I thought about that. Sometimes Stevie's schemes can be pretty harebrained and impractical, but I had to admit that this one made sense. We might actually find the pin, and even if we didn't, at least all that hard work would be a better use of time than worrying about how I was going to apologize when Mrs. Reg got home.

"It's worth trying," I said at last.

Carole agreed. "Then, after it's all over," she said, "why don't you plan to come to my house on Friday for dinner and a sleepover?"

I wasn't sure I was going to be in a partying mood once Friday rolled around—not unless we found the pin—but I didn't say so.

I'm not sure how Stevie managed to convince Max to let The Saddle Club take over managing the stable. Carole and I left that completely up to her, since convincing people to do crazy things is sort of her specialty. But she did it somehow, and before we knew it, all three of us were up to our eyeballs in work, work, work.

It's no secret that there's always a lot to do around a stable. Horses need to be fed every day. Their stalls must be mucked out regularly. Stable aisles have to be swept, feed needs to be mixed, tack needs to be cleaned, and about a million other things always seem to need doing.

It's one thing to pitch in and help. Max insists that all his riders do that—it keeps costs down, and it reminds us that there's more to riding than climbing in and out of the saddle. But in the past few days, my friends and I have found out that when you're running the whole show, all that work can become overwhelming pretty quickly. That first day, once riding class was over and our own horses were taken care of, we got ready to begin the *real* work—filling in for Mrs. Reg. Luckily (sort of), she'd left a list of what needed to be done. The first item read, "Painting, front of stable." That sounded like a pretty big job, but we figured we could do it if we all pitched in. After that was something about a new class of four beginners who were coming on Wednesday at eight o'clock. Fortunately Red O'Malley, the head stable hand, was scheduled to teach the class, so all we had to do was get some ponies ready for the students beforehand. Carole volunteered for that job, since her dad was dropping her off early on his way to work.

We went on with the list. The next item was "Buy food for Friday." We weren't sure what to do about that at first, but as usual Stevie came up with a plan.

"Whenever anybody delivers anything, there are papers," she pointed out. "Somewhere around here Mrs. Reg must have an invoice or something from the last delivery. I'll just call the same place and make the same order. If the stuff was okay last time, it's going to be fine this time, too. The hardest part may be getting it here by Friday."

"Nice thinking," Carole said admiringly.

I couldn't help agreeing with that. I also couldn't help thinking it was my turn to come up with some good ideas. After all, it was my fault we had to do all this work in the first place. "What's next on the list?" I asked.

And now I've come to the part of the story that still makes me blush (especially when I think about that silly note from my French teacher). "Wow," Stevie said as she checked the list. "We've got a VIP coming to Pine Hollow. The French ambassador himself! It says here, 'Thursday, eleven, Am. French. One-hour trail ride.' "

We were surprised we hadn't heard about that before, but we didn't really think about it much. Willow Creek sometimes seems like it's a million miles away from everywhere, but the truth is, it's really not far from Washington, D.C. That means there are always a lot of people around who work for the government (ours or somebody else's). Not too long ago, the ambassador from Brazil even came to Pine Hollow for a trail ride.

"I'll take care of that," I told my friends. "I got an A in French—"

"So what else is new?" Stevie teased.

I was a little embarrassed. I don't usually brag about my grades, but at that moment they actually seemed kind of relevant. "Well, this time it looks like it may do me some good. Anyway, I need some practice with my French. I'll go for a trail ride with the French ambassador."

"*Merci beaucoup*," Stevie said in her best French accent, which is actually pretty good. Then she turned to Carole. "And since Lisa is solving that problem, you get to cope with the fact that somebody named Jarvis is coming Thursday at one P.M. and wants his 'favorite horse.' That's what Mrs. Reg wrote."

I was glad that was going to be Carole's problem. After we talked about it a bit, we returned to *my* biggest problem—namely, the missing pin. We decided to search the tack room in case one of the cats had batted it in there.

It wasn't an easy job. By the time we'd examined every square inch of the room, cleaning it up as we went along, we were dirty and dusty and sweaty. We were also dejected, since there was no sign of the pin anywhere. The only good things about the task were that Max noticed what we were doing and seemed impressed, and Veronica noticed and seemed annoyed.

The next day—yesterday—was truly exhausting. One kind of funny thing did happen, though I could never tell Carole I thought so since she didn't see much humor in it. See, she had volunteered to tack up the horses for that beginner class. So naturally, she brought out four of the stable ponies. But it turned out that the "beginners" were actually four professional basketball players! Each of them was about twice as tall as the pony Carole had chosen for him! The basketball players thought it was hysterical, but Carole was really embarrassed. Stevie and I arrived at the stable just in time to help saddle up some tall horses.

"Thank you," Carole whispered as the four men rode off, still chuckling about the mix-up.

"No problem," Stevie said with a grin. "I got the feeling this was the funniest thing that had happened to those guys in a long time. They *loved* it."

Judging by the look Carole gave Stevie in reply, it was obvious that *she* hadn't loved it at all. I could understand her being a little embarrassed, but I didn't think it was that big a deal. After all, it was an honest mistake.

Not like my big blooper. I have no excuse for what happened today.

I guess I was kind of tired and cranky when I got to the stable this morning. The three of us had spent yesterday afternoon painting the front of the stable, and

18

we ended up accidentally dumping paint all over Diablo in the process. Luckily those basketball players returned from their ride in time to help us finish, but it still took an awfully long time. Plus I stayed up late last night boning up on my French vocabulary, and when I finally went to sleep I kept waking up from dreams of riding a horse straight up the side of the Eiffel Tower.

So I wasn't in the best mood on Thursday morning. For one thing, volunteering to ride with the French ambassador meant I would have to skip our jump class, and I really love jumping. But I knew it was the least I could do, considering that I'd lost Mrs. Reg's pin, so I tried to look on the bright side. At least I would get to practice my French, as I'd told my friends, and that would be fun. Not as much fun as jumping, maybe, but . . .

Anyway, while Carole was busy assigning horses to riders for the day and Stevie was figuring out how to order the feed, I was reviewing the French I'd studied the night before and feeling nervous. Even though Madame Smith always praised my work in her class, I wasn't sure that a real French person would be so impressed. I didn't think I'd have any problem with the basics—*Bonjour, je m'appelle Lisa Atwood*—but after that things could get tricky. What would a French ambassador want to talk about during a trail ride? Horses? International relations? Escargot? I had no idea. The only topic I'd really prepared for was the first one. For instance, I had memorized the French word for saddle, *selle*, and horse, *cheval*, along with some other useful words and phrases. But my stomach was in knots by the time a car pulled up to the stable at ten-fifteen and a distinguished-looking middle-aged man stepped out.

Still, I had promised my friends I would handle this. So I took a deep breath and stepped forward to greet the man. "*Bonjour*," I began. "*Je m'appelle Lisa Atwood.*"

The man looked surprised. Then he smiled and replied, "*Bonjour*, Lisa."

I was proud of myself, guessing that he was impressed that someone my age was talking to him in his native tongue. That made it easier for me to go on speaking as we got ready to head out on Barq and Delilah. Before long I'd lost a lot of my self-consciousness, and as we rode across the fields and entered a wooded trail, we chatted easily about this and that.

The man was so nice that I wanted to tell him a little about The Saddle Club. "*Moi et mes amies*," I began. "*Nous avons un*, uh, *une*—oh, drat—*une* . . ." This time my brain was failing me. "I just can't remember the word for *club* in French," I explained helplessly, shrugging sheepishly to convey my confusion.

"I can't remember it, either," the man replied in perfect English. "But I suspect it's something like *club* or *association*. Anyway, why don't we try English for a while?"

It took me about eight very long seconds to realize what was going on. The man's English was not only perfect, it was completely free of any trace of a French accent. In fact, the only accent he had was a slight, pleasant Virginia drawl.

I didn't know what to say. "You're not the French ambassador," I stammered. "You're not even French!"

"Of course I am," the man replied with a smile. "I'm Michael French. I thought you knew."

I felt like protesting. Mrs. Reg's list had said it was the French ambassador who was coming!

Then I realized it wasn't Mrs. Reg's mistake. It was mine—ours. Mrs. Reg had written, "Thursday, 11, Am. French." She hadn't meant anything about a French ambassador—The Saddle Club had assumed that. She had just written eleven A.M. in a slightly unusual manner.

"Oh no," I groaned, wishing the earth would open right then and there and swallow me and Barq. "I'm—" I'd been trying to think in French for so long that for a second I couldn't come up with the proper words in English. "I can't—I mean, it's so—"

"Don't worry," Mr. French said cheerfully. "I'm really very flattered. See, I work for the State Department. I would like nothing more than to be an ambassador. The fact that you thought I was one already—well, you can imagine. I've loved every minute of it. Besides, French is the language of diplomacy, and mine's been getting rusty. You gave me a chance to

21

speak in French, which was terrific. I only expected to learn something about horseback riding. I got twice the value for my money!"

"You're being awfully nice about this," I said, his kind words making me feel a tiny bit better. "In fact, I think you're giving *me* a lesson in diplomacy."

I meant it, too. If Mr. French hadn't been so wonderful about the whole thing, I really don't know if I could have survived it. As it was, I managed to forget the whole episode—mostly, anyway—as we continued our ride. But believe me, after the misunderstandings we've come up with so far—first Carole and the basketball players, then me and Mr. French, the "ambassador"—I'm really hoping nothing else like that happens before Mrs. Reg gets back tomorrow evening. I don't think I could stand it!

Hotel Zentrum
Vienna, Austria

Dear Lisa,

Greetings from Austria! I've been thinking of my favorite little sister a lot these past few days, because I've been visiting the Spanish Riding School here in Vienna. Mom keeps telling me how much you enjoy your riding lessons with your friends. You would really like the horses here. The riders and trainers are very interesting people, and the horses are really something—

probably a lot different from the ponies you ride there at Pine Tree Stable! They're all big and white, and they do lots of fancy tricks, sort of like circus horses. Sometimes they look like they're actually dancing! By the way, even though they call it the Spanish Riding School, it was started right here in Austria way back in the 1500s. They named it after the Lipizzaner horses they use, which originally came from Spain.

You're probably wondering why I'm spending so much of my summer vacation looking at dancing horses. I'm sure Mom and Dad told you I'm spending the summer traveling around Europe and seeing the sights. Since next year will be my last year of college, I want to start figuring out what I want to do after I graduate. I've been thinking about some kind of career in writing, so I've volunteered to write articles for a student-run paper at my school in London. I'm working on one about the Lipizzaners this week. Just imagine it—your brother, the famous journalist!

Anyway, I'd better go. I'm on a deadline!

Love,
Peter

Dear Diary,

Boy, am I sorry I ever complained about my life being boring! I have so much to write that I hardly know where to begin. I guess I'd better just start where I left off in my last entry, since everything happened pretty fast after that.

I had a big knot in my stomach when I got to Pine Hollow on Friday morning. It was the big day. The day Mrs. Reg returned.

I jogged all the way to the stable, and when I arrived I saw a huge eighteen-wheeler parked in the driveway. On the side were the words *Connor Hay & Grain*.

The driver was sitting in his seat looking at a piece of paper, so I figured he must have just arrived. I walked over. "Hello," I said. "You must be dropping off our feed order, right?"

"That's right." The driver scratched his chin and glanced at the paper again, looking perplexed. "But I'm wondering if there's some mistake. I deliver here all the time, and I can't figure out why there's so much more than usual this time."

I felt the knot in my stomach tighten a little more. The last thing The Saddle Club needed right then was another problem. "What do you mean?" I asked carefully.

The driver shrugged. "Take a look in the back. Tell me if you think what's inside will fit in your feed shed."

I did as he said, walking around to the big rear doors of the truck. They were propped open, and the bright morning sunshine lit up what was inside. Feed. A lot of feed. "This can't all be for us!" I exclaimed.

The driver had hopped out and followed me around to the back. "Sure is, young lady," he said, holding up the piece of paper. "I've checked and triple-checked the invoice. This is the order I was given." He scratched his chin again. "I can't figure it out. Mrs. Reg is always so careful about her orders."

I had no idea what to tell him. "Uh, Mrs. Reg didn't

place the order this time," I said. "Um, the person who did should be inside somewhere. I'll go get her."

"Thanks." The driver nodded pleasantly at me, then headed back to the cab of the truck.

I raced inside, wondering how this could have happened. Stevie had proudly explained to Carole and me how she'd found an old invoice and ordered the exact same rations. But judging by my quick peek into that truck, there looked to be three or four times what we needed. "Stevie!" I hollered as soon as I entered the stable building. I didn't know where she was most likely to be at that moment, and I didn't want to waste time searching. "Stevie!"

"Hold your horses!" Stevie's familiar voice called back. "I'm coming."

A second later she was hurrying toward me with a big smile on her face. I didn't bother to wonder what she was looking so pleased about—there would be time for that later. "Outside," I told her briskly. "Quick."

Stevie shot me a curious glance, but shrugged and did as I said. As soon as she stepped outside and saw the feed truck, her smile grew broader. "Oh, good, the order's here," she said, hurrying toward the cab.

The driver was inside again. He leaned out the window as Stevie approached. "Where does Mrs. Reg want me to put all this stuff?"

"In the feed shed, like usual," Stevie replied with an expression that said she thought the man must be a little slow.

"This won't fit in the feed shed like usual," the driver replied patiently. "This is a big order."

For once, Stevie was speechless. I could almost see the wheels in her head turning as she tried to figure out what was going on. She pulled a sheet of paper out of her pocket and glanced at it.

"Girls, why don't you go get Mrs. Reg so she can tell us what to do?" the driver suggested. He sounded less patient this time, and I gulped, guessing he was starting to get annoyed with the delay.

"Uh-oh," Stevie murmured, but she wasn't looking at the driver. I wasn't sure she'd even heard him. She was still staring at that paper. Looking over her shoulder, I saw that it was an invoice from the feed company. Finally she glanced up at the driver and smiled weakly. "This whole truckload isn't for us, right?"

"Every bit of it," the driver answered. "Just like you ordered. Now would you please go get Mrs. Reg?"

"I'll see what I can do." Stevie grabbed me by the sleeve and dragged me after her into the stable.

"What's going on?" I asked, hoping that Stevie had more of a clue than I did.

She did. She proceeded to explain it to me as we entered the office. It turned out that the invoice she had used as a guide had been placed exactly one week before the last big horse show at Pine Hollow. That was why the truck held enough grain, hay, and straw to feed and bed more than a hundred horses.

As soon as I understood what she was saying, I let

out a groan and sank down into the guest chair in front of Mrs. Reg's desk. "Oh no."

"Oh, yes," Stevie replied grimly.

"Why don't you just tell them we don't need it?" I suggested, figuring that was the only sensible solution.

Stevie was already shaking her head. "I ordered it; I begged them for it."

"But we can't keep an order that size," I pointed out. "There's no place to store it, and it'll go bad." I had no idea what we should do about this, but keeping the whole order definitely was not an option.

Stevie seemed to realize that, too. She picked up the phone and started to dial. "Hi," she said when somebody answered. "I'm calling from Pine Hollow."

I couldn't hear what the person on the other end of the phone was saying, so I just watched Stevie's face. For a moment or two she continued to look worried, and I guessed she was trying to figure out how to explain the goof. Then her expression changed. She looked happier and happier with every passing second. I leaned forward on my chair, practically dying of curiosity. Finally she spoke.

"You mean, you just want us to take a small portion of this gigantic delivery?" she asked.

I gasped. Stevie has truly amazing luck sometimes, but this sounded too good to be true.

It wasn't, though. It *was* true. Stevie told me the whole story as soon as she hung up. It seemed a nearby racetrack had just had a big fire that had destroyed most of their feed supply. They desperately needed a whole lot of feed right away.

Naturally, that made it a lot easier for Stevie to admit her mistake to the person at the feed company. Before long, everything had been straightened out. The driver unloaded the portion of the order that we actually needed before driving off to the track with the rest. It was all settled in time for us to tack up for jump class.

That piece of good luck kept my spirits up for a while. But by the time three o'clock rolled around, I was feeling anxious and panicky. Mrs. Reg would be back in two hours, and there didn't seem to be much chance of finding her pin before then. I wasn't sure what upset me the most—the fact that I was to blame, the fact that the pin was valuable, or the fact that it had been a very special gift to Mrs. Reg from her husband, who had died long ago.

I was thinking about all that as I groomed Diablo after our last class of the day. He still had some paint in his coat from the little accident earlier in the week, and I really wanted to get out as much of it as I could before Mrs. Reg saw him. She was going to be upset enough with me and my friends as it was.

Carole stopped by to give me a bottle of apple juice and leaned on the stall door to talk for a moment. "That stuff's really coming out, isn't it?" she commented, looking at the paint.

I just shrugged. Diablo was almost back to his normal bay self, but at the moment that didn't seem like much consolation.

"I'm going to run an errand," Carole went on. "Dad told me he wouldn't get to the store to buy the food for our lasagna tonight, so I brought the recipe with me. I'm going over to the shopping center to get the stuff."

I'd been so busy worrying about the missing pin that I'd completely forgotten we were all supposed to have a sleepover at Carole's that night. Actually, I was a little surprised that Carole was thinking about our dinner at a time like that. Wasn't she worried about what Mrs. Reg was going to say when she got home in just a couple of short hours? "You're really going shopping?" I said.

"I know it seems odd," Carole said. "I was thinking the same thing you're thinking now, but the fact is, worrying doesn't change anything. It won't help us find the pin."

Her words didn't change the facts, but for some reason they made me feel a little better. Carole can sometimes seem sort of scatterbrained about anything other than horses. But she's really a wise person deep down underneath all that.

"All right," I told her. "You do the shopping, and Stevie and I will search for the pin one more time. We'll go back to the locker area. I know we combed every inch of it, but it's still the most logical place."

"Good idea," Carole said. "I'll cross my fingers for you."

For the next two hours, every time I imagined Carole digging for a perfect tomato or grabbing a box of pasta with her fingers crossed, I couldn't help a secret smile. But there wasn't much else to smile about. Not only did Stevie and I have zero luck finding the pin, but Veronica diAngelo hung around while we were searching, smirking the whole time. She'd finally figured out what was going on, and she didn't want to miss seeing Mrs. Reg yell at us instead of her for a change.

I wasn't thinking much about Veronica, though, as Stevie and I finally gave up and walked back to Mrs. Reg's office to await her return. Stevie looked almost as glum as I felt as we dropped into the guest chairs.

Carole entered a moment later clutching two bags of groceries. She set them on the bookshelf next to Mrs. Reg's desk and shot us a sympathetic look. "No luck, huh?"

We filled her in on our search and on Veronica's annoying behavior. Before long Carole was looking just as depressed as we were.

But now that the moment of truth was almost there, I was starting to feel strangely calm. There really wasn't any other option—crying or yelling or running away wouldn't solve anything. We'd tried our best to fix our mistake, and we'd failed. That was all there was to it. "I think I know what I'm going to say to Mrs. Reg," I said.

"You've thought up a way to explain the mess we've made?" Stevie asked.

"Well, I haven't figured out everything I'm going to say," I replied, "but it's going to begin with the words *I'm sorry.*"

"That sort of covers it, doesn't it?" Carole remarked. "Beginning, middle, and end."

"Very sorry," Stevie agreed.

At that moment we all heard the unmistakable sound of a car pulling into the driveway. I suppose it could have been any number of people driving in for any number of reasons, but all three of us knew who it was without looking. It was just about time for Max to return from picking up his mother at the airport.

"Oh no," I said, a bit of my earlier panic returning. "I think I've forgotten my speech."

"It starts with 'I'm sorry,'" Stevie reminded me. "And if you forget, we'll say it for you."

Before I could respond, I heard an exclamation float through the open office window from the direction of the front of the stable. "Why, this is *beautiful!*" Mrs. Reg's familiar voice cried.

"What's that, Mother?" Max asked.

"The front of the stable! You painted it!"

"Stevie, Lisa, and Carole decided to paint it," Max explained. "I don't know why—but they took a turn at painting Diablo while they were at it!" He laughed.

I exchanged anxious glances with my friends.

We stood to welcome Mrs. Reg as she bustled into the office a moment later. She grabbed all three of us and gathered us in for a big group hug. "The front of the stable looks great!" she exclaimed before any of us could speak. "When Morris sees how much better it looks, he's going to love doing the painting for our living room! Don't you think so, Max?"

Max looked confused for a second, then his face cleared. "Definitely," he agreed.

Before we could try to figure out what any of that meant, Mrs. Reg turned to us with another big smile. "Whatever made you girls decide to take on that job?"

"It was on your list," Stevie said. "It said to paint the front of the stable."

Mrs. Reg raised her eyebrows in surprise. "No it didn't," she said. "Or maybe it did, but that wasn't what I meant."

"Did we mess up again?" I asked, feeling worse than ever.

"Again?" Mrs. Reg said. "This wasn't a mess-up. This was a case of mind reading. See, my old friend Morris is coming tonight, and he's staying with us for the weekend. He's an artist, and he offered to do a painting of the stable for our home. I was planning to ask him to spruce the place up a bit in his painting, but now I don't have to. He can make the painting look just like the real thing. Thanks!" She turned to her son. "Max, didn't you even look at that list?" she asked. "Did you just let these girls do absolutely *everything*?"

Max shrugged sheepishly. "They seemed to be doing a pretty good job of it," he said. "Actually, I came in here last night and took a look at the chart Carole made for assigning horses, and I was very impressed. You have to get her to show you how she did it. I think you'll want to use it, too. Can you show her, Carole?"

"Well, sure," Carole said. "But—"

"No buts," Mrs. Reg said, her eyes twinkling. "Because if you've gotten as good at assigning horses as Max says, you may just end up with the job permanently."

"Oh, no thank you," Carole said quickly. "Um, I'm sure you do a much better job of it than I ever could."

Max smiled knowingly at her. He knew as well as anyone that assigning horses was a tricky job. "Well, that may be true, Mother, but the fact is that these girls have been working some magic around here in your absence."

I was a little surprised to hear that. Max had been so busy all week that we'd hardly seen him. I didn't think he'd noticed much of anything we were doing, which seemed like a good thing when I remembered all of our embarrassing mix-ups and misunderstandings.

There was a knock at the office door, and Veronica diAngelo strolled in. "Can I speak to you and Mrs. Reg for a minute?" she asked Max. "In private?"

I gulped, guessing that she was about to spill the beans about the missing pin. It would be just like her to tattle on us before we even had a chance to confess.

33

"Not right now," Max told Veronica. "My mother just got back. Can it wait until morning?"

"It's important." Veronica isn't used to taking no for an answer, and she didn't look happy about Max's response.

He didn't notice. "A little later, then," he said, turning away to address his mother again. "You should have heard what some of the other riders said about these three," he told her.

I gulped again. Maybe Max hadn't been as clueless as I'd thought about what had been going on there lately. Had Mr. French told him what a fool I'd made of myself?

Max went on before any of us could say anything. "We've got a whole basketball team that wants to learn to ride," he told Mrs. Reg cheerfully. "Apparently their coach told them that horseback riding would help their balance. So four of them came and tried it. They loved it. I don't know what these three did, but the players just couldn't stop talking about how wonderful all the riders were and how much they loved the horses that had been assigned to them."

Mrs. Reg beamed. "It's awfully nice to know that when I'm gone, my shoes can be filled by young riders Max and I have trained so well."

I barely heard her complimentary words. I'd just checked out Veronica's face out of the corner of my eye, and she didn't look happy about all the praise being heaped on The Saddle Club. It wouldn't be long before she interrupted with her big announcement, I was sure.

Max was nodding. "But I can't claim any credit for the French lesson one of these young riders delivered," he said. "A new rider said he never had more fun or learned more on a trail ride than he did with Lisa. He said something about having a friend who wants to learn Arabic and wondered if we had any Arabian horses. I don't know what he was talking about, but he signed up for six months' worth of trail riding. For that, I'll learn Urdu! I don't know what you did, Lisa, but thank you."

I was stunned, to say the least. "It's a long story," I told Max. "But you're welcome."

"Max," Veronica whined, "I need to talk to you *now*."

"Not now, Veronica," Max replied. Then he continued to tell his mother about all the wonderful things we'd done that week. He was going on and on about how helpful we'd been to the people at Connor's when Veronica finally got fed up.

"Max, *now!*" she snapped peevishly.

Max shot her a slightly irritated glance. "Can't you see that my mother hasn't even taken her coat off?"

It was true. Max and Mrs. Reg had been so busy singing our praises that she was still wearing her light raincoat. Max finally reached to help her off with it. When it came off, I couldn't believe my eyes.

The pin! There it was, a little golden horse with a

diamond eye, fastened securely to Mrs. Reg's blue blouse!

There was stunned silence for a moment. Even Veronica was speechless.

"Y-Your pin—" I stuttered at last.

"I always wear it when I'm dressed up." Mrs. Reg didn't seem to realize that anything unusual was happening. She certainly couldn't have guessed that I felt as though a sixteen-ton weight had just been lifted off my chest. "Though, of course, it doesn't belong in a stable. I mean, look what happened last time I had it here. You girls did a wonderful thing by calming Prancer. I had to rush after I picked up the pin where you'd left it for me in the locker area, so I never had a chance to tell you how proud I was of the job you were doing. But I'm sure Max remembered to tell you, didn't he?"

"Max?" Stevie repeated.

"You did remember, didn't you?" Mrs. Reg asked her son.

Max's sheepish look was enough of an answer for all of us.

"You mean he never told you I got the pin?" Mrs. Reg asked.

I shook my head, not trusting my voice at the moment. I still could hardly dare to believe that the pin was there, safe and sound, let alone that it had all been a terrible mix-up.

Mrs. Reg turned to her son again. "Max Regnery,"

she began sternly, "is it possible that you knew that these girls were worried sick about my pin and you didn't tell them, just because you knew they'd be trying to do everything in the world to find it and to try to make up for losing it?"

Sometimes it's amazing how quick Mrs. Reg can be about figuring things out. How does she do it?

We don't get to see Max squirm too often, but he was definitely squirming just then. "Veronica," he said, sounding a bit desperate under his mother's steady gaze. "What is it you wanted to say to us?"

"Nothing," Veronica replied darkly. She spun on her heel and marched out of the office.

My friends and I weren't far behind her. Oh, and by the way—Mrs. Reg ended up taking Carole's bags of groceries, thinking Max had bought them for her. It turned out that when she'd put "Buy food for Friday" on her list, she was talking about food for *people*, not horses. She needed something to cook for her friend who was coming to visit!

We didn't bother to tell her the truth. Instead, we went out for pizza and ice cream. And that's how the day that started out looking like one of the worst of my life turned out just fine in the end!

Still, I don't ever want to go through a week like that again. We were just lucky that Mrs. Reg's pin wasn't really lost after all. It easily could have been. The next time I borrow someone's valuable piece of jewelry, I'll make sure I don't let it out of my grasp, no matter how many cats or mice or horses or elephants run through the room! If it hadn't been for that one mistake, we wouldn't have thought the pin was lost. And we wouldn't have been trying so hard to impress Max and Mrs. Reg that we ended up making a lot of assumptions and bad guesses that led to big misunderstandings.

Speaking of misunderstandings, I just remembered that I pasted in that letter from my brother a couple of days ago. I was so busy when it came that I hardly had time to skim it, but I just went back and looked at it. It made me feel kind of strange, actually. Almost sad, in a way. I mean, my brother has been living far away for so long—first he went away to college in Chicago, then he transferred to that university in England. And every summer he seems to have some kind of job or something to do that keeps him away from home, whether it's being a camp counselor or, now, traveling around Europe. In a weird way, I've almost started to feel as though I don't have a brother anymore at all. It's almost like all the years when Peter and I both lived here were just a dream, or something that happened to someone else. But that doesn't make much sense, because I still love him a lot, and I still miss him like crazy at weird times, like whenever I eat a peanut butter and banana sandwich (his favorite). It's hard to believe how long it's been since I've seen him or even heard his voice.

When we were younger, I thought he was the greatest thing—I used to follow him around every chance I could. I even used to beg to wear his old clothes! I know Stevie is always complaining about her three brothers, and maybe it's different when you're close in age like they are. But when I was eight or nine and Peter was sixteen or seventeen, I just couldn't spend enough time with him. He didn't seem to mind, either. He did lots of neat stuff with me, like playing detectives, baking a six-layer cake for Mom's birthday, or helping me build a scale-model Egyptian pyramid for my third-grade school project. He even taught me how to drive a car right after he got his license, and a couple of times he let me steer in the parking lot at the mall—not that I would *ever* tell Mom and Dad about that!

In any case, I'm starting to wonder if he really does still think of me as the little girl I was then, tagging along after him and impressed by everything he did. I mean, we haven't really had much of a one-on-one relationship for the past few years. He sends cards on my birthday and stuff like that, but usually I'm just included in his general phone calls and letters to the whole family. I mean, I never knew he was interested in writing, even though I am too. It's almost like we don't know each other at all these days. For all I know he might not like peanut butter and banana sandwiches anymore.

Anyway, I'm not sure how to respond to his letter.

He's probably not really expecting me to write back. I could just ask Mom if I can add a note at the end of her next letter.

But every time I think of doing that, I remember the look on Peter's face when he first showed me how to shift the car out of neutral. "Don't tell anyone about this, okay?" he told me with a wink. "It's a secret brother-sister thing."

I can't help thinking this letter should be strictly a brother-sister thing, too. Maybe it's a chance for us to get to know each other again.

Now, just one question remains: What should I write about? It's obvious that he doesn't realize how important horses are to me. Maybe I should start by telling him about some of the stuff that happened last week at Pine Hollow—all the work we did (though I think I'll skip the part about Mr. French). That should give him an idea of what the new, improved, grown-up me is like. And the best part is, I won't have a bit of trouble remembering everything that happened, since I've already written it all down here.

See? This diary is coming in handy already!

FROM:	HorseGal
TO:	LAtwood
TO:	Steviethegreat
SUBJECT:	What a week!
MESSAGE:	

Hi, guys! Now that I've finally had a chance to catch up on my sleep and rest my weary bones for a few days, I've been thinking about everything that happened last week. If you think about it, there really is a bright side to it all. I know we spent an awful lot of time worrying and feeling stupid (I'm sure I won't be able to watch a basketball game without blushing for at least a year!), but we also did a lot of good work. I'm not just talking about the obvious stuff, like painting the stable. We also got a lot of extra practice taking care of horses. Since Max always says we're learning anytime we're doing anything to take care of horses, I think we must have skipped forward at least a whole grade or two in horse school. Right?

FROM:	Steviethegreat
TO:	HorseGal
TO:	LAtwood
SUBJECT:	What a week! (2)
MESSAGE:	

Okay, Carole, I totally shouldn't be surprised that you've decided to look on the horsey side of all this. As for me, I'm also choosing to look on the bright side. Sure, we made fools of ourselves a couple of times, and we lost a little sleep. But it all turned out better than fine in the end, and do you know why? Because we're The Saddle Club, that's why. And when we put our minds to it, we can do ANYTHING!!!! :-)

Dear Diary,

I can't believe it's October already and I haven't written! So much for my vow about writing every week . . . I'll have to do better if I want to make this diary as good as the ones in that article. I guess my excuses for not writing are pretty lame, but after all the writing I did after the busy, busy week when we thought Mrs. Reg's pin was lost, I spent the next couple of weeks working on my letter to Peter. I had some trouble getting started, since I was worried about sounding too babyish or dorky. Also, it seemed kind of hard to explain everything that happened when Peter's never even met Stevie or Carole, or Mrs. Reg or Max, or Diablo or Prancer . . . I mean, airmail is kind of expensive, and I didn't want my letter to end up being longer than one of Peter's college textbooks. So finally I just went ahead and wrote down what happened and then sent it off before I could change my mind. That was almost two months ago, and I

42

haven't heard back from him. I'm not that surprised, really—I sent it to his college housing in London, and he probably didn't even get back there until a few weeks ago. And if he's half as busy with the new school year as I've been, well, let's just say I bet neither of us has had time to write to anyone!

First of all, it was back-to-school shopping time—with Mom in charge, that starts around the beginning of August. Then, of course, school started and I was busy getting settled, organizing my notebooks and supplies, making covers for my textbooks, and doing homework. I always like to put some extra time into my homework at the very beginning of the year. If you get started right, everything afterward is easier. Besides, teachers really notice the extra effort in those first few weeks and they usually remember it all year long.

But I'm planning to get back on track with my diary now. My creative writing teacher, Ms. Shields, says that when it comes to writing, the best practice is more practice. She says that along with reading a lot, the best thing to do if you want to improve your creative writing is to write as much as you can, any way you can think of. She told us that even a grocery list can be thought of as creative writing.

I don't know about that. When I think of creative writing, I think of stuff like short stories and poems, not "milk, bread, tomatoes." But I really like Ms. Shields—her class is a lot of fun. So I'll have to wait

43

and see what she means when she says she expects us to get very creative with our assignments this year. The first assignment was to write a short story, but she sort of hinted that we'll be doing all sorts of other things later.

Anyway, aside from creative writing class, school is pretty much the same as last year. I have Mr. Ramirez for math, Ms. McCormick for science, Mr. Mathios for history. Nothing too exciting there. Not much has changed at good old Willow Creek Middle School, or at Pine Hollow for that matter. Just about the best news there is that Prancer's leg is still improving. Max says he'll probably let people start riding her in a month or two if Judy Barker, the vet, says it's okay. I can't wait—Prancer is such a wonderful, lovable horse (with kids, at least—she's still skittish around most adults) that I'm sure she'll love being ridden again. The more I get to know her, the more I love her, and I know Carole and Stevie feel the same way.

Aside from that, as I said, not much new is happening. We've started a new season of riding lessons and Pony Club, of course, but most people have been so busy with school and everything that we haven't been doing anything too interesting. (I hope Max never reads this, or he'll have me mucking out stalls for hours! Ha ha!)

FROM:	Steviethegreat
TO:	LAtwood
TO:	HorseGal
SUBJECT:	The night when Evil is released and the Dead walk upon the Earth (a.k.a. Halloween)
MESSAGE:	

Hi, girls! I just wanted to remind you that the most wonderful holiday of the year is coming up in a couple of short weeks, and we haven't even talked about it yet. I've been thinking about costumes, and it occurred to me that the three of us should try to do some kind of three-way costume. I just had the idea, but I can already hear Carole saying it should be something horse-related. So how about the Headless Horseman? It would be kind of complicated to build, but I bet it would look fantastic. Carole could be the front of the horse; Lisa, you could be the rear end plus work the body in the saddle. I'm sure Max would let us borrow a real one, by the way (saddle, not body), and we could build the body out of straw, like a scarecrow, and dress it in one of my dad's suits. As for the horse costume, I think I could talk Miss Fenton into lending us the one from last year's senior class play. Oh, by the way, in case you're wondering where I would fit into all this, I was thinking I would be dressed as a giant severed head. (You know, the one that the Headless Horseman is missing.) I could sort of pop out from behind the horse and scare people. Wouldn't that be cool?

If you don't like that idea, here's another one: a jump. You know, like in a horse show. Carole, you and I could be the two ends. We could dress all in white, or maybe red-and-white stripes, with a sort of wooden hat thing that would square off our heads. Naturally, we'd have to paint our faces to match. And on our hands, we could make some kind of mittens or something that would look like cups. Lisa, since you're the lightest, I thought you could be the middle part of the fence. One of us would hold your feet and the other would hold your head, and you would stretch across the middle. I haven't really decided what kind of jump we should be, exactly—maybe a brush fence, with Lisa all covered in branches. Or just a plain post-and-rail . . . The possibilities are endless!

While we're on the subject of endless possibilities, I just saw my devious brothers whispering together in the kitchen. I'm sure they're already planning some lame Halloween pranks to play on me, and I want to make sure I'm ready to give as good as I get. Does either of you know where I could get a real human skeleton? I could also use some glow-in-the-dark paint and a pulley. Also, do you think Max would mind if I borrowed Topside for an evening? He's a pretty calm horse—he probably wouldn't be spooked by rattling chains or howls.

Let me know what you think. Happy haunting!

FROM:	HorseGal
TO:	Steviethegreat
TO:	LAtwood
SUBJECT:	Bar None trip (what else?)
MESSAGE:	

Hi, you two! It's too late to call, but Dad just told me he talked to Colonel Devine about what time we need to be at the airstrip the day after tomorrow. If you want to meet at my house at nine, Dad said he'd drive us over there. Kate's not coming along on the plane with her dad this time, but she'll be at the airfield near the Bar None to pick us all up when we get there.

Okay, I just read over what I wrote, and I can still hardly believe it's true. We're really flying off to the Wild West to spend Halloween at the Bar None Ranch with Kate and her family! It's almost too good to be true.

Isn't it funny how you can just be going along with your daily life, not even suspecting that such a huge, wonderful thing is coming? I mean, when Dad and I were sitting in the den watching *Psycho* the other night and the phone rang, it just seemed like an unfortunate interruption. But then it turned out to be Kate calling, begging the three of us to come out and stay at her family's dude ranch so that we can help her mother throw a Halloween party.

And not just any Halloween party—but a fund-raising fair to help create an after-school program for the Native

American children at the local reservation school to replace the activity center that burned down. Who could ask for a more worthy cause?

I guess it's lucky for us it's so worthy. Otherwise I doubt any of our parents would have agreed to let us miss three whole days of school for this trip, even if Kate's father is flying his private plane east specially to pick us up! I can't wait to see him—and I can't wait to see the Bar None Ranch again, either. It was so beautiful the last time we were there. I'm dying to take a trail ride through the desert, maybe over to Christine Lonetree's house to say hi. I can't wait to sit in a Western saddle again and practice my reining and say "lope" instead of "canter." And after a hard day in the saddle, I can't wait to stuff myself with Mrs. Devine's delicious home cooking!

But the first thing I'm going to do when we arrive (well, after I say hello to the Devines and to Berry and Chocolate and Stewball and the other horses) is make Kate tell us exactly what she meant when she said there was "something else" she was going to talk to us about when we got there. Kate is so straightforward most of the time—if she's being mysterious, there must be a really exciting reason. And I bet it has something to do with horses!

Secrets or no secrets, though, I guess we have a lot to look forward to. I mean, we already have so many fantastic ideas for the Halloween Fair that it's sure to be a huge success. Everyone is going to love the costume contest and the pumpkin-carving table and the horror house and all the other fun things we have planned. And I absolutely love Stevie's idea that the three of us dress up as three blind mice for the costume parade!

Speaking of costumes, Stevie, I forgot all about your Halloween e-mail until I just went into the computer to write this. But I guess it doesn't matter now anyway—now we know exactly what our Halloween plans are, and I can't wait!

FROM: LAtwood
TO: Steviethegreat
TO: HorseGal
SUBJECT: Bar None trip (what else?) (2)
MESSAGE:

I'm with you, Carole—I can't wait for our trip to start, either! Nine o'clock sounds fine. Stevie, call me tomorrow if you want a ride over to Carole's house.

By the way, just in case spending time with Kate, going on trail rides in the desert, and helping a worthy cause aren't good enough reasons to look forward to this trip, I have one more to add to the list. It saved us from having to talk Stevie out of dressing us up as a brush jump for Halloween!

Dear Diary,

As you can see from the above e-mails I just pasted in, things are getting exciting around here again. I could hardly believe it when Carole called with the news that Phyllis Devine actually wanted The Saddle Club's help with her fund-raising party. It's going to be great to see Kate again, and Christine, too—they're two of my favorite out-of-town members of The Saddle Club. And helping with the Halloween Fair should be lots of fun. Planning stuff like that is one of Stevie's natural talents, and when she drags Carole and me into her plans, we almost always end up having a blast, too.

I can hardly believe all our parents and both our schools agreed to let us go. I'm a little worried about missing three whole days of classes, but I'm sure if I work hard before I go and after I come back I'll be okay. Stevie isn't worried about that sort of thing at all, naturally. She's thrilled to be missing school, even though she has to write an extra-credit report for her headmistress on the value of community service while she's away. That's the only way Miss Fenton would agree to let her out of school.

Carole keeps wondering about Kate's little surprise or secret or whatever. I guess Kate mentioned it on the phone but wouldn't tell her anything more—but naturally, Carole is completely convinced that it must be about a horse. She could be right, too. Kate is just as horse-crazy as the rest of us. As for me, I don't mind waiting to find out what her secret is all about, horse or no horse. There's plenty to look forward to as it is!

I'd better go get some sleep. We leave the day after tomorrow, and if this visit to the Bar None is anything like the others, I'll need to be well rested. I won't be writing again until we get back—I'm sure I won't have time—but don't despair, Diary. I'll fill you in on the trip as soon as I return!

Dear Diary,

Well, I'm back! If I'd had any idea how much was going to happen on this trip, there's no way I would have left this diary at home. I have some homework to do—luckily my teachers didn't assign anything extra like Stevie's headmistress did, and I did get a lot done before I left, but I still have some math problems to finish and a poetry assignment to do for my creative writing class. The poem is supposed to be about something "active" in my own life. That means no sonnets about love or urns or anything like that.

I have no idea what to write about, but I figured I could do something about my trip out West. And the best way to get inspired is to start putting down my thoughts here. Right? So here goes . . .

Okay. Normally I know I would start at the beginning and write about the trip in order. But there's one thing—well, one person—I can't seem to get out of my head. I mean, it's not really just a person. It's a person, and what he had to say about a horse, and then what happened . . . Basically, I'm talking about John Brightstar. He's the son of the Bar None's new head wrangler. At first I wasn't sure what to think about him. I mean, after the things he said to Kate about that stallion . . . Well, I guess I really am getting ahead of myself here. But I'm just trying to say that John is confusing. Unusual. And I'm still not sure what to think of him, even after everything that happened, although I definitely wasn't lying when I told my friends I thought he was nice . . .

Oh dear. I'm not making much sense, am I? Maybe I should get to that homework after all. In fact, thinking about John reminded me of the white stallion he told us about, which gives me an idea for my poetry assignment. I'll have to write about the trip later when my head is clearer.

Moon Stallion
a haiku by Lisa Atwood

Gleaming 'neath the moon
White horse rearing to the sky
Free, forever free.

Dear Diary,

Okay, I've been home from the trip out West for a few days now, and I think I'm finally ready to write about it. I have some time before dinner, so I thought I'd at least get started now.

This time I'm going to do the sensible thing and begin at the beginning. That would be our flight cross-country with Colonel Devine. We spent most of the flight talking about the party, going over the plans we'd already made and coming up with more. Stevie was really excited about her horror house idea—she had all sorts of tricks up her sleeves for gross things to scare the kids with, like cold pasta that would feel like brains in the dark, peeled grapes that would feel like eyeballs, stuff like that.

Kate was waiting to pick us up at the airfield as promised, and we spent a few minutes greeting, hugging, and telling each other how wonderful we all looked. It was true, too—Kate looked great. Her reddish brown hair was a little longer than it was the last time we saw her, but otherwise she looked just the same as always, right down to her dusty cowboy boots and wide smile. After a few minutes, though, I guess we remembered how much work was waiting for us. We all piled into the truck, and before long we were back at the ranch. Stevie immediately began bombarding Mrs. Devine with her ideas, and Mrs. Devine totally loved it. Soon they were both sitting at the Bar None's big kitchen table, making notes and planning away.

I was watching them, smiling at Stevie's boundless enthusiasm, when I heard a thump behind me. "Where do these go?" asked a voice I'd never heard before.

I turned to see who it was. Standing there, our suitcases on the floor beside him, was a boy a little older than me. He had dark hair that kind of fell over his forehead, and really dark, intense-looking eyes.

"This is John Brightstar," Kate told us, waving a hand at the boy. "His father, Walter, is our new head wrangler." She turned to John. "Thanks for bringing the bags in from the truck, John. These guys will be staying in Bunkhouse One. Would you mind taking their stuff over there?"

"I'll help if you want," I offered quickly, stepping forward. I figured Stevie was already so lost in her plotting that she wouldn't miss me. And I was equally sure Carole was going to drag Kate off and question her about her secret the first chance she got. That meant I had a little time on my hands—why not try to make myself useful?

John nodded. "Thanks." He didn't say anything else, but he waited as I came over and hoisted my suitcase in one hand and my duffel in the other. I felt a little embarrassed about having so much luggage for such a short trip—that's Mom for you. She wants me to be prepared for anything when I travel. It's easier just to let her pack what she wants than to try to explain that there's no way I'll ever need a long skirt and a pair of velvet flats at a dude ranch!

Anyway, I soon realized that John wouldn't have any idea how many of the bags were mine. That made me feel a little better. But I still wasn't sure quite what to say to him as we left the main building and headed across the dusty yard toward the row of bunkhouses. I pretended to be very busy looking around, and there really was a lot to look at—the big familiar barn, the corral with a herd of horses grazing near the fence, and of course the gorgeous Rocky Mountains circling the ranch on the horizon. Finally, though, as we approached Bunkhouse One, the silence started to get to me. That was probably my mother rubbing off on me. She thinks silence is impolite. As she would say, "Nice young ladies should be able to make courteous conversation with anyone, at any time."

I glanced over at John. "Um, how do you like living here at the Bar None?"

"It's nice," John replied. "The Devines are nice people."

I nodded. "They sure are." It wasn't much of a conversation, but for some reason I couldn't seem to think of anything more interesting to say. Anyway, we had reached the bunkhouse's small front porch by that time. "Um, you can just leave the bags here. I'll take them inside."

"That's okay." John stepped onto the porch and opened the front door. He glanced at me with a slight smile. "I've been here long enough to know that you dudes aren't used to hard work like carrying your own luggage."

I could tell he was kidding, so I grinned. "Thanks," I joked back, following him inside the cozy, welcoming bunkhouse and tossing my duffel bag onto the nearest bed. "While you're at it, could you fluff my pillow for me, too?"

John chuckled. Then suddenly he stopped and tilted his head to one side, listening. "That sounds like Dad calling," he said abruptly. "I'd better go. See you."

Without another word, he disappeared through the door. I was kind of disappointed—it was too bad he'd had to go just when we were really starting to communicate. But then I shrugged and snapped open my suitcase, digging around for my riding clothes, which Mom had buried under a pile of button-down shirts and two pairs of pantyhose. I had plenty of other things to think about.

A few minutes later Kate, Carole, Stevie, and I were at the barn, getting ready to go for a ride. We had our favorite horses already picked out from our previous trips, and Kate had alerted Walter to have them ready for us.

I was really happy to see my horse, Chocolate. She's a sweet, gentle bay mare who's really easy and fun to ride. Carole, as usual, was riding a strawberry roan named Berry. And Stevie was paired up with Stewball,

56

a mischievous skewbald with a personality that almost matches Stevie's.

As I took hold of Chocolate's halter, John Brightstar appeared at my side. "Do you want me to bring you your saddle?" he offered.

I smiled. "Thanks. That would be great." Western saddles are heavy and hard to handle, so I was grateful for the help—until John showed up carrying a tiny pony saddle!

Kate giggled. "Uh, John," she said.

I had spotted the twinkle in his dark eyes. "I just thought these fancy English-rider types might prefer a little saddle to a real one," he explained, straight-faced.

Stevie burst out laughing. She's usually the first one to appreciate any kind of joke. I smiled, too. I could already tell John was a nice guy. "Thanks," I told him. "I think we can handle the real thing."

Just then John's father, Walter, bustled into the ring. He spotted the pony saddle immediately. "John!" he barked. "What's going on?"

Kate answered for him. "We were just joking around, Walter," she said calmly. "John's helping my friends saddle up."

"It doesn't look like he's being much help," Walter said sternly.

I was a little surprised by his tone. I thought he was being kind of hard on his son. We really weren't in a big hurry, and John had only been kidding around.

I shot John a sympathetic look. He wasn't looking

at me, though—he was staring sheepishly at his father. He didn't say another word as he helped his dad saddle up our horses and Kate's Appaloosa, Spot.

Once I was in the deep, comfortable Western saddle, riding out of the corral with my friends, I quickly forgot about John and Walter Brightstar. I love riding in any form, and I especially love the kind of riding we do at Pine Hollow. But riding at the Bar None is special, too. We weren't riding through fields and hilly woods. Instead, we were riding through the desert on dusty trails, passing tall cacti and scrubby bushes, with the imposing Rockies always in view in the distance. It was so open and wild and unique—it almost felt as though we'd been dropped into an old Western movie, with cowboys and stagecoaches and all the rest of it.

I was thinking about that when I realized Kate was talking about her secret. She'd already told us that she planned to adopt a beautiful white (well, actually a very light gray) wild stallion she'd seen running free nearby. The Bureau of Land Management runs a program that allows people to do that, and their next adoption was coming up in a week. Kate was really excited, though she was a little worried that someone else would get the horse she wanted before she did. He sounded like a special horse—Kate's eyes positively glowed every time she talked about him.

"So when can we see your stallion?" Stevie asked as we rode along the edge of a small canyon.

"The herd has been collecting by the rise across the

58

creek every afternoon recently," Kate replied. "We should find them there about now."

It took a while to get to the spot Kate meant. But finally we reached a small green valley where Two Mile Creek ran, and we found that she had been right. The herd was there.

I couldn't take my eyes off them. It was amazing. I'd seen hundreds, maybe even thousands of horses in my life. But I'd never set eyes on one that didn't belong to someone, didn't live in a stable or a field, didn't wear horseshoes and halters. These horses were different—they didn't belong to anyone but themselves. They were completely wild, completely free, wandering wherever they pleased and eating whatever they could find. It took my breath away.

"They're beautiful," Stevie whispered, sounding as awed as I felt.

"Where's the gray?" Carole asked Kate softly.

"Watch," Kate said.

The wind shifted and carried our scent toward the herd. Some of the mares lifted their heads and sniffed. And then a pure white head rose, sniffed, and looked. The horse's ears twitched like antennae, reaching to pick up any sound. We were silent, but the horse found us anyway. The stallion called the alert to his herd, and as if by magic, they sprang into motion, galloping off with a thunder of hoofbeats, the magnificent stallion urging them along.

Moments later, all that was left to mark their presence was the cloud of dust they'd raised. "Oh," I said breathlessly, still hardly believing what I'd just seen.

Stevie nodded wisely. "Just what I was going to say."

Soon we began the long ride back to the Bar None. I pulled Chocolate up alongside Spot on the trail. "You've just got to have him," I told Kate, the image of the white stallion still dancing in my mind. "He's so beautiful . . ."

"Did you notice the nick in his ear?" Kate asked. "It's very distinctive. It's like the imperfection that makes him absolutely perfect."

At first I wasn't sure that made much sense. But as I thought about the horse, I saw what she meant. Part of what made the stallion so beautiful was his wildness, and the scar was a symbol of that. It always would be, even after Kate adopted and trained him.

Carole and Stevie joined in the conversation as we rode along. "Will you train him yourself?" Carole asked Kate. "Do you know how to do it?"

"Training a wild horse has got to be different from training a domestic one," Stevie pointed out. "I mean, that stallion has never stood still for a human in his life. It's hard to imagine that he ever will."

"Walter said he'd help me," Kate said. "He's had lots of experience with wild horses."

Her mention of Walter reminded me of what happened with the pony saddle a little earlier. I guess my friends were thinking the same thing, because Stevie asked Kate if Walter was always that serious. "He came down pretty hard on John," she added.

Kate nodded. "I think Walter feels he has to prove himself. See, he's got some kind of odd reputation. There's something mysterious about his past. Neither John nor Walter will talk about it, but it has something to do with John's mother. She's dead, I think. I overheard some parents talking about it at school, but as soon as they saw me, they stopped talking."

"Too bad," Stevie commented. Eavesdropping on other peoples' interesting conversations is one of her favorite activities.

"It doesn't matter," Kate said. "It's all just gossip. Walter is a hard worker, and John works even harder. Sometimes I feel sorry for them because they work so hard and nothing ever seems to get better. Walter is always grim and determined. John? Well, he's nice and helpful, but he's hard to get to know."

"He seems lonely," I commented, thinking of those deep, dark eyes. I guessed that his jokes were his way of trying to be friendly.

After that we changed the subject to dinner (which we were definitely ready for by then) and the party. I didn't think much about John again until after dinner that evening. We were playing Pictionary with some of the other guests in the ranch house when I noticed my watch wasn't on my wrist. I remembered that I had taken it off after our ride when I was giving Chocolate a bath.

While the others were arguing good-naturedly about something or other, I slipped out of the room and headed to the kitchen to grab a flashlight and a jacket. It got awfully cool out there in the desert at night.

I didn't even need the flashlight as I walked to the barn. The sky was clear, and the moon and stars provided plenty of soft, silvery light. The barn was another story. It was pitch black, and I didn't remember where the light switches were, so I flipped on the flashlight. It cast weird shadows all around me, making the familiar barn seem strange and almost frightening. I shivered slightly, telling myself that I was getting spooked because it was almost Halloween. The sudden stomp of a horse's foot on the wooden floor made me jump, but when it was followed by a whinny, I relaxed. The sound was so familiar that it was comforting.

"There, there, girl," came a human voice.

That startled me even more than the stomp. I'd thought I was alone in the barn.

"Who's there?" the voice called softly.

"It's me," I called back automatically. Then, realizing that wasn't much help, I added, "Lisa Atwood. Who are you? Where are you?"

"It's John. I'm with the mare over here."

I followed the sound of his voice to a big box stall at the end of the barn. When I got closer, I noticed the warm glow of a portable lantern. John was sitting on a stool inside the stall. A mare, almost ready to foal, stood nearby.

"She seemed restless," John explained softly when he saw me. "I don't think she's ready yet, but she calmed down when I came in. I figured she just wanted company." He patted the mare on the forehead. "What are you doing out here?"

"I think I left my watch out here this afternoon," I said.

"Gold watch, white face, black leather band?"

"Yes."

"Haven't seen it."

I couldn't help laughing. John really had a great sense of humor. He grinned, then fished my watch out of his pocket. "Thanks," I said, slipping it on.

John stood up then and stepped out of the stall. He closed the door softly behind him so as not to disturb the mare, who seemed to be asleep. As I glanced up at him, I found myself suddenly very aware of him. Of how close he was. How tall he was. Of the way his eyes seemed to see everything.

I shivered again. Not wanting John to guess what I was really thinking, I quickly commented, "It's a little spooky out here in the dark."

"Don't worry," John teased. "I'll fend off any bats or gremlins who try to attack you or drink your blood."

"What a relief you're here," I teased back.

"I'll also walk you back to the main house," he offered. I was surprised to find that it was exactly what I'd been hoping he'd say.

As we left the barn, John asked about our ride that afternoon.

"We went out and found the herd of wild horses," I told him. "You know, the ones that are going to be put up for adoption. Kate has her heart set on the stallion. What a beauty he is—pure white, with a nick in his ear."

"No," John said abruptly.

I glanced at him, surprised. "Sure. It's his right ear."

"No," he repeated. "She can't."

I was startled by the sharpness of his voice. Suddenly the gentle, caring guy I'd seen in the mare's stall had disappeared. I could feel his tenseness—or was it anger? He halted and faced me squarely, and as I met his grim look, for a second I almost felt afraid.

"What's the matter?" I asked.

"The stallion. She can't have him. You can't let her do it."

"Why not?" Then I had an idea. I wondered if John wanted the stallion for himself. But when I suggested that, he just shook his head.

"I don't want the stallion," he said. "And Kate can't have him, either. Don't you see? He's where he belongs. It's where he's got to stay."

I replayed the scene from that afternoon in my mind. I remembered how the stallion had looked standing in the middle of his herd, king of all he surveyed, untamed, unowned. But then I remembered what Kate had told us earlier—that it was necessary to thin out the herds once in a while so that they wouldn't become too large for the land to support them.

"I know why they put horses up for adoption," John said, as if reading my mind. "It's a great program and it's well done. The problem isn't that, it's the stallion with the nick in his ear. Kate can't have him. Nobody can. Don't let her do it."

Without another word, he spun on his heel and disappeared into the darkness. I turned and hurried toward the house, my mind spinning. What had that been all about? And while I was at it, what was John Brightstar all about? I just couldn't figure out what to think of him.

Later that night, Christine Lonetree—Kate's neighbor and another out-of-town member of The Saddle Club—joined the rest of us in the bunkhouse for a Saddle Club meeting. We talked about all sorts of things, including a special dollhouse Christine's mother had made. Mrs. Lonetree is an artist as well as a high-school history teacher, and the dollhouse sounded incredible. It was a miniature adobe home with traditional Native American furnishings and decorations. She was donating it to us to use as a prize at the Halloween Fair. We were sure it would be a big hit.

We discussed details of the party plans for a while before Stevie suggested some ghost stories. We turned off all the lights, lit a candle, and the spookfest began.

Stevie was just finishing one of her usual creepy, complicated tales when a sudden gust of wind blew through the cabin, extinguishing the candle. I screamed—I couldn't help it. I'd been completely caught up in Stevie's story. I screamed again when I heard footsteps stomping across the bunkhouse porch. I think Carole screamed, too, or maybe it was Kate. Anyway, a moment later the ceiling light flipped on.

"Are you okay?" John Brightstar asked, squinting at us with concern.

Stevie, Kate, and Carole started to giggle. But I felt a little embarrassed. "We're fine," I said quickly. "We were telling ghost stories. Stevie's very good at it, and she managed to scare me. Then when the candle went out, well, it just startled me."

Suddenly it occurred to me to wonder what John was doing there, anyway. Before I could ask him, he spoke again.

"Ghost stories?" he said eagerly. "Great. I have a story I want to tell you."

He began to speak. And I don't think I'll ever forget a word of the story he told. I'm going to try to write it down now, without interruptions, just the way he told it to us that night.

The Legend of the White Stallion

Many years ago, so many my grandfather does not remember it, there were two tribes who lived and battled one another in these lands. They had warred for so long that nobody could remember when they had not warred. Neither could anyone remember why they warred. So deep were their hatred and fear that it was forbidden for members of one tribe to speak to members of the other.

One year, on the night of the first full moon after the harvest, a baby was born in each of these tribes. In the tribe to the north it was a girl, daughter of the chief. He named her Moon Glow for the first natural beauty he saw after gazing at her face for the first time. In the tribe to the south it was a male child, son of a mighty warrior. His father named him White Eagle, after the great bird which had soared majestically above his home at the moment of his son's birth.

When Moon Glow was fifteen, she was betrothed to her father's bravest warrior. As a wedding gift, she chose to make him a cloak of pure white leather, embroidered with eagle feathers in the image of a bison—his totem. She traveled from her village to find the most perfect feathers for the cloak.

At that time, White Eagle was being prepared for the rigors of war. His elders had sent him out in the mountains with only his clothes, his knife, and a flint to make fire. He had to live alone and survive for half the life of the moon—two weeks—with only those tools. He could not see anybody or talk to anybody until he had completed his test. While others before him had died alone and in shame, White Eagle was determined to survive. In the wilderness he had made the weapons of survival—a bow and many arrows, even a spear. He had eaten well, he had slept warmly. He was sure he would survive his test.

White Eagle had been in the mountains for ten days. His only companion was a white stallion who roamed the mountains near his camp.

The horse ran whenever White Eagle tried to touch him or capture him, but he seemed to like being near White Eagle. The boy knew that the horse was wild, now and forever, and somehow the horse's very wildness was a comfort to him.

One day Moon Glow walked in the mountains alone, hunting for an eagle from which she could pluck feathers for the cloak. She did not see the mountain lion that stalked her, nor did she hear him. But the mountain lion saw her. Without warning he attacked, howling and shrieking in victory as he landed on her back. Moon Glow screamed, knowing it would do no good and hearing in response only the slow, sad echo of her own voice.

White Eagle heard the cry of the mountain lion and leaped up from his fire. Then he heard the cry of Moon Glow and he ran. He was only vaguely aware of the presence of the white stallion—a shadow at his side in his flight toward destiny.

When he found Moon Glow and the mountain lion, the girl was struggling bravely against the overpowering force of the wild creature. Without hesitation, White Eagle drew an arrow from his quiver, slipped it into his bow, pulled it back, and let it fly. But he had drawn too quickly. The first arrow sped right past the lion and the girl and struck the ear of the white horse, who watched from beyond. The horse flinched momentarily but stood his ground bravely as the arrow passed right through his ear and landed harmlessly beyond him. Then White Eagle shot again, taking more careful aim. His arrow met its target. The mountain lion fell limp and dead. White Eagle ran to Moon Glow and took her up in his arms. She was almost unconscious and bleeding badly. White Eagle knew she was near death.

All thoughts of himself fled from his mind. He knew only that he must save this woman and the only way he could do so would be to return her to her people. He did not think of the consequences; he thought only of the woman who needed him. He began the long walk to the north, carrying the chieftain's dying daughter in his arms.

As he walked, White Eagle became aware that the wild white stallion walked with him. It surprised him because it was White Eagle's arrow that had wounded the stallion, but the ear showed no blood—just a nick that looked like an old wound, long healed. The stallion matched the boy step for step, never straying more than a few feet. And when a rock in the mountain caused White Eagle to stumble, the horse was there for him to lean on. It was the first time White Eagle had ever touched the horse. He was certain the

69

horse would flee from his touch, but the stallion did not. The horse waited. Then White Eagle understood. The horse was offering to carry them to the north.

White Eagle lifted himself and Moon Glow onto the stallion's back. He cradled her in his arms as the sleek stallion made the journey.

It was an arduous trip, for Moon Glow had traveled far to search for feathers. When they arrived at her village, the chief took his daughter but would not speak to White Eagle. The chief recognized him immediately as a son of the people of the south. White Eagle knew that his thanks was his life. He returned to the mountains.

Time passed. Moon Glow healed and White Eagle survived the rest of his test. But neither could forget the other.

Then, one day, the stallion mysteriously appeared at White Eagle's village and seemed to invite White Eagle to ride him. White Eagle climbed onto the horse's sleek back. The stallion took off immediately. Soon White Eagle found himself in the mountains once again. This time he was not alone. Moon Glow was waiting there for him. She was well and beautiful. At the moment they saw one another, they knew they would love each other for eternity and that the stallion understood their love and had brought them together.

Many times after that, the stallion carried the two lovers to one another. Moon Glow delayed her marriage by insisting that she finish the cloak she was making for her future husband. She sewed the feathers on the soft, white leather, but try as she did to make it the pattern of a bison, it was an eagle, soaring grace-fully. Though she knew she was being disloyal to her father and to her tribe, Moon Glow loved the design she had crafted, as she loved the man it stood for. She would present the cloak to White Eagle, rather than to her promised husband.

Finally the day came that Moon Glow and White Eagle had always dreaded. On the day that Moon Glow planned to give the finished cloak to White Eagle, Moon Glow's betrothed trailed the white horse to the mountains. When he found the lovers together, the warrior was angry and jealous. Hatred for this enemy of his people filled his heart. Vowing that the pair would be punished, he seized them both, bound their hands, and made them walk back to the village in shame. There was no sign of the white stallion as they walked. There would be no rescue this time.

The chief was shocked to learn of his daughter's treason. He immediately condemned White Eagle to death and offered his daughter to any of his braves who would still have her.

All hope was lost for the lovers. There was no escape for either, and to both death seemed preferable to separation. At the moment of White Eagle's execution, Moon Glow swallowed some poison. She lived long enough to watch the flames consume her beloved White Eagle and the flowing white cloak he wore to his death. As the smoke drifted up to the pale blue sky, she saw the distinct outline of a soaring eagle take flight. She gasped—whether in pain or surprise, nobody knows.

Then, at that moment, there was a thunder of hoof-beats. A pure white stallion came galloping through the village. He paused at the weak and dying Moon Glow. With her last ounce of energy, she reached upward, clutched the stallion's mane, and was swept up off the ground. Magically the horse rose in the air and flew skyward. Then, as the tribe watched, there appeared behind her on the horse the pure white leather cloak she had so painstakingly made. On it was the perfect image of an eagle.

They say the horse still roams the wilderness, riderless, on an endless quest to help others whose love transcends hatred and bigotry. He carries the nick in his ear as a reminder of White Eagle's sacrifice, for the moment the brave performed the selfless act of saving Moon Glow, his fate was sealed. Our people call the horse after him—White Eagle.

It was an incredible story. I thought it was so sad that the lovers were separated for such a stupid reason. But they still stayed true to each other. . . . I guess it just goes to show that when love is true, it will live on, no matter how far apart the people are. It's sort of like how we (my parents and I, I mean) still love Peter just as much even though he's so far away. Speaking of Peter, I'm beginning to wonder if he's ever going to write back. Maybe my letter got lost in the mail or something, or maybe he's so busy with his studies and his newspaper reporting and the rest of it that he doesn't have time to write. I guess I could understand that. But it would be nice to hear from him . . .

Anyway, as I was saying, John's tale was quite a story. After he'd finished, he left the bunkhouse as quickly as he'd come, and we were left talking about it. Stevie and Carole thought the tale was very romantic, and Christine said her mother had told her a similar story once, though she hadn't told it as well as John had.

"He *is* good," Stevie agreed. "I mean, his story made me shiver, though not in the way my story scared you guys, right?"

"His wasn't supposed to be a scary story," Carole said.

"Oh, yes it was," I said. "It was meant to scare Kate from adopting the stallion."

"I know. And it's not fair," Kate added.

We talked about it some more, trying to figure out what John was really up to and why he'd come to tell us that story. Whatever he'd meant it to do, in the end, I think his tale just made Kate more determined than ever to adopt the stallion. After all, the story was just a story.

It took me a while to fall asleep that night. My mind was full of John, the stallion, and all sorts of other things. But the next day I didn't have much time to think about any of it. There was too much to do to get ready for the Halloween Fair. Stevie kept us all busy— hanging decorations, peeling grapes, and so forth.

That evening we saddled up our horses for a moonlight ride over to Christine's house. Her mother was going to help us put the finishing touches on our three blind mice costumes. She was even going to come up with a costume for Kate as the farmer's wife!

It was during the ride that it happened. It started with a howl: *How-ooooooo!* I had never heard the sound before, but I knew immediately what it had to be. A coyote. It was a spooky sound, dangerous and lonely in the clear, cool night. I found myself shivering as it came again. *How-ooooooo!*

"Let's go," Christine said. Coyotes don't usually attack humans, but they are dangerous animals, and it made sense for us to hurry on our way in case there were more of them about.

"No, wait." Kate was staring off to one side. "Look!"

We all turned and saw what she had seen. Some distance away, a cloud of dust rose from the dry earth. "It's the herd," Carole said. "They must have been startled by the coyote. Look at them!"

We hadn't even noticed the horses until they started moving, though they weren't all that far away. But now we couldn't miss them. The mares and foals were milling frantically, letting out frightened whinnies and snorts.

"We've got to help them!" Carole said.

"By doing what?" Christine shook her head. "What's going on here is what's been going on for thousands of years. There's nothing for us to do."

74

I could tell Carole wasn't happy about that. But a moment later, just as the moon slipped behind some clouds and the unseen coyote let out another long howl, the horses suddenly stopped their panicky movements. After a moment, the stallion emerged from the center of the pack, his gleaming, silvery coat shining in the dim light from the stars.

I squinted at him. There was something about him—something odd about his shape. "Did you see that?" I whispered to the others. I couldn't believe what my own eyes were telling me, and I wanted someone else to confirm it.

"What?" Stevie asked as the stallion led his herd behind a rock outcropping. Within seconds, the horses had disappeared from our sight.

"It was a rider," Kate said breathlessly.

I nodded, glad that she'd seen it, too. "Pure silvery white, just like the horse."

"And just like White Eagle," Christine added.

Stevie looked at us skeptically. "Come on, you guys," she said. "It's just John, playing another joke on us."

I wasn't too sure about that. But there didn't seem to be any way for us to know the truth for sure one way or the—

Oops, I just realized Mom's calling me from downstairs. I guess I'd better sign off for now—she probably wants me to set the table for dinner. I'll have to finish this later!

LOCAL HALLOWEEN FUND-RAISER A SPOOKY SUCCESS

HALLOWEEN, TWO MILE CREEK. All Hallows' Eve is a time for ghosts and goblins and ghouls, for spooky sounds and horrifying howls, for vampire bats and black cats, for . . . pony rides?

That's right, pony rides were an important part of the Halloween spirit this year, as any of the hundreds of youngsters who enjoyed the Halloween Fair at Two Mile Creek High School could tell you. The fair, headed by local ranch owner Phyllis Devine, was planned as a fund-raiser to help sponsor an after-school youth program. Held last Saturday afternoon and evening, it featured a pumpkin-carving table, a candy corn counting contest, a haunted house, and numerous other activities along with the aforementioned pony rides. In the end, the event raised plenty of money for its cause and provided lots of fun for its young attendees.

We can only hope that Mrs. Devine and her gang of ghoulish helpers will be back for more spooky fun next Halloween!

Dear Diary,

When I reread the article I just pasted in, which Kate sent us from her local newspaper, I realized what my writing teacher, Ms. Shields, means when she says you can say a lot with a few words or a little with a lot of words. The article has quite a few words, but it

76

doesn't even scratch the surface of what really happened at the fair. That's why I've decided to write my own "newspaper article" that tells the whole story. (I'm sure Peter would be impressed after all his newspaper reporting this summer!)

PHONE FAILS; SPOOKY STALLION SAVES STEVIE

HALLOWEEN, BAR NONE RANCH. Little did Stevie Lake know what a long, strange ride she would have last Halloween night!

Miss Lake was one of the co-planners of the fabulously successful Halloween Fund-raising Fair at Two Mile Creek High School. As such, she was responsible for arranging transportation for the amazing door prize, a beautiful handmade adobe dollhouse. Miss Lake, a resident of Willow Creek, Virginia, is a very intelligent young lady with many fine personal qualities. However, in this instance her memory failed her and she was left at the eleventh hour with the prized dollhouse several miles across the desert from where it was supposed to be. She had to find a way to move it from its creator's home to the high school—pronto.

Miss Lake first attempted to telephone the house in question, but she quickly deduced that the local phone service had been disrupted and was out of service. Not wanting to waste any more time, Miss Lake hurried outside, mounted her trusty steed, Stewball, and prepared to ride to the rescue. She alerted her friend, Miss Christine Lonetree, of her intentions. Miss Lonetree loaned Miss Lake the white cloak from her costume as protection against the chilly desert evening, and Miss Lake set off.

Among Miss Lake's other fine qualities is a vivid and sometimes overactive imagination. As she rode across the moonlit desert, she found her mind overrun with thoughts of all the spooky ghoulies that were supposed to roam on Halloween night.

Then, breaking into her thoughts of imaginary dangers, a real threat appeared. A coyote howled nearby. Miss Lake's horse, spooked by the sound, took off. Unfortu- nately, Miss Lake was left behind, flat on her—well—behind.

Obviously, the situation was already rather grim for poor Miss Lake. She was stranded, on foot, all alone at night, miles from where she was supposed to be.

Then things got worse. Somewhere nearby— way too close, in fact— Miss Lake heard a familiar, menacing sound. The sound of a rattlesnake.

She froze immediately, aware that the slightest movement could attract the deadly snake's attention. She tried to determine where the sound was coming from, but the night was dark and the surrounding rocks threw too many echoes. Before long it seemed as if a whole pack of monster snakes surrounded her, and Miss Lake understandably began to panic. She screamed in terror, loud and long.

Then another sound broke through the echoes of her screams. The sound of hoofbeats. Miss Lake felt a flicker of hope. Had her horse returned for her?

But it wasn't her faithful skewbald coming toward her. It was a stallion—a silvery white stallion with a nick in his ear. There was a rider on his back, cloaked in white. A long, strong arm reached toward her, and in one smooth motion she was drawn up behind the rider. They raced across the desert, away from the snake, away from all danger.

Miss Lake clung to the rider with all her strength, not speaking a word. She was so grateful that she hardly knew how to thank her rescuer.

He never gave her a chance. After depositing her safely at her destination, the horse and rider whirled before she could speak and disappeared into the night. It was a Halloween Miss Lake would never forget.

Dear Diary,

Okay, I decided writing newspaper articles is harder than I thought. It was impossible to work in everything that happened that night and have it make sense in that "who, what, when, where, how" kind of way that reporters do. Because you see, so much of what happened didn't make sense in that factual way. I can't explain it. I can only write down what happened and hope that someday, somehow, I'll figure it out.

First of all, before I even get to the fair, I should mention what happened the night before when I was trying to get a rock out of Chocolate's foot. It was wedged in there pretty tightly, and I guess I looked like I was having trouble, because John came over to offer his help. I managed to get the stone out myself, but then we started talking. After a few lame comments about decorating for the fair, John reached over and took my hand. Yes, took my hand as if it were the most natural thing in the world.

"I want to show you something," he said. "Come with me."

I was feeling a little off balance, having my hand in his. John seemed to have that effect on me a lot. I sort of forgot about that, though, when I saw what he wanted to show me. It was the mare—the one he'd been with the night before. Standing at her side was a tiny, wobbly, adorable little foal!

"Oh, when was it born?" I asked breathlessly. The foal stared at us curiously with liquid brown eyes that seemed almost too large for its head.

"This afternoon," John replied. "Isn't she cute?"

She definitely was that. We chatted about the filly and her mother for a couple of minutes. John said the mare hadn't had any trouble delivering the foal, but he'd been there with her the whole time, just in case.

"How did you learn so much about horses and foaling?" I asked.

John hesitated for a minute. "My mother was a horse breeder," he said at last. "She taught me everything I know. It's part of the legacy she left me."

"Left you?" I repeated, not really understanding.

"She's dead," he said bluntly. From the way he said it—and the way a sort of curtain seemed to fall over his dark eyes, making them impossible to read—I knew I shouldn't ask any more questions about his mother. I felt a little hurt that he trusted me so little, but I didn't want him to see that. I decided it was time to change the subject.

"We saw the stallion again tonight," I told him.

"Still running free?" John asked.

"As you very well know," I replied with a bit of a smirk. After the incident with the coyotes, when Kate and Christine and I had been sure we'd seen a rider on the stallion, we'd talked it over and decided it had to have been John playing a trick on us. We already knew he had a sense of humor and liked to use it on us. And what other explanation was there?

I guess I'd sort of hoped to one-up John by showing that I knew about his trick. But he just looked puzzled at my comment. "Why should I know?" he asked. "I don't know when they round up the horses for adoption."

"Nice try," I said. "But we saw you. You were there

when the coyotes were calling." I told him how we'd seen a rider on the stallion's back.

John was silent for a moment. "You saw somebody," he said. "I believe you. But you didn't see me. I was here. I came home on the school bus, and I never left the mare's side. The filly was born at five o'clock this afternoon, and I stuck around to keep an eye on her."

That stopped me cold. I stared at the filly, knowing that he had to be telling the truth. I hadn't known John very long, but I felt certain of one thing. There was no way he would have abandoned the mare just to play a trick on us. No way at all.

That was weird enough. But when Stevie told us about what had happened to her out in the desert, it seemed even stranger. She'd assumed the rider who helped her escape from the snake was John, out playing pranks again. But John had been at the fair with us the whole time. So how do you explain that? I guess you don't, at least not in any way that makes sense.

Another thing that's still kind of hard to explain about that whole trip is John himself. I spent quite a bit of time talking with him as we all cleaned up after the fair. It was really nice—he's smarter and funnier than most guys I know, and there was something else. Something that happened while we were talking.

I don't quite remember how we got on the subject. We were just chatting about stupid things like costumes and crepe paper, and suddenly John was looking very serious and telling me the truth about his family.

82

"I had a sister," he said. "Her name was Gaylin. She was wonderful, always happy, always laughing. Then one day Gaylin got sick—very sick. My father had to drive her and my mother to the hospital. I came along, too. I sat in the front seat with Dad. Mother was in the back. Gaylin lay on the backseat with her head on Mother's lap. She was so sick she was sweating with her fever. Dad knew it was bad, and he drove as fast as he could. But it turned out to be too fast, because when a deer ran across the road, Dad tried to stop and swerved to avoid it. He missed the deer but ran the car right off the edge of the road and down a shallow ravine. He and I were okay. We'd had our seat belts on. But Mother and Gaylin weren't so lucky."

I gulped, suddenly understanding why he had looked so strange when he'd mentioned his mother the day before. Poor John!

He told me the rest of the story. Some people thought his father had been drinking before the accident, and there were lots of rumors. That was why Walter seemed so somber and serious all the time.

My mind wandered back to John's mother and sister. "You must miss them both."

"I do," John replied. "But in some ways I still have them, here in my heart. Every time I see a happy child, I feel I am with Gaylin again. And my mother? I remember her through the stories she used to tell us. She was the great-granddaughter of a chief, and it was her family's responsibility to carry the traditions to each succeeding generation."

"You mean like the story about the stallion?"

"It was her favorite. She swore it was true, too. She believed that no matter what else happened, there was always the stallion to help those who tried to do good things for our people. Sometimes I'm sure it was White Eagle who carried her and Gaylin out of the car . . ."

"How beautiful," I breathed, amazed by the thought.

Suddenly I noticed that John was looking at me deeply. There was no curtain blocking the emotion in his eyes now. I felt my heart start to pound as he moved a little closer.

"Got one!" Stevie shrieked at that moment, totally interrupting the moment as she rushed over to blab at us about the candy corn counting contest. I was more than a little annoyed with her, even though I knew she had no idea what was going on between John and me. Still, the moment was ruined . . . but only for that particular moment.

You see, we made up for it later. It was in the barn, just before I left to come back home. As my friends were doing some last-minute packing (well, actually, just Carole was packing. Stevie was frantically scribbling some notes for the essay she was supposed to write during the trip, which of course she hadn't even started yet), I went to say good-bye to the new little filly. I was hoping a certain wrangler's son would be around for good-byes, too—I hadn't seen much of him since Stevie's interruption.

I wasn't disappointed. John was leaning on the stall door when I arrived. He looked happy to see me. Nobody else was around—it was just us and the horses. We chatted a little bit about this and that, and then he reached out to take both my hands in his.

I looked down at our clasped hands, suddenly feeling strangely shy. It wasn't that I'd never been close to a boy before, but John was . . . well, he was different from most boys.

"I wish you didn't have to leave so soon, Lisa," he said.

I looked up at him then. His gorgeous dark eyes were so close. "Me too," I managed to squeak out. His face came closer, and closer . . .

As soon as our lips touched, I wasn't nervous at all anymore. It just felt natural. Really nice, actually. Am I blushing? Well, I don't care. It's not like anyone is ever going to read this except me.

Anyway, that was our good-bye. It was a wonderfully perfect end to a fun, exciting, action-packed, sometimes confusing, always interesting trip.

Dear Diary,

I'm pasting in a letter we all got from Kate today. Actually, she sent it to Carole. But it was meant for all three of us, and Carole said I could keep it if I want. Here it is:

Dear Carole, Lisa, and Stevie,

You're hearing from the proud adoptive parent of a beautiful wild horse. She's a mare—mostly quarter horse, I think, and she's got a foal, too! They're both sorrel. I've named the mare Moonglow. She's so beautiful! I can't wait to show her to you girls. You've got to come back and meet her. Walter says we should start gentling her—that means getting her used to a halter and a lead rope—within a week or so. After that, we begin the real training. She's got wonderful lines. I know she's going to be a fine riding horse for me someday, and her foal is a beauty, too.

I suppose you want to know about the stallion, and, frankly, so do I. I can tell you what happened, but I certainly can't explain it.

Dad and I went to the adoption, looking for the stallion. We'd even spoken to the man in charge of it to warn him that was the horse we wanted. He said he didn't know the horse we meant, but since we'd had our application in for so long, we should have a good selection, as long as we got there early.

It was the stallion's herd all right. I recognized some of the mares. You would have, too. But there was no sign of the stallion. There was a stallion with the herd, but he wasn't silvery, and he didn't have a nick in his ear. In fact, he was a kind of ugly skewbald pinto.

Dad and I asked all the Bureau of Land Management people about the silvery stallion with the nick in his ear. Every single

86

one of them said they'd never seen such a horse with this herd. Never even seen a horse like that around here. So, what do you think?

Your friend,
Kate

Dear Diary,

As I was turning in a history essay today in school, for some reason it made me think of that report Stevie promised to do for her headmistress during our trip to the Bar None the week before last. I realized I'd never asked her if she finished it or what Miss Fenton thought. When I mentioned it at Pine Hollow today, it turned out she'd just gotten it back. It was crumpled up in her backpack, but she took it out and showed it to me. When I asked if I could have it to paste in here, she said I could. Actually, what she said was something like, "Be my guest. I certainly don't ever want to see it again." I guess that's because Miss Fenton gave her a stern lecture about thoroughness or something when she handed it back (and she didn't even know that Stevie wrote most of it at the breakfast table the morning it was due!). After reading it myself, I could sort of see Miss Fenton's point. Not that I would ever tell Stevie that, of course!

THE VALUE OF COMMUNITY SERVICE
by Stevie Lake

Community service means doing good things for other people, whether you know them or not. That's what my trip to the Bar None Ranch was all about. I was busy, busy, busy for the whole trip making other people's lives happier and more fulfilled and even more educated, too. It was very gratifying for me to help so many, many, many people so very, very, very much. I didn't even mind sacrificing my own time to help others, even though it meant I didn't have much time to work on this essay. I had to make a decision—help others by concentrating on the Halloween Fair that would benefit a whole community, or help myself by selfishly spending valuable time working only for my own purposes and grades?

It wasn't an easy decision, but I think it was the right one. I chose to devote myself to others, and that's why this essay is shorter than it was supposed to be. That in itself makes an important point about the value of community service, don't you think?

Thornbury Hall
London, England

Dear Lisa,

It was great to find your letter waiting for me when I got back
to my dorm after the summer! Thanks for writing back. It's been
a long time since we've seen each other, and it was terrific to
hear your voice again (well, you know what I mean . . .). I'm
sorry it's taken me so long to reply. I never realized how busy my
last year of college would be—it's nothing like my senior year of
high school, when there seemed to be plenty of time for hanging out and doing nothing!

Anyway, how is your new school year going? Actually I guess
it's not so new anymore—by the time you get this it will probably be almost Thanksgiving. I wish I could come home for the
holiday this year, but as you know the Brits don't celebrate it, so
I don't have any time off. Maybe I can get Mom to FedEx me
some turkey and stuffing. (On second thought, I'd better not
mention it to her, even in jest. Knowing her, she'd actually do it!)

It was nice to hear that you were having an interesting summer, riding a lot and hanging out with your friends Steffie and
Carol. I hope I get to meet them sometime—they sound like
nice girls. By the way, how is Francine Potts doing? Do you still
see much of her?

In any case, that business you wrote about—I think you called
it the Mystery of the Missing Pin—gave me a terrific idea. I
might have written last time about how I was doing some newspaper reporting this summer, right? Well, after a couple of

months on the job, I decided that journalism probably isn't for me. I liked the writing part well enough, and the traveling was fun, too. But I just couldn't get comfortable with interviewing strangers all the time, asking them all sorts of personal questions. I don't think I have the personality for it, you know?

So ever since I got back to school, I've been trying to figure out what else I could do for a living once I graduate. Mom and Dad (well, mostly Mom) are already on my case about starting to look for a "real" job. I guess they didn't like my idea of working part-time as a waiter or something and writing at night. I had to promise to send out a few resumes just to get them off my case.

But now I think I have a better answer. I've sort of been thinking about trying my hand at screenwriting—you know, writing scripts for movies. And I know movies for kids your age are a big thing right now, and when I got your letter and realized how interesting your life is, I got inspired. So now I'm hoping you'll agree to write back whenever you can and fill me in on more of what you and your friends do. That way I should have enough straight-from-the-horse's-mouth (ha ha) info on people your age to come up with a really great script. And if I finish by the end of the school year, maybe our parents will actually believe I can make a living by writing and they won't tie me up and shove me, kicking and screaming, behind a computer in some insurance or accounting office somewhere!

What do you think? Write back soon and tell me!

Love,
Peter

Dear Diary,

Well, I'm glad Peter finally wrote back. I was beginning to think he'd forgotten all about me. I'm also glad he seems to have gotten the hint that I'm not an infant—this letter actually sounded more like an ordinary one between two mature people. Of course, it was still a little weird realizing how out of touch we've actually been lately. I'm sure I must have mentioned Stevie and Carole at least a million times in notes and phone calls (not to mention in my last letter), but he still got both their names wrong. Hasn't he been paying attention? I guess not, or he'd know that Francine Potts moved away three years ago—not that I cared much, since we haven't been good friends since second grade!

Still, I guess it takes two to lose touch, right? Maybe I haven't been communicating that well with him, and that's why he doesn't seem to know what my life is really like these days. Ms. Shields says it's important to be clear when you're trying to convey information in your writing. She had us do an exercise in technical writing the other day, where we weren't allowed to include any judgments or emotions, but simply reported the facts.

I don't know if this is the same kind of thing, though. I mean, shouldn't Peter and I be better at communicating with each other? After all, we're brother and sister. If we can't understand each other, who can?

But his idea about becoming a screenwriter is exciting. It would be cool to have a big brother who's some kind of Hollywood mogul. Maybe he could fly me and my friends out to the West Coast to "do lunch." Just about the only thing cooler than that would be to see The Saddle Club immortalized on the silver screen. I can't wait to tell Stevie and Carole about that when I see them tomorrow!

Still, I'll have to be careful. Whatever our communication problems in the past, I'll have to be extra clear about whatever I write to Peter from now on, since it could end up in his script. Even though his letter was a lot more normal this time, I don't want him getting any wrong idea about what "kids your age" (to use his own words) are like. I don't want his screenplay messed up because he thinks I'm still some kind of baby.

FROM:	Steviethegreat
TO:	LAtwood
SUBJECT:	Hooray for Hollywood!
MESSAGE:	

Hi, Lisa! I've been thinking about what you told us this afternoon about your brother's screenplay. I still can hardly believe that The Saddle Club could be *coming to a theater near you* someday soon! How cool is that???

Anyway, I was also thinking about something else. You

know how you're always seeing articles and shows about screen tests, where directors look for the next hot young star for their movies? Well, you should tell your brother that if they do anything like that for our movie, he should let us know. Because with our talents and natural charm, who better to play ourselves than ourselves? (Plus, I'm sure Carole would insist that no horse could play Starlight better than Starlight himself—ha ha!)

Dear Diary,

I just had a great idea. I was still thinking about what I wrote the other day about wanting to be clear when I write to Peter again. And suddenly I remembered Ms. Shields's favorite two words in the English language: *rough draft*. Maybe I'll do a rough draft of my next letter right here in my diary, just to make sure I get it exactly right before I send it. I want to try to keep it as clear as I can, sort of like that technical writing exercise we did in class. No emotions, no judgments . . . Here goes!

Dear Peter,

Thanks for writing back. ~~It was good to hear from you.~~ Your new screenwriting plan sounds very ~~exciting~~ interesting. I will write to you as often as I can to tell you about me and my friends.

School is fine. I'm taking a special elective creative writing course along with my other classes. ~~It's really interesting.~~ So far my grades are fine.

My friends and I have been riding as often as we can. We have meetings of our Pony Club, which is called Horse Wise, on Saturdays and lessons twice a week. We've been working on jumping lately, ~~which is one of my favorite things to do.~~

I don't know if Mom told you, but I got back from a trip out West a few weeks ago. Kate Devine and her parents invited us to their dude ranch to help them plan a Halloween ~~fair~~ fund-raising event to benefit local Native American kids. We spent several days planning the event and then worked hard to make it ~~fun~~ a success. We ended up raising quite a bit of money for the cause. Kate also adopted a wild mustang just after we left.

I'll write more soon when something else happens.

Love,
Lisa

P.S. Francine Potts moved to Kentucky three years ago.

FROM:	HorseGal
TO:	Steviethegreat
TO:	LAtwood
SUBJECT:	Prancer
MESSAGE:	

Hi, guys! I just got back from making the rounds with Judy Barker, and Dad's on the phone gabbing away with one of his Marine Corps cronies, so I thought I'd drop you a note because Judy looked in on Prancer when she dropped me off at Pine Hollow. She says her leg is doing really well, and she thinks she'll probably be ready for riding by sometime next month! Of course, she said she'd want to check her leg again in a couple of weeks just to make sure, but I think it's just because she's a good vet and good vets have to be cautious when it comes to stuff like that. But I'm sure it's going to happen—Prancer looks so healthy she practically glows, and she's not favoring that leg anymore at all. Isn't that exciting news?

Speaking of exciting news, Lisa, have you heard from your brother since you sent that letter last month? Any word on his screenplay? You can tell him I'd be happy to teach him anything he needs to know about horses, since you said he doesn't ride himself. I'm sure he'll want all the details to be accurate.

Dear Diary,

Good news from Carole! I can hardly believe Prancer is almost ready to be ridden. It's so exciting! When she first came to Pine Hollow, I sort of thought of her as Carole's horse. I mean, I know Starlight is Carole's horse—I'm not talking about actual ownership here or anything. It's just that Carole is the one who kind of discovered Prancer. If not for her, Prancer might not be at Pine Hollow at all. But lately I've sort of stopped thinking that way. Actually, when I think about it, it's sort of like the way things are with me and Peter. Just the way I've finally started having a relationship with him separately from the rest of the family (or trying to, anyway), I'm also starting to spend time with Prancer apart from the rest of The Saddle Club. And it's been wonderful. She's a sweet, calm horse—anybody could see that—but you have to spend some time with her to realize that she has a feisty personality all her own, too. For instance, the other day I stopped by her stall after lessons and gave her some carrots I'd brought for her, but I guess I missed one. Prancer didn't miss it, though—she reached right into my jacket pocket and took it out while my back was turned! It was really funny, especially when she gave me that innocent look when I turned around. She just stood there munching on that carrot as if nothing unusual had happened!

I don't think I've liked a horse so much since Pepper. I mean, I've ridden several horses since Pepper retired, and I like all of them in their own way. And I've learned a lot from riding Barq in class lately. But Prancer is really something special. I can't wait until she's back in action. I just hope Max thinks I'm good enough to ride her someday!

Oh well, I'd better finish this entry now. I want to start my next assignment for creative writing class tonight, or at least start thinking about it. It's due in less than two weeks, and I'm not sure what I want to write about yet. Ms. Shields is still talking about clarity. She wants us to write a one-paragraph essay on any factual topic we want. Only this time it doesn't have to be all facts. She wants us to include our own feelings or opinions on the topic without sacrificing any clarity in the facts or making it too long. Maybe I could write something about Prancer's leg or some other horse-related topic.

A Day at a Horse Show
an essay by Lisa Atwood

There's nothing like a day at a horse show, whether you are a competitor or simply a spectator. A horse show is a way for a horse and rider to demonstrate their abilities in various areas, such as jumping, equitation, and conformation. It's also a way for a person who loves horses but has not actually entered the show to spend a day watching the best of the best perform. For instance, I am hoping to attend the Briarwood Horse Show, which will be held in this area soon. I know that seeing all those accomplished horses and riders will help me in my own riding education. I am especially interested in watching the hunter jumper classes, which usually feature obstacles inspired by those that a foxhunter might encounter in the field. I have always loved jumping, and there are sure to be a number of hunter jumper classes at Briarwood. For me, like many other horse show fans, a day at a show like Briarwood is a real treat.

Dear Diary,

What an exciting day this has been! I left the stable hours ago, but my head is still spinning from everything that happened.

I knew it was going to be a special day from the beginning, because it was the day Judy Barker had decided that Prancer could be ridden for the first time since her accident. So Carole, Stevie, and I were in a great mood. I was especially thrilled because they'd elected to let me take the first ride on her. They thought that was only fair since I was the only one of us who'd never ridden a Thoroughbred—Carole rode Prancer once before her accident, and Stevie usually rides Topside in class. And I wasn't about to argue with their logic!

Judy was already giving Prancer a final check when we arrived at the stall. We were carrying her tack with all our fingers crossed, hoping that the vet wouldn't find any last-minute problems.

"How does she look?" Carole asked.

"Looks just fine," Judy said with a smile. "I'd say she's as ready as can be for her test drive."

I was happy to hear that. We started tacking up the

mare. It didn't take long—as usual, Prancer behaved perfectly. I couldn't be sure, but I thought she seemed happy to have a saddle on her back again.

Riding Prancer was just as wonderful as I'd imagined it would be. She was eager, almost frisky, as I signaled for a walk and we rode into the outdoor ring. She picked up an easy walk and within a few steps was trotting. I could hardly believe how smooth and fast her trot was. It was amazing!

Judy and my friends were watching from outside the ring. "Try a canter now," Judy called as we trotted past.

I started to slide my outside foot back to give the signal, but Prancer obviously knew what the word meant. She began cantering all on her own. And it was even better than her trot!

After a couple of turns around the ring, Judy called to me again. "Now walk again."

I tightened up on the reins and sat more deeply in the saddle. I guess Prancer was having too much fun cantering to pay attention to my signal, though. She kept going. It took a little extra effort to pull her up— she was really enjoying herself.

"That was *wonderful*!" I declared as I rode back to the gate.

"She was a little hard to control, though, wasn't she?" Judy asked.

I shrugged. "Not really," I said. "Poor old Prancer's been cooped up for so long, she just wanted a chance to let it all out. I can understand that, can't you?"

99

"Sure," Judy said. "I can understand it, but you can't let her get away with it."

"I know, I know." One of the things I both love and hate about horseback riding is that everybody always seems to notice everything I do wrong. I know that most riding mistakes are mistakes made by riders, not horses. Prancer didn't make those mistakes, I did. But I'm not too worried. I'll do better next time—and there are going to be a lot of next times!

That brings me to the other exciting thing that happened today. Max stopped by the ring to see how Prancer was doing, and Judy told him that she appeared to be perfectly fit.

"I declare Prancer ready for a full load of work," she said. "Riding and a lot more training."

"Well, that's wonderful news," Max said. "And that means this is a day just full of good news . . ."

"Yes?" Carole said expectantly.

"I've just heard from the Briarwood Horse Show. They've invited me to send some of my students to compete the week after next."

"*Young* students?" Carole asked. I knew what she was thinking, because I was thinking the same thing. Was Max talking about his adult riders—or about us?

He didn't keep us in suspense for long. "Yes," he said with a smile. "Young students. All the junior riders are there by invitation, and they said I could pick four riders."

Four wasn't very many. I was sure he'd pick Carole,

and probably Stevie. But I haven't been riding nearly as long as they have, or as long as some of the other intermediate riders. Still, sitting tall in Prancer's saddle, I felt bold. "Any idea who you'll send?" I asked.

"Well, I've had to think about it for a long time," Max said. "There are lots of considerations. First of all, I need to send riders who have something to offer a competition. Then, I also want riders who will learn something from it. I told the man at Briarwood that I have this obstreperous threesome who think they know everything and who are always coming up with wild schemes and who get themselves into trouble and that they also talk a lot in class, but he said to send them along anyway."

"You mean us, don't you?" Carole asked, looking a little confused by Max's rambling.

"Of course he means us!" Stevie snapped. "Who else is obstreperous and talks a lot in class?"

Max couldn't help laughing at that. Then he told us to meet in his office after our riding class to talk about the details.

I hated to dismount from Prancer for class, but I was supposed to ride Barq, so I went and got him ready. My friends and I didn't have a chance to talk about the exciting news before we got to Max's office after class.

That was when we got the only tiny piece of *bad* news of the day. We found out that Veronica diAngelo was the fourth member of the Briarwood team. I guess I shouldn't have been surprised. Veronica is a terrible snob and a pretty unpleasant person most of the time, but she is a better-than-average rider. And Max is nothing if not fair. Carole and I weren't thrilled that she was included, but Stevie was really peeved. She takes anything good that happens to Veronica as a personal affront.

Max started telling us how the Briarwood show would work. "You are all intermediate riders in the Junior Division," he said, tapping his pencil on the desk in front of him. "There are five different classes for you each, and each class stresses different skills and talents. Don't assume that because you're good riders you will do well in all the classes. That's not always the case."

I felt myself nodding slightly. I suspected Max was thinking of me when he said that, and it made me feel more confident about being there. He was saying that even though I was the newest rider in the group, it didn't mean I couldn't succeed at the show—we all had our strengths and weaknesses as riders, no matter how long we'd been riding.

"Your first class of the day," Max went on, "will be Fitting and Showing. You'll lead your horses into the ring without saddles on them. The judges will be looking for grooming, conformation, and manners. The second class is Equitation. In that, you'll be showing your riding skills. You'll follow instructions about gaits, directions, turns, and gait changes. Next will be a Pleasure class. That's just what it sounds like. There are no tricky maneuvers expected, just good, solid riding and a good relationship between horse and rider. If you work well with your horse and if you both enjoy it, you'll do well in this one."

Max went on to talk about the next class, Trail class, but my mind was wandering. The mention of the Pleasure class had made me think of Prancer—riding her a little earlier had certainly been a pleasure!

I did my best to tune back in as Max described the last class, the Jumping class. "I'll schedule some special prep classes for the four of you before we go so that you can each put your best foot forward at Briarwood," he finished. "I want you to remember a few things, though, and one above all. This may be a chance for you to show off skills and win a ribbon or two, but most of all it's a chance for you each to learn. You will learn from your own mistakes, and you will learn from other people's talents and skills. Keep your eyes and your minds and your hearts open at all times."

Max's words then inspired me to do my very best at the show. So what if I'm the newest rider? I just might surprise everyone. Especially since I've decided to ride Prancer at Briarwood. Max looked a little surprised when I told him, but he said it was okay.

My friends, however, were another matter. The three of us went to TD's after the meeting to celebrate, but we weren't even halfway there when Stevie started jumping all over me, telling me all the reasons she didn't think I should have chosen Prancer for the show. At first I tried to be patient with her, figuring she was just surprised that I hadn't picked Barq. But after a minute or two I started to get kind of annoyed. She obviously thinks I'm not ready for a show like Briarwood or a horse like Prancer, and that kind of stings. I mean, shouldn't best friends believe in each other?

I tried not to get too mad, though. Stevie doesn't always think before she speaks, and I figure this was one of those times. She'll see that she was wrong when she sees me and Prancer at Briarwood.

And here's the last bit of great news for today: My parents actually agreed to sign the permission slip Max sent home with us! I wasn't sure they were going to. Mom's never quite understood why I like riding so much, even though she's the one who made me take lessons in the first place. But once she heard Veronica was involved, Mom was convinced. For some reason she's *almost* as impressed with the diAngelos as they are with themselves. I don't care about the reasons, though. I'm just glad she agreed to sign.

Nothing can stop me now—not with wonderful, perfect, incredible Prancer on my team!

Hi, guys! Lisa, I was thinking about Briarwood and everything else and thinking how cool it would be to have a horse show in our movie. In fact, don't you think a scene set at Briarwood would make an awesome opening? I can picture it all in my head, and I thought I'd write it out here before I forget. You can send it to your brother if you want. He doesn't even have to give me half the screenwriting credit—just a listing in the opening credits would be fine. (He can even use my title idea if he wants.) Here goes . . .

HORSING AROUND

a screenplay scene by S. Lake

FADE IN:
INTERIOR a stable, early morning
CLOSE UP on STEVIE, a stunningly lovely and obviously extremely intelligent middle-school girl, braiding the mane of an attractive bay Thoroughbred horse, TOPSIDE. Stevie is dressed in spotless white breeches and a dark riding coat,

and her hair is neatly braided with not a hair out of place. Topside looks good, too.

STEVIE
(humbly)
This is the big day, Topside. I hope we're good enough to compete here at the Briarwood Horse Show. Oh, I know my very discerning riding instructor, Max Regnery, says I'm the most naturally talented rider he's ever seen, but still . . .

There is the clatter of FOOTSTEPS from the aisle outside, and a moment later LISA and CAROLE appear in the doorway. They are dressed like Stevie.

LISA
Hello, Stevie. Are you ready for our big day?

STEVIE
(even more humbly)
I hope so. I just want to do my best.

CAROLE
(sincerely)
I'm sure you will. You always do. After all, you are the most naturally talented rider Max has ever seen.

That's all I have so far, but I could write more if you think it would help Peter. What do you think? Pretty brilliant, huh?

Thornbury Hall
London, England

Dear Lisa,

I got your last letter. Thanks for writing. I'm sorry your trip out West wasn't more of a vacation—sounds like you didn't have much time for fun. Still, what you wrote gave me some more good inspiration for my screenplay. I'm hoping to start putting some thoughts on paper soon. Keep writing if you can! The more stuff you send, the better.

I guess by the time you get this, Mom probably will have told you that I got a job offer. It was in response to one of the resumes I sent out, to a real estate office here in London. I was actually only interested in a position working on their company newsletter, since that would at least be writing-related. Instead, they want me to work in the contracts office. It doesn't sound like the most exciting job in the world, but the money's good. And I'm sure Mom and Dad will be thrilled to know that their son won't be sleeping in some London gutter this summer, right? Ha ha!

Anyway, since it looks like I'll be staying in London, I'm going to start bugging Mom and Dad about bringing the family to visit. You'd like it here, I think—there are lots of beautiful old buildings and interesting museums and things to see.

I'd better go—I have an exam tomorrow. But write again if you can. And I hope you've cheered up since your last letter. You know what they say about all work and no play!

Love,
Peter

Dear Diary,

Well, I guess that mature, factual letter I wrote Peter last time didn't quite do the trick, either. He totally missed the point of what I was saying, and when I look back at the draft of the letter I wrote here in my diary, I can't blame him. I know Ms. Shields says that even a grocery list can be creative, but the description I gave of our trip out West was less exciting than any grocery list I've ever read. It's a little embarrassing, actually. But all I can do is try again. Maybe my next creative writing assignment will help—it's a letter, of all things, and it's due right before winter break. Naturally, I've already decided to make my next letter to Peter my assignment. Maybe I'll try drafting it in here again.

But not right now—I got a little distracted looking back at the last few pages of my diary, but I didn't open it to write about Peter at all, let alone homework. There are too many other things to write about, like Briarwood, which is coming up in just six days now. Believe it or not, even Stevie's silly screenplay thing gave me shivers, just because it reminded me that the show is coming up soon!

I've hardly been able to think about anything else since Max gave us the news. I guess that's why I had that incredible dream last night . . . But before I write about that, I want to jot down a few notes about what's been happening lately, since I haven't written in almost a week and a lot has been going on.

The more I ride Prancer, the more thrilled I am with her. We had our first trail ride together the Monday after we found out about the show. It was wonderful, even though she was a little frisky and fidgety. She fought the bit a little and kept switching to faster paces without my permission. Once she actually started to gallop on the trail! I was pretty embarrassed when I finally pulled her up—I knew I had messed up in a big way.

"I just broke every rule the most amateur rider in the world knows and let my horse run away with me," I told my friends ruefully.

"Prancer, you bad girl!" Stevie scolded my horse.

"It wasn't Prancer, it was me," I reminded her, even though I was sure she was joking. "I never should have let her trot without signaling her."

"Well, maybe," Stevie agreed. "But it seems to me that you paid too high a price for a little slip. I mean, you did make a mistake, but at some point before a gallop, Prancer should have listened to you. You gave her every signal in the book. She just wasn't paying attention."

"I can't blame her," I replied. "I wasn't doing it right."

My friends seemed kind of surprised—I guess they've both been riding for so long that they've forgotten how complicated everything can seem sometimes when it's still new. I wasn't sure exactly what I'd done wrong, but obviously I'd messed up somehow, and I know I can do better. I *have* to do better if I expect to keep riding a valuable, beautiful horse like Prancer.

By the way, before I forget to mention it, Carole has been thinking about something other than horses, horses, horses for once. Well, sort of, anyway. She met this girl Cam on a computer bulletin board thing for riders, and they've been e-mailing back and forth for a little while now. I guess Cam must know almost as much about horses as Carole does, because Carole keeps talking about her. It turns out that she's going to be at Briarwood, too, so she and Carole will have a chance to meet in person. Isn't that nice?

Anyway, back to Prancer. I've been working with her all week. And yesterday before our riding class, Max called the four of us (me, Carole, Stevie, Veronica) into his office to talk more about the show.

"There's one other aspect of Briarwood I wanted to discuss with you," he told us. "It's not official from Briarwood's point of view, but it is from mine. As you know, I believe all my riders must meet certain standards—nothing unreasonable, mere excellence . . ."

I smiled along with my friends at that, feeling kind of nervous. Max's tone was light, but I knew he was only half joking. I also knew that riding an excellent horse like Prancer would challenge me even more than usual.

"I believe that excellence comes from within," Max went on. "I also believe that one person's excellence cannot be judged by another's standards. So here's what I want you to do. I want each of you to think about what your own goals are for riding, especially for riding at Briarwood. You'll each be in five classes, and that means you should be thinking about your goals for each class. For instance, in the Fitting and Showing class, one of you may think of her goal as keeping her horse calm. Another may feel that there's progress to be made in hoof cleaning. When you've decided what your personal goal is, you are going to write it down on a piece of paper and put it in an envelope—one for each class. Then you are going to seal the envelopes and give them to me. After the show we'll meet again. I'll return the envelopes to you, and you can open them to remind yourself of what you thought was important before the competition. You then get to grade yourself. I won't ask what your goals were; I'll simply ask you if, in your opinion, you met them. I will then give you whatever ribbon you tell me you deserve."

I thought that was kind of an interesting idea. While my friends (and Veronica) asked Max some questions, I started thinking about what my goals might be. I was still thinking about it when I started tacking up Prancer for class. There were so many possibilities—I still sometimes have trouble keeping my legs perpendicular to the ground and my heels down; sometimes I lose track of which diagonal I'm supposed to be posting on; stuff like that. But somehow, when I looked at Prancer, none of those things even seemed worth writing down.

Prancer was still pretty frisky in class, though I'm sure it was just because she'd been cooped up in her stall for so long during her recovery. She was eager to go faster than Max was letting us go a few times, and when we started jumping she practically sailed over the low jumps, clearing them by yards (well, it seemed that way to me, anyway). It was kind of hard to keep up with her sometimes, but it was fun, too. She's such a great horse! I'm sure she'll settle down in time for the show next Saturday. And by the way Max kept paying extra attention to us in yesterday's lesson, singling us out to try things while the others watched, I'm pretty sure he's expecting big things from her at Briarwood.

And so am I. Actually, by the time I got home from the stable last night, I wasn't too sure anymore that Max's idea about writing down goals made much sense. When I thought about it, wasn't that what the judges were there for? Still, if he wanted us to do it, I'd do it. I got ready for bed and then settled in against my pillow with pen and paper. I closed my eyes to think about everything I'd learned so far about horseback riding. I guess the long day at the stable caught up with me then, because I fell asleep before I'd written a word. And that's when I had the dream.

It started out kind of scary. It was sort of like one of those dreams where I walk into class and find out there's a big test that day and I haven't studied any of the material for it. Only in this case, I found myself riding Prancer into a show ring where a jump course was set up, and I realized I had no idea what the path was. I almost panicked, but then I realized that Prancer knew what she was doing and there was nothing for me to worry about. We started the course at a smooth canter, and we cleared every jump perfectly. Prancer made her way easily through the complicated course as if she'd jumped it a thousand times before. All I had to do was focus on my own form, keeping my head up, eyes forward, legs in, heels down, hands firm but not tight, and so on. And I was doing it all right as if it were the easiest, most natural thing in the world. When we finished the course, Prancer drew to a halt in front of the judges' stand while the judges tallied the scores. Then the judge in the middle stood up. "Ladies and gentlemen," he announced, "there is no point in continuing this competition. This rider, Miss Lisa Atwood, is simply the finest rider any of us has ever seen. And her horse, Prancer, defies all description. This may be just a local horse show, but you have been treated here to a performance that could take the blue even at the American Horse Show. We don't need to see any other riders, we have our winner right here!" The audience broke into loud applause as I rode forward, knowing that we deserved every word of praise. And that wasn't all. When the judge clipped the blue ribbon to Prancer's bridle, I suddenly remembered that we'd already won the blue in every other class we'd entered. That meant there was just one prize left. I leaned forward to speak to the judge. "Does this mean that I'm—" The judge didn't even let me finish. She smiled. "Champion," she said. "Yes, you are the champion." The audience went wild at that, making an incredible amount of noise . . . and a moment later I woke up to the buzz of my alarm clock. But the wonderful feeling of the dream still lingered. It's still with me now, actually, as I write this.

That feeling made it easy to know what to do about Max's little assignment. As soon as I woke up, I realized I was still clutching five pieces of white paper. My pen was beside me, and I picked it up and wrote the same word on each piece of paper: *Blue*.

With a horse like Prancer to ride, what other goal could I possibly have?

FROM:	LAtwood
TO:	Steviethegreat
TO:	HorseGal
SUBJECT:	It's almost time!
MESSAGE:	

Just a reminder—let's meet at Pine Hollow a little early so we can help each other check all our tack and stuff like we discussed, okay? I know we went over everything today before we left, but better safe than sorry, right? We wouldn't want a worn stirrup leather or a dusty saddle to cost us any ribbons!

See you tomorrow—I just hope I can manage to sleep tonight. I'm not sure I'll be able to, though. I'm too excited!

Dear Diary,

What a difference a day can make. It's Saturday night, and I'm writing this by the night-light in the hall outside Carole's room. Carole and Stevie are both sound asleep, and so is Carole's dad, but I'm wide awake. I just can't stop thinking about everything that happened today—so much happened, so many things, so many emotions and thoughts and everything . . . I thought maybe if I wrote it all down here it would start to make more sense, and then I could stop thinking about it and go to sleep.

This morning I woke up with butterflies in my stomach. I remembered right away that it was the day of the show, and I hopped out of bed immediately, not wanting to waste a second. I met my friends at Pine Hollow, and after that the next hour or two were a blur as we got our horses and equipment ready and loaded onto the van for the ride over to Briarwood. Even Veronica was on time for once, and the trip came off without a hitch. Soon we were set up in our temporary stalls at the show grounds, and I set to work on Prancer's grooming. I wanted to make sure she looked her very best, especially since she would be judged partially for her grooming in the first class, Fitting and Showing.

By the time the class was about to start, there was no doubt in my mind that Prancer was going to be the most beautiful and best groomed horse in the ring. Her coat was gleaming, her mane and tail lay perfectly smooth and flat, and her incredible breeding and conformation showed in every move of her muscles. I led her out of her stall, following my friends to the east ring, where we would wait until it was time to enter the show ring. Most of the other horses looked good, too, but none of them could hold a candle to Prancer.

As we waited, Prancer fidgeted a bit, stomping her feet and looking around at all the other horses. Figuring she was a little nervous, I patted her neck to put her at ease. She nodded her head and then shook it, mussing her mane. I smoothed it quickly and soon she looked perfect again.

"This way, riders!" a woman announced, calling everybody in the ring to the gate that led to the show ring.

With her words, everything in the world faded to gray for me—everything, that is, except for myself, my horse, and the judges. I held Prancer's reins firmly and followed the horse in front of me into the ring, visions of blue ribbons dancing in my head.

We were asked to line up in front of the judges'

stand. I did so as quickly as I could and then stared at the flag hanging from the center of the stand, not wanting to look like I didn't know what I was doing. I faced straight forward, standing at attention. I think I sort of noticed that Prancer was tugging at the reins, but I didn't look around at her. My eyes were focused on that flag.

I don't know how long I stood there. I was vaguely aware that the judges were bustling around the ring, checking over the horses, asking questions, and doing I don't know what else.

After a while, the boy standing in front of the horse next to us glanced over at me and spoke. "Uh-oh, here comes the judge," he joked.

I didn't laugh. I didn't think there was anything to laugh at. I just stood a little straighter, still keeping my eyes on the flag.

The boy noticed. "Relax," he said. "They're looking at your horse's conformation, not your posture."

I hardly heard him. I gripped the reins tightly, determined not to let anything distract me. I didn't want to take a chance of messing up somehow, of ruining Prancer's chances of getting the blue ribbon I knew she deserved.

Suddenly I felt Prancer tug hard at the reins. I was a little worried, but I didn't dare turn around, because a judge was approaching us.

"Hi there," she said. She glanced at Prancer. "Your horse seems uneasy."

"She's fine," I assured her, still gripping the reins tightly.

"I don't know about that," the woman said. "She keeps shifting around. She's as nervous as you are."

"Oh, I'm not nervous," I said. It was true. I was being careful not to mess up, but so far I was sure I was doing everything exactly right. I was sure it was only a matter of minutes before that blue ribbon was fluttering from Prancer's bridle.

The judge stepped forward. "I'm going to check out the mare's conformation. Hold her steady, okay?"

"Yes, ma'am," I said. I kept my tight grip on the reins, not daring to watch as the judge examined Prancer. I was afraid if I watched, the judge might think I wasn't confident about our chances, so I focused my eyes on the flag once again.

I felt the reins tighten and guessed that Prancer had moved quickly away as the judge approached her. Suddenly I remembered that while Prancer loved every kid she met, she wasn't crazy about most adults. As the thought crossed my mind, I heard a commotion behind me. I didn't see what happened, naturally, since my eyes were still on that stupid flag. But other people told me about it later.

As the judge ran her hand along Prancer's flank and then down the mare's leg, Prancer finally lost it. She'd been nervous all along, but this was too much. She bucked. She simply lifted her hindquarters off the ground and kicked back. That wouldn't have been so bad if the judge hadn't been crouched there by her hind legs at the time. Prancer wound up kicking the poor woman right in the rib cage.

When the judge howled in pain, it finally broke me out of my trance. I turned and saw the judge sitting on the ground holding her ribs while Prancer skittered away from her nervously. Half the people around us were staring at the judge in concern.

The other half were scowling—at *me*!

Another judge was already hurrying toward us. "Move that horse," he told me sternly.

"I-I'm sorry," I stammered when I realized what was going on. Could Prancer really have done that? Could she actually have kicked the judge, knocked her down?

"You're excused," the second judge said.

I was a little surprised that he had accepted my apology so easily. I felt that I should do more to help the injured judge. "Can I do something?" I offered.

"You can leave the ring," the second judge said coldly before bending over his colleague.

At that, it felt as though all the blood in my body suddenly rushed to my face. Leave the ring? I realized that "You're excused" didn't mean the man had accepted my apology. It meant that I was excused from the class. I was done. Out. No blue. No ribbon at all. No chance.

If any doubt remained in my mind, what came over the public-address system a second later cleared it up

119

completely. "Competitor number two seventy-three has been disqualified. Lisa Atwood, please remove your horse from the ring."

I don't think I saw or heard anything around me for the next few minutes. All I was aware of was my own humiliation. I could hardly believe it was over almost before it had begun. But it was true. The horse show was over—for me and for Prancer.

Somehow I led Prancer out of the ring and back to her stall. My mind was a jumble of thoughts and feelings. The biggest emotion was disappointment, though somehow that word doesn't seem strong enough for what I was feeling just then. The main thought was that it couldn't possibly be our fault. Prancer and I hadn't done anything wrong. That judge must have done something to provoke Prancer, to make her kick like that. There was no other explanation. And now all my dreams were shattered.

The worst part was that I couldn't even leave, rush away from the show and that horrible word *disqualified*. Mom and Dad weren't coming until later in the day, and there was no way to reach them. I had to stay. But I didn't have to stay where anybody could see me or talk to me. I felt completely alone, and I wanted to stay that way for a good long while. Even the thought of facing my best friends, seeing their sympathetic faces, practically made me sick to my stomach.

I wandered down the temporary aisle and then into Briarwood's main stable building. Finding a staircase, I climbed up into the loft and found it was empty of anything except bales of fresh, sweet-smelling hay. I sat on one bale and leaned back against another.

I tried to shut out the sounds of the horses below me and the show continuing outside, but I couldn't. The amplifier for the public-address system was mounted just outside the upper door to the loft, and the sounds of the judges' instructions blared at me, echoing off the wooden ceiling. I crammed my fingers into my ears, but it didn't do any good. So I just gave up and listened.

When the amplifier went silent at last, I crawled over to the window to see what was going on. I found I had the best seat in the house. I could see the ring perfectly, but nobody looked up and saw me watching.

Fourteen horses were lined up in the ring, a rider beside each one. As they waited for the judges to reach a decision, some of the kids chatted with each other. Others patted their horses. None of them were standing at attention, which made me wonder. If nobody had really good form, would the judges actually award the blue ribbon to anybody?

But they did. They awarded it to Veronica diAngelo and her horse, Garnet! I couldn't believe it. Garnet was a purebred Arabian, but she wasn't anywhere near as well bred as Prancer. And how could someone as awful and undeserving as Veronica win the blue when I had worked so hard for it?

It just didn't seem fair. A wave of jealousy washed

over me as I watched Veronica accept her ribbon. The first tear rolled down my cheek, quickly followed by others. I watched the judges award the rest of the ribbons through a blur of tears. Carole came in fourth and Stevie came in fifth.

Eventually my tears stopped, but I was still sitting there, staring blankly out the window, when the competitors entered the ring for Equitation a short while later. I watched my friends ride. They were both doing really well, but I was sure that Prancer and I could have done better. If only . . .

I watched that whole class and the next from my spot in the loft. Stevie ended up winning the Equitation class, while Carole took the blue in the Pleasure class. During the Pleasure class, I noticed that Stevie was having some trouble with Topside. After watching her carefully for a few minutes, I was pretty sure I'd pinpointed her problem. She was simply trying too hard. Instead of looking like riding was a pleasure, it looked like a terrible effort, and that meant that Stevie and her horse just weren't working well together.

I wished there was some way I could get her that message. After the class ended, with Stevie coming in a distant sixth, I realized I could still help her. Maybe it was too late for the Pleasure class, but I knew Stevie. I knew when she's unhappy, she sometimes gets so caught up in her feelings that she can't look at things logically. I guess that's true of anyone, but Stevie is so super-competitive that it's even more true of her. She really has a temper, and I was afraid it was going to cost her any chance of doing well in her last two classes.

I knew I had to talk to her. I was sure that if I explained what I'd seen, it would help her see what she was doing wrong.

I found her at Topside's stall. She looked just as angry and upset as she had a couple of minutes earlier as she rode out of the ring. "Oh, Stevie!" I called to her.

"What do you want?" Stevie muttered coldly, hardly glancing at me.

"I saw it," I began.

"You saw me blow it, you mean?"

"I saw you make a mistake," I said. "That's all it was—a mistake."

"I blew it." She didn't even seem to have heard me. "I got one blue ribbon, and suddenly I think I'm the champion of the world. Well, I was kidding myself. I'm no good."

"That's not true!" I exclaimed, shocked that she would say such a thing even in a fit of temper. "You're very good, and Topside is, too. You just made a mistake."

"And you know what it was?" she challenged. "All of a sudden you're an expert?"

"I didn't say that," I said. "I just said I knew what you did wrong."

"Maybe, but don't bother to tell me. It won't make any difference. The judges aren't going to change their minds."

"Maybe not for this class, but you can do better in the next one," I reminded her.

"You think I'm going to go out there again, after that experience?" she snorted. "I go from a blue ribbon to sixth place, and then I'm going to go for it again?"

I couldn't believe my ears. Stevie never gave up when she wanted something. And I knew she wanted to do well today. "Of course!" I exclaimed. "You have to!"

"Says who?" she said sharply.

I could tell she was just upset enough that she was looking to pick a fight. But I wasn't about to get distracted. I love Stevie too much to let her make a mistake like the one she was about to make. "Just because you messed up in one class doesn't mean you can just quit," I told her firmly. "The trouble was you were trying too hard. You completely forgot to have fun—"

"It wasn't fun," Stevie interrupted icily.

"Maybe not," I said. "But that doesn't mean you can't make it *look* like it's fun. You're good at pretending, Stevie, and I just know that when you get into the next class, you'll remember to relax, and then you will have fun. The next class is the Trail class. You love trail riding. All you have to do is pretend you're in the woods behind Pine Hollow and you'll do great."

Stevie hesitated, her expression wavering between

annoyed and thoughtful. "You mean it, don't you?" she said at last. "You really think I can do better?"

I nodded. "I honestly do."

Stevie looked over at her horse. "What about you, Topside? Think we can improve from sixth place this time?"

Topside sort of bobbed his head a little. I'm sure Max would think we were crazy, but both Stevie and I would have sworn it was a nod. After all, Topside *is* a very smart horse.

"All right, I'll take your advice," Stevie said, looking calmer already. "I'll try again. I won't quit. On one condition."

"And that is?"

"That you take your own advice."

She hurried away, mumbling something about saddle soap, before I could ask her what she meant by that. I honestly had no idea. I hadn't quit—I'd been disqualified. It wasn't my fault.

Before I could think too much about Stevie's words, though, I saw my mother approaching. Having her there reminded me afresh of my awful, terrible, unbelievable morning. Ever since the judge had excused me, I'd wanted nothing more than to have my mother there. There's something about a mother at times like that—there's just no replacement. I knew I could count on Mom to take my side, to understand that the judge had made a horrible mistake, to comfort me and make it all better.

125

As I rushed forward to hug her, the tears started again. When I could speak, I led her to a quiet spot, away from the bustling crowds that had descended on the stable during the half-hour break between the last class and the next. Then I told her the whole story. When I described what the judge had been doing just before Prancer bucked, Mom looked shocked.

"The judge ran her hand down the horse's leg? Well, no wonder the horse bucked! What right did the judge have to do that? She must have had it in for you. There certainly is no excuse to send you out of the ring for something your horse did, and it's clear that the judge did something very improper."

"It wasn't really improper, Mom," I said. "The judges do that to all the horses. It's a way of checking the horse's conformation and making sure she's in good condition."

"It is? But it must be very annoying to the horse."

"She did it to all the other horses," I said. "None of them seemed to mind it."

"Well, she must have done it wrong to your beautiful horse," Mom said firmly. "Otherwise just give me one good reason why your horse would have hurt her."

"I don't know." I shrugged. "Prancer has always been a little odd and unreliable around adults. We don't know why; it's just a character trait of hers. If the judge had been a young person, maybe Prancer would have been okay."

"Well, why didn't they have a young judge for Prancer, then?"

It was such a crazy idea that I might have laughed if I hadn't been so upset. Who ever heard of a horse show choosing their judges according to the entrants' quirks? "It's not their job to have a special judge for a horse," I told Mom a little impatiently. "It's the rider's job to have the horse ready to be inspected by the judge."

"But your horse was ready," Mom insisted. "I know you groomed her more carefully than anybody else, and she's so beautiful!"

I nodded. "She's the most beautiful horse I've ever seen. But beauty isn't all that goes into being fit for a horse show. She has to have manners, too. Prancer doesn't have her manners yet." I hadn't really thought about that until I said it. I guess it should have been obvious. But it hadn't even occurred to me until that moment.

"Manners?" Mom said. "How can they expect a young rider like you to teach a horse manners *and* control it? The judges are out of their minds if they blame you for something your horse does! I ought to give them a piece of my mind!"

On the one hand, it was wonderful. Mom was doing exactly what I'd known she would—taking my side, sticking up for me against everyone and anyone else. On the other hand, her ideas about what was important in a horse show were so wacked out that I just had to try to explain. I couldn't have her going off and telling the judges they'd been mean to me!

With that thought, in some weird way, my memory of what had happened began to change. I didn't realize how much until I heard my own voice speaking the undeniable truth.

"No, Mom," I said. "You don't understand. It's the job of the person showing a horse to keep the horse under control. All the other riders managed it. I should have been able to do it, too. Prancer is a beautiful, wonderful horse, but she's young and inexperienced. She hasn't learned good manners. A horse needs to learn manners, or it can't be trusted. A horse that can't be trusted shouldn't come to a horse show."

For a second I could hardly believe what I'd just said. But when I stopped to think about it, I couldn't believe I hadn't realized it earlier.

It was obvious that Mom still wasn't following me. "But Prancer is so valuable!" she said. "I mean, isn't she a Thoroughbred racehorse?"

I did my best to explain that whatever Prancer's breeding, whatever she had done in the past, whatever potential she had, it didn't automatically make her a good show horse. "I was wrong," I said, struggling to find the right words to fit what I was thinking, how I was feeling about the whole day. "She isn't a champion yet. She will be, but not yet. Right now, she's like a young girl who's never been in a horse show before and doesn't understand what's really important until she loses it." I shook my head sadly. "I thought that being in a horse show was about winning and that Prancer was the secret to winning. Now I know that Prancer wasn't ready to show. I had no business bringing such a green horse into a show ring."

I could tell that Mom still didn't quite understand, but that really wasn't so surprising. I hadn't understood any of what I'd just said myself until about two minutes earlier. Still, she was there to listen and offer comfort, and that was what I'd really needed.

She hugged me. "Now let me take you home," she suggested. "You can take a nice hot bath, and then maybe we'll go to a movie . . ."

It was tempting, but I knew I couldn't do it. I had unfinished business right there. Even if the show was over for me, I had to stay and support my friends.

Mom looked uncertain when I told her. "But how will you get home?"

I didn't want her to have to stay when I wouldn't even be riding. "Max will bring me," I assured her. "Or maybe Stevie's parents. Don't worry. I'll find a way."

"No problem, Mrs. Atwood," Max said from just behind us. I was a little startled, since I hadn't even known he was standing there until he spoke. "I'll bring her home. Lisa's right to stay. She's got some work to do."

"I do?"

"Yes, you do," he said.

"Well, your father and I have our tickets already,"

Mom said. "Maybe I'll just stay around here and watch some of the show. Maybe I'll learn something."

"You might," Max agreed. "There's a lot of learning going on here today."

After Mom hurried away to find her seat, I turned to Max, feeling ashamed. "I really blew it, didn't I?"

He smiled kindly. "Yes, I think you did. But I knew your mind was made up when you asked to ride Prancer today. And I think you've learned from the experience." He put his arm around my shoulders and gave me a quick hug. I was relieved, because I knew then that he wasn't mad. He understood.

"Thanks," I told him. "I needed that. Now I think my friends need me. I'm going to go help them get ready for the Trail class."

"No, there's something else you need to do," Max said. "According to the Briarwood rules, your disqualification applied to Prancer, not necessarily to you. I would like to see you compete in the last two intermediate classes here today."

"Me too," I said, meaning it with all my heart. I really wanted a chance to prove what I'd learned. "But I think the Briarwood rules require that I be on the back of some sort of four-footed animal . . ."

"Like Barq?" Max said with a twinkle in his eye.

Half an hour later, it was all settled. It turned out that Barq was there for some of the adult classes later, but he was free until then. After a short talk with the judges, the switch was official, and I was back in

130

the saddle. Barq and I were all ready to compete in the Trail class.

I had fun in the class, and my friends did, too. There was a world of difference between competing on Barq—a well-trained, experienced horse—and Prancer. I still think Prancer is wonderful, and I want to keep riding her as much as Max will let me, but I realize now that she still has some learning to do. So do I, though maybe not quite as much as before the horse show!

Anyway, Barq and I must have looked as good as we felt, because we ended up with the second-place ribbon! It was amazing. Almost as amazing was that we won fourth place in the Jumping class. Carole came in first, and Stevie was third. Carole's friend Cam won second place.

Oh, that reminds me. Carole got a big surprise when she finally met Cam, that girl she's been writing—because it turns out that Cam isn't a girl, he's a guy! Actually, he's a really cute, really smart guy our age. I think Carole was *really* stunned and a little confused by that. It's sort of cute, really. Carole spends so much time thinking about horses that I wasn't sure she'd ever start to notice boys. But I think she's noticing this one, though I can't help wondering how much of it is his big brown eyes and nice smile and how much is his riding ability and knowledge about horses! Oh well, I guess there's no way Carole could ever fall for anyone who wasn't a rider—that would be like Stevie liking

131

someone with no sense of humor, or Max dating a woman who'd never seen a horse before. Ha!

But back to Carole. I just remembered something else that happened to her today. When we came back here to her house after the show for our sleepover, her dad brought us in some cookies. And then he gave her the big news. They're going to Florida to visit some relatives over winter break! Carole will get to hang out at the beach and go to Walt Disney World and see her relatives and all sorts of other fun stuff. Isn't that cool?

FROM: HorseGal
TO: Steviethegreat
TO: LAtwood
SUBJECT: Stevie the Screenwriter
MESSAGE:

Hi, you two. I was just going through old e-mails and realized I never deleted that "screenplay" you (Stevie) sent a while ago. As I was looking at it again, I realized that you (Lisa) might actually have sent it to your brother. If you did, you ought to warn him that it's not very detailed or even accurate as far as the horse-related aspects are concerned. For one thing, Stevie said that we were all wearing white breeches, which we would never do unless we were entering a formal third-level dressage test or something, which obviously we weren't. Also, you make it sound like we're just about to step into the ring, so there's no way you would still be braiding Topside's mane at that late hour. (Not even you, Stevie—Max would kill you!) Also, I think if it's going to be the opening scene of the movie, we should talk about something more substantial, don't you? Maybe something more like this:

HORSING AROUND

a screenplay scene by C. Hanson and S. Lake

FADE IN:
INTERIOR a 12 X 12 box stall lined with straw in a stable, early morning
CLOSE UP on STARLIGHT, a mahogany-colored bay gelding with a lopsided six-pointed star on his face. His mane is done up in neat high plaits and his tail has been carefully pulled so it looks just perfect. His owner, CAROLE, is standing just outside the stall with her friends STEVIE and LISA. They're dressed in buff or other solid-colored breeches or jodhpurs (not white) and navy or tweed riding jackets.

CAROLE
Well, girls, here we are at the Briarwood Horse Show. I am really looking forward to our first class, Fitting and Showing. I know it might not seem like a very exciting event to some people, but it is certainly important. After all, it

demonstrates not only the horse's conformation, but also the rider's skills in grooming. And of course, the horse's manners are very important. An unruly horse shows that a rider is not in control, and that is a very serious thing.

LISA
You're right, Carole. It is very important.

STEVIE
Yes.

And so on. They (I mean we) could go on to discuss the other classes we've entered, and then maybe give a little bit of general information about horse shows in case all the moviegoers aren't horsepeople.

Hope this helps Peter. See you both tomorrow at the stable!

Dear Peter,

I'm sorry my last letter was so weird. I was trying to make it sound important and grown-up, but I think all that happened is I sounded dull and cold. It's hard—really hard— writing to someone I haven't seen in so long, even though we're brother and sister. At first I thought that meant there was something wrong with me, or maybe with us. But now I realize it's only natural. Even siblings can fall out of touch. And the only solution is to write more and try to get back in touch with each other that way. So that's what I'm going to do. From now on I'm not going to try to impress you with how much I've grown up since you saw me last or anything like that. I'm just going to tell you what's going on with me, and I hope you'll be interested and do the same in return.

I guess you could say I've learned my lesson. Actually, this has been a week of important lessons for me. I entered a horse show last weekend, and at first I didn't do very well. You see, I somehow became convinced that just because I was riding a beautiful, blue-blooded Thoroughbred, I was automatically going to win every ribbon in sight. It didn't turn out that way. Actually, I had a pretty miserable time for a while—I even managed to get my horse disqualified. But Max—that's Max Regnery, my riding instructor—let me ride another one of his horses, and in the end I won a couple of ribbons, including a red one for second place. It ended up being a good day, because I learned a whole lot.

Before the show, Max had asked us to write down some goals for each class we entered. He said that afterward, he was going to ask us what ribbon we thought we deserved—in other words, whether we thought we had lived up to the goals we'd set. He wouldn't ask what the goals were or any other questions. It was up to us to judge ourselves. Well, I'm embarrassed to admit it, but the only goal I wrote down was the word blue, as in blue ribbon. I wrote it five times, once for each class.

Needless to say, I didn't come close to meeting that particular goal. At first I was going to tell Max to award me the booby prize. But after talking with my friends, I realized that wasn't right. I certainly didn't deserve a blue ribbon, but I thought that maybe I deserved something just for the fact that I'd figured out why my goals were wrong. So when I had my meeting with Max, I told him I thought I deserved a "most improved" ribbon, and that's what he gave me. He didn't ask me any questions about my goals, just as he'd promised, though from the way he smiled at me I think he sort of suspected what had happened. He's a pretty smart man.

The show was this past Saturday. Next week is my winter break from school, so maybe I'll have time to write more then. In the meantime, good luck with your writing. Please let me know how the screenplay is going and also if you need to know anything in particular from me. I told Carole and Stevie about it, and they're both just as thrilled as I am at the thought that we could inspire a movie!

Love,
Lisa

P.S. Do you still like peanut butter and banana sandwiches?

Dear Diary,

Three more days until winter break! And my creative writing assignment is finished already. I decided I'm definitely going to use my letter to Peter. I'm going to turn it in tomorrow. I hope Ms. Shields likes it. But even more, I hope Peter likes it. I feel as though I've finally figured out how to be myself when I write to him. I'm glad about that for a couple of reasons. For one thing, it means we may finally be able to start really communicating with each other—maybe even get back to being as close as we were when we were kids. Closer, actually. I mean, back when I was following him around everywhere, it was more like hero worship than a real, equal relationship. The other reason I'm glad is that my letters from now on should give Peter a much better idea about how people my age really think. That should help him a lot with his screenplay.

Let's see, what else is happening? Carole and her father are getting ready to leave for Florida in three days. Carole is looking forward to seeing her relatives and everything, but I think she's also a little bit sad that she'll miss a whole winter break of riding every day at Pine Hollow. Oh well—I can't feel too sorry for her. Going to sunny Florida, hanging out at Disney World and lying on the beach, sounds like a pretty good way to spend winter break to me! Still, Stevie and I will miss her.

What else? Today in riding class we worked on balancing, and then in jump class—

Oh! I almost forgot to mention that we had a new student in class today. Her name is Alice Jackson, and she's from Ohio, but she's visiting her grandmother, who lives here in Virginia. She'll be riding at Pine Hollow for a week during her school's winter break. (Alice, that is, not her grandmother!) She's very nice, and she's a good rider, too. There's just one thing about her that's kind of strange—she didn't want to stick around for jump class, even though she seemed to enjoy herself in the flat class. She was very definite about it. She just kept saying she didn't want to stay, and when we tried to find out why, she said, "I don't jump," without any other explanation.

Still, I guess she's probably in a pretty weird mood, and I can't blame her for that. The reason she's staying with her grandmother is that her parents are having some problems. Alice is afraid they're going to get a divorce. She's really upset and worried about it.

I can't even imagine what she's going through. It gave me a sort of unhappy tingling feeling in my stomach just listening to her talk about it. Having your parents get divorced must be just about the most awful thing in the world. I only wish there was something I could do to help her. We talked about it a little at TD's after lessons, but the only thing we decided was that we wanted to know why Alice didn't want to jump.

I'll have to think about it some more. Maybe we can make helping her a Saddle Club project. I guess it will just be a two-thirds Saddle Club project, though, since Carole is leaving on Friday and Stevie and I won't see Alice again until our next riding class on Saturday.

Dear Diary,

Today's riding class was fun. Alice came again, just as she said she would, and Stevie had the great idea of having her ride Starlight, since Carole is away. We were sure she would approve, and as it turned out, Max approved, too. He came over to talk to her just before the start of class.

"I watched you in class on Tuesday, Alice," he said, "and I know you're a good rider. Starlight has a mind of his own, though. You'll have to be a little careful."

"I will be. I promise," Alice said. "Besides, I always am careful."

"She'll do fine," Stevie told Max reassuringly. "As a matter of fact, I'm so sure she'll do fine that I think she should come along on the trail ride that Lisa and I are planning to take this afternoon."

She was just full of good ideas! That's Stevie for you. I waited to hear what Max would say.

He looked amused, as he often does when Stevie is around. "We'll see how she does in class," he said.

But Alice was shaking her head. "I can't do it," she said. "I have to do something with my grandmother this afternoon."

"Tomorrow?" Stevie said, not missing a beat.

"Great!" Alice replied with a smile.

Max looked at his watch, which meant the discussion was over for the moment. It was time for class to start.

Alice loved Starlight, of course. She didn't have any trouble controlling him at all, which didn't surprise me a bit after what I'd seen of her riding skills on Tuesday.

139

Then, about halfway through the class, something weird happened. We started a new exercise where we were supposed to ride in and out between some cones, jumping over a few very low obstacles along the way. The first time, we did it at a walk. Since the obstacles were only about six inches high, getting over them at a walk involved more of a high step than a jump. We all did fine at that, including Alice, though I noticed that she slowed Starlight down to a really slow walk right before he reached the little jumps.

Then we moved up to a trot. This time there was definitely a difference when Alice reached the jumps. Even though she'd ridden effortlessly through the little course marked out by the cones, she took Starlight back to a walk again right before she reached the jumps. She had him step over them slowly, just like the first time.

She was just a guest at Pine Hollow, so nobody said too much. But it was very strange, and Stevie and I were both wondering about it in a big way. After all, we'd ridden through the same course ourselves. It really wasn't very hard, and Alice is a good rider. There was no reason we could imagine for her behavior.

And if I was curious, Stevie was . . . well, what's a word that means curious times about a thousand? Because that's what she was.

We decided to discuss it during our trail ride after class. As soon as class was over we grabbed our brown-bag lunches and headed out, starting down the trail leading to our favorite picnic spot by the creek. We didn't talk much on the way, knowing that we could sit back and discuss Alice's weird behavior much more easily once we were settled on the banks of Willow Creek with our food.

Along the way we came across a small tree trunk that had fallen across the trail. It was windy last night, and it must have toppled over then. In any case, it made a perfect natural obstacle where we could practice our jumping, and we proceeded to do so. It was fun—for some reason, jumping the obstacles that Mother Nature sets up is always more fun than jumping the ones that plain old humans have constructed in a ring or field.

When we were almost to our lunch spot, we slowed our horses so they could cool down, and then we started to talk about Alice.

"I wonder if she's ever even tried to jump," I mused, the memory of flying over that fallen tree trunk still in my mind. "Or if she's had a bad experience with it. Maybe she's just afraid. Some people have fears that don't make any sense, you know."

"Like my fear of exams?" Stevie asked.

"Not exactly," I replied with a grin. "Your fear of exams isn't irrational. See, if you don't keep up with your homework or pay attention in class—"

"Spare me!" Stevie exclaimed, breaking into giggles. "I'm on vacation."

"Anyway," I went on more seriously, "it's not the

same thing as with Alice. Somehow, for some reason, she's convinced that she shouldn't jump. I wonder if it could be connected with her family situation—like maybe she's afraid of what's happening with her parents and that makes her afraid of other things, too, like jumping."

I thought it was a pretty good theory, and Stevie agreed. That led us to talk a little about Alice's parents, how scary divorce was, and serious stuff like that. Soon after, we reached the creek, so we spent the next few minutes settling the horses in a grassy clearing and taking out our lunches.

"I've been thinking," Stevie announced when we were comfortably seated on a big rock at the edge of the creek. "About Alice."

I guessed one thing she might be thinking, because I was thinking it, too. "Should we bring her here tomorrow when we go on our trail ride?"

"Yes, I think so," Stevie said. "It's such a pretty place, even in this cool weather, that it always makes me feel better. It will probably have the same effect on her."

"Good idea." I bit into my sandwich, imagining Alice's reaction to the pleasant little spot. Maybe a babbling brook and majestic trees couldn't help her family stay together, but at least it might help her have a pleasant afternoon without worrying too much.

Stevie wasn't finished, though. "And I also think," she said slowly and carefully, "that we should bring her the same way we came."

"The same way?" I said. "But there's that—"

I didn't finish the sentence. I suddenly realized what Stevie was thinking. That fallen tree—it was perfect! It formed a natural obstacle that was only about two feet high. Any well-trained horse would simply jump it as a matter of course. And any experienced rider would have no trouble managing the jump.

"It's going to be perfect," Stevie said. "It'll just be there. I'll be in front, so she won't be able to see it until I've been over it, and she'll be just a few feet behind me. Starlight's the best jumper in the stable. He won't be able to resist it, no matter what Alice says, especially if she doesn't have much warning."

"And I'll be behind her," I said thoughtfully. "So in case anything does happen, I'll be right there. She's such a good rider, she's sure to react naturally to the jump, and she'll go over it smoothly."

"With some help from Starlight," Stevie said. "I wouldn't trust any other horse to do this, you know."

"I know. He's the perfect choice," I agreed. I was feeling excited about our plan. "Alice is sure to realize how silly she's been about jumping. It's like we're opening up a whole new world of possibilities for her on horseback. She's going to love it!"

"It won't exactly make up for the fact that her parents are splitting," Stevie pointed out.

"But it will give her something else to think about," I concluded.

After we finished eating, we spent the rest of the afternoon fixing up the jump to make it perfect. I know I just said the best jumps are straight from Mother Nature, but in this case we decided she could use a little help. We moved the fallen tree trunk a little way down the trail so that it's just around a bend, impossible for Alice to see ahead of time. We also made sure it was nice and low and perfectly safe.

I can't wait to put our plan into action tomorrow. It's great to think that we found a new friend who has a problem and that we can do something about it. That's what The Saddle Club does best! I only wish Carole could be here with us . . .

I wonder how Carole's doing in Florida? I miss her already, even though she just left yesterday. She probably hardly has time to miss us at all, though. She told me and Stevie that she's staying with her father's sister, Aunt Joanna, and her husband and daughter. The daughter, Carole's cousin Sheila, is sixteen years old, and she has a pony. I think she's had the same pony for a long time, actually—so long that she's pretty much outgrown him. At least that's what it sounds like to me.

But what do I know? I only have one cousin whom I've ever met, and she's only nine years old. It would be cool to have cousins who shared my interests, the way Carole and Sheila share a love of horses. And it would be cool to have a big family like Carole's. Besides about a million relatives on her dad's side down in Florida, she has a whole bunch of relatives from her mother's side who live in Minnesota and North Carolina and I don't even know where else. It must be nice to have so many people related to you.

Oh well, I guess I'll have to settle for the family I have. Speaking of family, I mailed my letter to Peter the same day I turned it in for my writing assignment. I'm sure I'll get a decent grade on the assignment, but now that it's in the mail, I'm not so sure how Peter is going to react to his copy. I'm a little nervous, actually. I mean, I want his screenplay to be good and interesting and true to life. But do I really want all my most serious innermost thoughts and feelings—not to mention my big, embarrassing blunders, like what happened with Prancer—splashed up on the silver screen for all to see?

Oh well—too late to start worrying about that now, I guess.

Dear Diary,

Wow, I guess it's been a couple of weeks since I wrote last. I've been so busy I've hardly had time to think about it, but I really want to write down what happened with Alice Jackson.

I have a little time to write today, since Mom's off at her job at the mall and my homework is finished except for my creative writing assignment. This time it's what Ms. Shields calls creative nonfiction. The topic is people helping people. I'll have to figure out what to write about soon.

But back to Alice for the moment. I'm trying to think back and remember exactly how it happened. I remember that Stevie and I were super excited that Sunday when we got to the stable. We couldn't wait to put our little plan into action, but we were careful not to give Alice any hints.

Well, I was careful, anyway. Stevie couldn't resist entirely. "You're going to love the trails here," she told Alice as we set out. "They're beautiful and fun to ride. They always seem to have surprises for us, too."

Alice seemed a little nervous at that. I think she was afraid we would get lost. But we hurried to reassure her. Then we just rode along comfortably, chatting about this and that. Alice was really nice and friendly, which made me feel even better about what we were trying to do.

Little did I know how badly it would backfire. Don't get me wrong—the plan worked exactly as we had wanted it to. We moved into a canter about fifty yards before the bend in the trail. Alice and Starlight were about twenty yards behind Stevie and Topside. I was bringing up the rear as planned. I came around the curve just in time to see Starlight clear the jump with no trouble at all. The only thing that didn't come out right was Alice's reaction.

"Wasn't that wonderful?" Stevie called to Alice as she brought Starlight to a halt past the jump. "You did it perfectly. We knew you would. You're a natural jumper!"

Barq jumped easily over the log and I urged him forward to join the others. "Jumps in a ring are fine, but the best ones are the natural obstacles," I told Alice happily. "Starlight knew just what to do, didn't he?"

Just then I started to realize that Alice hadn't said anything at all since the jump. That was my first indication that maybe something was wrong.

"Are you all right?" I asked her.

"Of course she's all right." Stevie waved a hand as if to dismiss the question. "She jumped like the champion we knew she would be."

Finally Alice spoke. "You planned this?" she asked us. "You intentionally put that log where I wouldn't see it so Starlight would just go over it?"

"It took a while to find the right place," Stevie said, still oblivious to Alice's expression, which I noticed was growing stormier with every second. "But we obviously picked the perfect one, right?"

"Perfect for what?" Alice said so sharply that even Stevie looked at her in surprise.

"Perfect to show you that jumping is wonderful and you have all the skills you need to do it very well," Stevie answered, sounding a little defensive.

"And who asked you to do it and said it would be okay?" Alice demanded. By now there was no mistaking the fact that she was very angry. "Max Regnery wasn't behind this, was he?"

"No," I said quickly. "Max didn't know anything

about it. It was our idea. We thought it was a good one."

"You thought wrong," Alice said bluntly. Without another word, she turned Starlight around and began walking him back down the trail in the direction we'd come. She had him step back over the tree trunk very carefully.

"Alice?" I called after her, still not quite sure what we'd done wrong.

"Leave me alone."

"We just want to help," Stevie tried.

"Then leave me alone from now on," Alice retorted. That was the last word she said to us. I was kind of worried about her, and I thought maybe we should go after her. But Stevie reminded me that we ought to move that tree trunk off the trail first. Besides that, I think she was a little hurt by Alice's reaction to what we'd thought was a good deed. I know I was.

We talked about it as we cleared the path. "We were just trying to help," I mused sadly. "Why is she so angry with us?"

"I've been thinking about it, and I've decided she's probably not all that angry," Stevie said. "It's just that we surprised her. Maybe she's really angry with herself for letting so many jumping opportunities go by without trying it before now. The way I figure it, by the time she gets back to Pine Hollow, she'll be really glad we tricked her and ashamed she rode off alone."

148

"Maybe," I said, though secretly I couldn't help thinking that Stevie, with her naturally optimistic nature, was getting a little carried away. Alice had looked really angry as she rode off. She had looked really angry at *us*.

"I bet she's waiting for us right now so she can apologize," Stevie went on. "She's probably talked to Mrs. Reg and signed up for a zillion jump classes for the rest of the time she's here."

"Maybe," I said again.

But Stevie was wrong. When we got back to the stable, there was no sign of Alice. And when we tried to call her, she didn't want to talk to us. In fact, just about the only thing she did tell us was that she was going to quit riding!

We definitely weren't expecting that. For the next couple of days, I couldn't get Alice out of my mind. By Tuesday, the day of our next riding lesson, she was all I could think about. The one thing that bothered me even more than the idea that Alice was angry with Stevie and me was the idea that she might actually have meant it when she'd said she wasn't going to ride anymore. Horseback riding is the most important thing in the world to me, and I couldn't bear the idea that somebody else might never do it again because of something I'd done—even if I'd meant well. I felt positively terrible.

Finally I called Stevie to talk about it. She was having the same sorts of thoughts as I was.

"I can't believe she means she'll never ride again," she said.

"But what if she did mean it?" I asked. "That means we caused it even if we don't know why."

"Then maybe we *ought* to know why," Stevie said.

"Maybe the why is none of our business," I suggested. It was something I'd been thinking about a lot that morning.

There was a long pause on the other end of the line. One of the strongest parts of Stevie's personality is her insatiable curiosity. She tends to forget that some things just aren't her business to know. But I was starting to see that we might have made a big mistake. We'd just assumed that Alice's reasons for not jumping weren't important and needed to be overcome. What if we were wrong? What if Alice had serious reasons for not wanting to jump and serious reasons for not wanting to talk about it? I explained what I was thinking to Stevie.

"But what kind of serious reasons could she have?" Stevie asked.

"None of our business," I replied.

Stevie finally seemed to catch on. "You mean we were just meddling?"

"I guess that's the word," I agreed.

"How soon can you get here?" Stevie asked.

I was used to Stevie's quick changes of direction. She's a girl of action, and it can be a little hard to keep up with her sometimes. But I just answered the question. "Fifteen minutes," I said. "I have to get changed and pack my stuff for riding class."

When I rang Stevie's doorbell fifteen minutes later, she was waiting for me. "We have to talk to Alice," she announced. "We have to get her to come to class today. If she makes good on her threat and misses just one riding class, it may take a lot longer to get her back into the saddle."

I agreed wholeheartedly with that. We knew we had some major apologizing to do, and we had to do it fast, before it was time for class. We walked over to Alice's grandmother's house.

Alice answered the door. "What are you doing here?" she demanded through the screen door.

"We came to say we're sorry," I began.

"You should be," Alice said.

"We are," Stevie chimed in.

"We thought we were being helpful," I said.

"You weren't."

"We know," Stevie said. "We were just meddling."

"It isn't any of your business whether I want to jump or not," Alice told us.

"We know that now," I said, and Stevie agreed.

"But if you don't ever ride again and we caused it," Stevie went on, "then it is our business. You don't have to jump and you don't even have to talk to us. But we know that you love riding just as much as we do, and we can't stand the idea that you might not ride because of something we did that we shouldn't have done."

"Even though we were just trying to be helpful," I added.

"We're sorry," Stevie said sincerely. "Really, we are."

Alice didn't say anything for a long time. She just stood there behind the screen door. Then, as we watched, her eyes brimmed with tears.

I wasn't sure what to say. Luckily Stevie spoke up. "Class starts at two," she told Alice.

"Please come," I added softly.

Alice stepped back and closed the door, and there was nothing for us to do then but go to Pine Hollow, catch up on some chores, and hope that Alice would show up for class.

She did, thank goodness. We didn't have time to talk to her before class, but she caught up to us afterward.

"I—uh," I stammered. Stevie and I had both been dying to talk to Alice, but now that she was there, neither of us knew what to say.

Alice spoke up and saved us from trying to figure it out. "I just wanted to thank you two."

"Thank us?" Stevie sounded surprised. "For what?"

"For making me come back," Alice replied with a small smile.

This time I knew exactly what to say. "You're welcome," I said, meaning it with every fiber of my being. It was nice to know that we'd finally done something right.

And that was that. Alice left at the end of the week,

and we still don't know why she doesn't jump. I guess we'll never know. But that's okay, because it really is none of our business. Some things just need to stay private, and no matter how curious we are, we need to respect that.

Yikes! I just realized I've been writing for ages. And I haven't even gotten to the scary stuff that happened to Carole while she was in Florida. I guess I'll have to put that off for another day, though. Mom will be home from the mall soon, and I really want to start thinking about my writing project before it's time for dinner.

To help remind me that I still have to write about Carole, I'm going to paste in the postcard she sent us from Florida. Unfortunately Stevie left it sitting on the edge of Topside's stall, and I barely saved it in time—I had to yank it out of his mouth. That horse loves to taste absolutely everything! It got a little blurred by his slobber in the process, so I'm not sure if the picture on the front is supposed to be Mickey Mouse or a horse and buggy on Main Street. Knowing Carole, though, I'm betting on the horse and buggy . . .

Hi, guys!

This place is fantastic. And tomorrow may be even better. I'm going riding on the beach with Sheila. Can't wait. And can't wait to see you!

Love, Carole

FROM: LAtwood

TO: HorseGal

SUBJECT: A favor . . .

MESSAGE:

Hi, Carole! I just tried to call, but your line was busy. I need to do an assignment called "People Helping People" for my writing class, and I was wondering if you'd mind if I used the story of what happened to you in Florida. I think it would be the perfect example of PHP, don't you? So would you mind? Can I write about you? Pretty please?

FROM: HorseGal

TO: LAtwood

SUBJECT: Favor granted

MESSAGE:

Of course you can write about me for your project! I'd be honored. If you want to talk to my relatives, just let me know and I'll give you their phone number.

I can't wait to read your assignment when you're finished! Although if you ask me, the title should be "People and Ponies Helping People." Just a thought! :-)

People (and Ponies) Helping People
an essay by Lisa Atwood

I believe it's important for people to help other people however they can. Sometimes this means explaining homework to someone who doesn't understand. Or it could mean volunteering at a soup kitchen or reading to younger kids or unloading the dishwasher without being asked.

But sometimes helping can be even more important than that. Sometimes it can literally mean the difference between life and death.

My friend Carole learned about that firsthand recently. She was visiting relatives in Florida, and one day she and her cousin Sheila decided to ride their horses along the beach and have a picnic. It was a perfect afternoon, and they had a lot of fun riding, eating, and napping on the warm sand.

Then they decided to go swimming. As they waded out through the gently lapping waves, Sheila gave Carole a warning that she will always remember: "Never turn your back on the ocean."

The two girls frolicked in the surf for quite a while before Sheila decided to go back to shore and bring out a flutterboard. As she watched her cousin return to their picnic spot, Carole noticed that it seemed to have moved about fifty yards down the beach. But she didn't think much about it.

She started to swim out toward the place where the waves began to crest. She wanted to be ready to use the flutterboard as soon as Sheila got back with it. A nice-sized wave came. Carole jumped up into it, enjoying the frothy lathering she got as the crest passed her by. But the next wave broke so quickly that she didn't have time to take a big enough breath, so she ended up with a noseful of salty water. She coughed and tried to clear out her nose, and she rubbed her eyes, which were stinging from the ocean water.

She was so busy with the problems the last wave had caused that she never saw the next wave coming. Only instinct caused her to take a deep breath when it hit.

In an instant Carole was completely submerged in the surf. This time, instead of propelling her upward and toward the shore, the water pulled her down, tugging fiercely at her feet, dragging her down toward the sandy bottom.

Carole had never felt a force like that. It was mightier than a team of horses, stronger than anything she'd ever known. Her body scraped the bottom, and the rough sand scratched her skin while her lungs screamed for air.

Carole didn't know how far she traveled or how long she stayed underwater, but finally she found herself near the surface again and was able to fight her way up to the precious air. She gasped with relief, coughing and sputtering. For a second she was so glad to be able to breathe again that she didn't notice what else was happening to her.

Then she looked around and realized that she was out beyond the line where the waves broke. And she was being pulled farther away from the shore at every second! She could breathe all right, but she could still feel the water pulling at her feet. If it pulled her under again, she wasn't sure she would have the strength to fight it. She was totally exhausted.

She looked toward the shore, hoping to spot her cousin. When she saw her walking down the beach with the flutterboard tucked under one arm, Carole waved at her frantically.

Sheila waved back.

Carole cried for help, but Sheila was too far away to hear. When Carole waved again, Sheila just held up the flutterboard. It was obvious she had no idea that Carole was in trouble.

Carole realized she wasn't going to get help from Sheila. What could her cousin do, anyway? If she came out to help, both of them might be killed.

Carole tried swimming toward shore. It took all of her might to pull her feet up a bit and begin kicking. She moved her arms, though it felt as if they had lead weights attached to them. Carole was a good swimmer—she'd been swimming all her life. But she'd never had to swim like that. No matter what she did, how hard she tried, with each stroke she found herself farther from shore.

Soon Sheila reached the water and waded in. When she looked at Carole again, she finally saw what was happening. Carole wasn't playing in the waves. Carole was caught in a riptide, and she was being carried out into the ocean, out where there was nothing but danger for swimmers.

Sheila was terrified and panicked. "Help!" she cried, but

there was nobody else close enough to hear her. The life-guard tower was empty at the moment, and all the other beachgoers had left the area.

Sheila looked around desperately. All she saw was the peaceful beach where they'd had their picnic and where their horses were now enjoying the shade of a coconut palm. Her own pony, Maverick, looked up when she looked at him.

Maverick, her beloved pony. Could he help? Sheila didn't know, but she knew there was no other possible answer. She dropped the flutterboard and ran to her horse. Unhitching his lead rope, she leaped onto his bare back.

"Let's go, boy," she said. And they went.

Meanwhile, Carole was still struggling against the current. Every inch of her body told her she must not allow herself to be dragged out into the ocean. She kicked, she used her arms, she kept moving . . . and she kept going farther out.

Suddenly there was a tug at her feet as the water tried to suck her under again. She filled her lungs with air just before she went under. Again, she was relentlessly pulled by the force of the water, down and out. She was swirled around as if by water going down a drain. Then, as suddenly as she'd gone down, she popped up. She gasped for air and looked around. The beach was very far away now, the few people farther down the beach looking very tiny in the distance.

There was one figure that was bigger, though. Carole squinted against the glare, trying to figure out if she was seeing right. Someone was entering the water. Not just a person; a horse. It was a horse she'd seen before, she was sure of that, but just at the moment she couldn't remember where. And the rider—she knew the rider. Definitely. But who was it? Before she could remember, the water tugged again, and she took another deep breath as it pulled her under once more.

On the beach, Sheila urged Maverick forward. The brave pony entered the water fearlessly, trotting straight into the powerful surf. He didn't flinch when the water was at his knees or splashing on his chest. Sheila gripped tightly and prepared for the onslaught as they approached the area where the surf might grab at them, too. She spoke to her pony with her legs and he answered with his heart and all his strength. Soon he was jumping against the oncoming waves just as Sheila and Carole had been doing only a few minutes earlier. This time, however, it wasn't for fun.

Sheila sat as tall as she could on her pony's back and searched the deep blue water ahead for a sight of Carole. At first she couldn't find her. But finally she spotted her, bobbing helplessly almost a quarter of a mile away.

While Maverick moved forward toward Carole, Sheila considered the circumstances. She knew what was going on, though she suspected that Carole did not. Carole was caught in a riptide, an incredibly strong surface current that was pulling her down into the ocean and away from shore. There was no way a single swimmer could defeat the force of the riptide. Fighting it would surely only lead to exhaustion, and exhaustion led to a place Sheila didn't want to think about.

The only way to defeat the riptide was to get out of its force. Since it could be a mile or more long, straight away from the beach, the only option was to move parallel to the shore, beyond the section affected by the riptide. Somehow Sheila had to convince Carole to stop swimming toward the beach and start swimming parallel to it.

Carole saw Sheila then. She knew who it was. It was her cousin Sheila and Sheila was riding a horse. It was her horse. It was . . . She couldn't remember the horse's name. He had a name, she was sure of that, but she just couldn't remember it. But she knew she wanted to reach them. She lifted one arm, put it in front of her, and kicked weakly. Her arm didn't really feel much like her arm anymore, though. It was more like some sort of very heavy attachment to her body. It just fell back in the water and hung limply by her side.

Sheila was waving at her. Carole wanted to wave back, but her arm weighed too much. What did she want, anyway? It didn't look like she was waving hello. It was more like she was waving at Carole to go away.

Carole wasn't sure, but she thought maybe she *was* going away. Far away. She started thinking about her mother, who had died a couple of years earlier. The water tugged at her feet again. It was cold, but so was she.

Sheila could tell that Carole didn't know what she wanted her to do. Carole just had to swim sideways. It was the only way—unless Maverick could get to her, and then all three of them would go sideways together.

She shifted Maverick's direction. They had to go down

the shore beyond where Carole was. They would have to be beyond the force of the riptide and make Carole swim toward them. She urged her horse on faster, and he obeyed. When the water got too deep for him to stand and walk, he simply swam, strongly and bravely, as she sat on his back.

With every stroke, Maverick brought her closer to Carole. Sheila didn't know what would happen if she and her pony got caught in the riptide, but she knew what would happen if they didn't reach Carole, so there didn't seem to be any choice. They swam on, Maverick never faltering as he swam and swam and swam, snorting now and then to get the water out of his nose.

Suddenly Carole didn't feel any more pulling. The torturous tugging stopped. She was vaguely aware of the motion of the ocean around her, rocking, reassuring water everywhere. But no more tugging. Carole rolled over on her back, laying her head on the water and looking up at the blue sky above. She closed her eyes. She was tired. Very, very tired. She thought she might sleep now.

Sheila saw Carole floating on her back, rising and falling with the swell of the ocean. She didn't know what was happening, but she knew that, one way or another, Carole was no longer being held by the riptide. It meant that it might be safe to swim near her now.

"Over there, boy," she told Maverick, aiming the pony toward Carole.

It took another few minutes for the pony and rider to reach Carole. Although Sheila and Maverick were both exhausted by the difficult swim, Sheila knew that they had more strength left than Carole, who seemed barely aware of where she was.

Sheila checked her balance, leaned over, and grabbed her cousin's arm. "Come on up here, girl," she commanded.

"Wake me later," Carole said. "Later. I'll sleep now." She closed her eyes again.

Sheila pulled. She pulled as hard as she could, drawing Carole up out of the water. She finally managed to get her onto Maverick's back in front of her. Carole slumped forward. Sheila didn't know how well she'd stay there, but it was the best she could do. It was time to begin the long journey back to the beach.

Carole felt the pony's mane in her face. She didn't know what horse it was, but it was a nice horse. It smelled of the ocean, but it smelled of horse, too. That was a good smell.

"Nice horse," she mumbled, hugging the horse tightly.

Sheila wasn't sure why Carole was holding on to Maverick so tightly, but she was glad. It was keeping her from sliding off into the ocean again.

Maverick seemed to understand that he had to get back to shore. Sheila knew he couldn't have much energy left, nor did she. She didn't want to think about what might happen if they didn't reach land soon.

One of the first rules of riding is that you always look where you want your horse to go. On dry land a horse might misunderstand the slight changes in balance caused by a turned head and shift his own direction. Sheila didn't know if it was the same in the water, but that seemed logical. She stared at the shore ahead as it drew closer and closer. She was only barely aware of their progress as Maverick swam through the surf that was now helping to carry them to safety. The pony pushed himself up and rode on the force of the waves, grasping for footing each time the ocean set them back down again, each time a little closer to shore.

Sheila saw people gathered on the beach. She thought she saw some men wading into the surf with life preservers and ropes. She thought she saw an ambulance. Then she thought she saw her father and Carole's father.

But she was too tired to be sure. She knew only that she and her pony and her cousin were going toward the shore. They were going to get there.

Maverick's feet struck sand. He was walking now, not swimming. He struggled with the weight of the two girls on his back; he struggled with his own exhaustion. He took more steps. He paused. Without any signal from Sheila, he walked forward again toward the beach, the dry sand, and safety.

Sheila heard voices. She saw hands reaching for her and for Carole. She felt Maverick snort weakly and then stumble. That was the last thing she remembered for a long while.

Sheila and Carole ended up in the hospital, but they both recovered quickly and completely from the ordeal. Thanks to Sheila's quick thinking and her pony's courage, they're perfectly fine today. Maverick will be fine, too, though it will take him a little longer to recover. He's got some lameness, and the vet said there was some strain on his heart. But I think he proved that his heart is big enough to handle just about anything. Sheila probably won't ride him as much anymore—she was outgrowing him anyway, and her parents just bought her a new, larger horse—but she will always take care of him and always love him. Because no matter what the size of Maverick's body, the size of his love was never in question.

That's why he was able to help his owner when she needed it, and why he was able to save Carole. It was the same with Sheila herself. She didn't hesitate to lay her own life on the line to save her cousin's. And Maverick didn't hesitate to do whatever his beloved owner asked of him, never wavering, no matter what the cost to himself. Because of their generous, brave, wonderful spirits, Carole is alive and well today. It all just goes to show the true power and value of people—and ponies—helping other people.

FROM:	LAtwood
TO:	Steviethegreat
SUBJECT:	Your favorite: HOMEWORK!!!
MESSAGE:	

Hi, Stevie! It's too late to call, but I wanted to tell you I just finished my "People Helping People" essay. I decided not to write about what happened with Alice after all. Instead, I asked Carole if I could write about what happened to her in Florida. I even talked to her cousin on the phone to get her side of the story, and I think the essay turned out pretty well, if I do say so myself. You can read it sometime if you want.

Anyway, I just wanted to let you know that I think your idea to write about Alice was a good one. And I thought I could just use what I wrote about it in my diary, more or less. But I thought my teacher might not be interested in every little detail about Pine Hollow and the rest of it, and when I wrote down what was left it was too short—the essay had to be at least five pages long and the Alice essay was barely three.

Still, I think the last paragraph of the Alice essay was pretty good, and I couldn't stand to just delete it. So I figured I'd put it in my diary, and I thought you might like to see it, too. Here it is:

People Helping People

an essay by Lisa Atwood (abridged version)

(First five paragraphs: description of what happened with Alice, which you already know, Stevie . . .)

In the end, Stevie and I realized two very important things. The first was that you can only help someone who wants to be helped. We thought we could help Alice learn to jump just because *we* wanted her to jump. But it didn't work because *she* didn't want to learn. She didn't want our help, as she told us in no uncertain terms. That leads me to the second lesson we learned, which is that sometimes you just have to learn to mind your own business. It's nice to want to help everyone, but you don't always know what's best for other people, and you shouldn't force your own opinions on them. That's what we did with Alice. We assumed that just because we love jumping, she should love it, too, and we didn't bother to stop long enough to ask her if she wanted our help. That wasn't right. It didn't help her one bit. And that's the most important lesson of all: Everyone is different, and you can only be a truly helpful person if you always remember that.

Thornbury Hall
London, England

Dear Lisa,

I just got your last letter, and I wanted to write back right away. I think I really understand what you're saying—you know, about our falling out of touch and your trying to sound mature and everything. I guess I never thought much about it before, but I do kind of still have this picture of you in my head. You're about eight years old and you're showing me a picture you painted of me in art class. It's one of my favorite memories and probably always will be, but I know I have to start remembering that you're not that little girl anymore, right? I mean, I'm going to try to remember that.

It's kind of tough being away from home for so long and missing that sort of stuff, like you growing up and everything. I mean, I wouldn't trade any of my experiences in college for anything. I don't think I could have stayed closer to home—I needed to get some distance from Mom and Dad and figure out how to be my own person. Or something like that. Do I sound like some kind of pop psychologist or what?

But anyway, being on my own, making my own choices, living my own life has been really great. Of course, it's a little scary to think about how much more on my own I'll be in a few months when I graduate. I mean—REAL LIFE. It's a weird thought in a way. I guess I'm sort of glad that I have that real estate job lined up. It makes things a little less uncertain. But in another way I can't help wondering if it's really what I want to do. Maybe I'm just copping out, taking the first "real job" that comes along because Mom and Dad keep bugging me about it.

Sorry to sound like such a downer. I guess your letter kind of made me think about things, but now that I look back over what I've written, I'm tempted to chuck this whole letter in the Thames and start again.

But maybe I won't. You're a big girl now, right? I guess you can handle a big brother who's not perfect. Anyway, I'm glad you wrote me about what you're really thinking and feeling. Not only does it help me with my screenplay, but more importantly it shows me what you're really like these days since I can't be there to see for myself. But just because I can't be there doesn't mean we can't be friends as well as brother and sister. Right?

Oh, and by the way—I still love peanut butter and banana sandwiches as much as ever. In fact, I wish I could have one now, but peanut butter isn't big here.

Write back soon.

Love,
Peter

167

Dear Diary,

I'm really glad I took a chance and opened up with my brother. This time I'm not nervous at all about writing back. In fact, I'm looking forward to it. And this time, I'm not even going to bother with a rough draft!

I'm also going to beg him to send me part of his screenplay whenever he has something written. I'm dying to see how my friends and I come out in it!

FROM:	LAtwood
TO:	HorseGal
SUBJECT:	Congratulate me . . .
MESSAGE:	

Guess what? I got my "People (and Ponies) Helping People" essay back today. And I got an A+! My teacher said it was one of the most exciting essays she's ever read. She said her phone rang while she was reading it, and she couldn't put it down—she just let the answering machine take the call. Isn't that cool?

So thanks again for letting me use your story. Actually, I rushed right over to Pine Hollow to show you my grade after school today—I forgot you had that dentist's appointment. So you'll just have to come over and see it sometime. I may even have it framed! Ha ha! Oh, and I'm definitely going to enclose a copy in my next letter to my brother. I'm sure he'll want to use it in his movie.

Dear Diary,

Sorry I haven't written in a few weeks. It's harder than I expected to keep up with this diary—my homework has kept me pretty busy lately. But I just turned in my big science report and we don't have any creative writing assignments due for a couple of weeks. It's a good thing, too, since my friends and I are up to our necks in other sorts of work!

It all started at our Pony Club meeting this morning. No, actually, it started just before that—in Stevie's room. The three of us were hanging for a little while before we had to leave for the stable. As usual, her room was a disaster area, with clothes, books, papers, and who knows what else scattered everywhere. I guess Mrs. Lake noticed, too, because she stopped by to tell Stevie that she couldn't leave for Pine Hollow until she'd cleaned it all up. There was no way one person was going to be able to do that in time, so Carole and I pitched in to help. It wasn't easy, but we all made it to the meeting in time. Barely.

Oh, and one other thing. While we were working, we somehow ended up talking about Dorothy DeSoto's wedding. It really is pretty romantic—I mean, I guess it only makes sense for a famous former competitive show rider like Dorothy to marry a member of the British

Equestrian Team like Nigel Hawthorne. But it still sounds like something out of a fairy tale—a horsey fairy tale, since they're having the wedding at Dorothy's stable. I just feel lucky that Dorothy used to ride at Pine Hollow and that that means we know her.

Anyway, the meeting was fun. We played games on horseback, then Max made an announcement. "We're going to have a visitor next week," he told us. "Dorothy DeSoto will be here. She's bringing a friend—a *special* friend . . ."

My friends and I exchanged glances. I couldn't believe it. We had just been talking about Dorothy earlier this morning, and now she's coming for a visit!

". . . a gentleman who is a member of the British Equestrian Team," Max went on, "Mr. Nigel Hawthorne. Mr. Hawthorne is coming here because his team is competing in the Washington Horse Show."

Everybody was excited about that, because the Washington Horse Show is a major event on the horse-show calendar, and it's held very close to Willow Creek. But I had another question.

"Aren't they about to get married?" I blurted out, remembering our conversation. "I mean, shouldn't there be parties and dress fittings—stuff like that?"

Max smiled. "Yes, they are about to get married, but business has to come before pleasure. This is going to be Nigel's last show before the wedding. His team is going on to Italy for a show after this. He and Dorothy will have their wedding the following weekend."

170

"You mean Nigel won't go to Italy?" Stevie asked. "What's his team going to do?"

"They'll manage," Max assured her. "All these teams have a couple of alternate riders so that if one member has to be someplace else or if a rider's horse is lamed and can't compete, they'll still have a full team. Nigel has somebody to stand in for him while he and Dorothy get married and have a honeymoon. Anyway, Dorothy will be here for our meeting next week. I've asked her to talk with you all about training championship show horses."

That was exciting news. Not only is Dorothy one of the nicest people in the world, but she knows just about everything there is to know about training. I'm sure her talk will be really interesting.

What Max told Carole after the meeting was pretty interesting, too. She was going to tell us all about it when we got to TD's, but getting there took a little longer than usual, because Mrs. Reg stopped us as we were leaving and insisted that Stevie clean Topside's tack for real, not just with the "lick and a promise" method she'd obviously decided to use that day. Naturally, Carole and I pitched in to help—again.

Anyway, sitting around cleaning tack together gave Carole the perfect opportunity to tell us Max's other big news. It seems that part of the reason Dorothy's coming is because she has a stallion she wants Max to buy. She'd been training him for another stable, but he had an accident that will keep him out of the ring for

171

a long time—too long, as far as his owners are concerned. Dorothy told Max that the stallion's bloodlines are excellent, and I guess Max had mentioned to her that he's been thinking of doing a little more breeding at Pine Hollow.

"You mean we're going to have a lot of baby horses around here?" I asked excitedly when I realized what Carole was saying.

"Sometimes," Carole said. "Breeding horses can really be a big business. If this stallion is good enough, Max can probably make a lot of money with him."

"Then why doesn't Dorothy want to keep him?" I asked.

"Dorothy owns his full brother and already uses him for breeding. She doesn't need another horse with identical bloodlines," Carole explained.

"Another wedding," Stevie mused.

"Huh?" Carole said.

As usual, Stevie was looking at things in her own, well, *Stevian* way. Horses don't really marry each other the way people do, and Stevie knew that as well as anyone.

"It's always seemed to me that there should be a little more romance to it," she reasoned. "Of course, we don't even know who this stallion would marry, do we?"

After talking about that a little bit, we hit on the perfect answer. Delilah. She's one of the nicest and most beautiful mares at Pine Hollow, and she's already foaled successfully, which is very important. She would be the perfect "wife" for Max's new stallion—if he decides to buy him.

Actually, that wasn't our only discussion about Delilah today. Carole told us a funny story about her. It seems that one of Max's new adult riders, Judge Gavin, isn't quite as good a rider as he thinks he is. He had some trouble with Comanche the last time he rode, and this time he demanded a different horse. Carole somehow managed to convince him that Delilah is much more spirited than she is, and I guess the judge was so dazzled by her beautiful palomino looks that he didn't notice that she's actually a gentle, obedient sweetheart. He had a wonderful time on his ride, and I'm sure he'll want to ride Delilah again. Max stopped by the tack room while we were working on Stevie's tack to thank Carole for helping him with the judge.

He also told us something else, something much more exciting. "One of the events that Nigel is going to be competing in is called the Gambler's Choice," he told us. "It's really exciting. Mom and I are planning to go with Dorothy, although there's so much work to be done around here that I'm not sure we'll be able to take the time off. Anyway, if I could get some extra tickets, would you three like to come along?"

I could hardly believe my ears. It sounded incredibly wonderful. I guess the looks on our faces answered Max's question, because he went on before any of us could speak.

173

"I'm not sure, though," he sort of muttered. "There is a lot to be done." He looked at us seriously. "I know I'd need some help from you all—I mean like major chores, not just the routine stuff."

"We'll help," Carole said.

"Promise," Stevie added.

"Whatever it is," I promised.

"I'm not actually certain that I'll have time to call about the tickets," Max said, looking worried. "I do have to sort and catalog all the specialized riding habits in the attic. Mom says it *has* to be done this week . . ."

"We can do it," I said quickly. "I'm good at cataloging stuff."

"And I'm good at organizing closets and storage places," Carole said.

"And I'm good with messy rooms," Stevie added. Everybody laughed at that, including Stevie.

"Whatever you need done, we'll do it," Carole told Max. "Promise."

"I'll try, then," he said. "I know you girls would enjoy the show. The Gambler's Choice is on Friday. Mother has a complete list of chores."

"Just give it to us," Carole said. "We'll see to it that it all gets done."

"Sounds like a good deal to me," Max said. "And as I said, I'll see about tickets. If I have time. I've got to get going now. And you're about done with Topside's tack, aren't you?"

"Almost," Carole said.

"You know," Max mused, "one of the problems with one really clean saddle is that it makes all the other ones around it look dirty. Well, see you!" With that, he left.

We took the hint. By the time we stumbled out of the tack room for that well-deserved snack at TD's, the gleam of clean leather was practically blinding.

So we have our list of chores, and it's pretty long. But we definitely don't want to miss out on the horse show, so we're determined to get everything done. I even volunteered to make a list so we can keep track of how we're doing. I created it on the computer and printed out copies for each of us. I also printed an extra copy to paste in here.

PINE HOLLOW CHORES TO DO BY FRIDAY

sort specialized riding clothes (Max's house—attic)
check bales of hay in hayloft for mold
mix grain rations for the week
mix special grain ration for Garnet
clean and check all leather tack in tack room
sort through spare irons bucket; arrange bits by size
    and match stirrup irons in pairs
sort riding hard hats by size
sort out medicine cabinet in tack room; discard out-
    dated medicine and organize remaining contents
clean stall for new stallion

Dear Diary,

I don't want to sound like a bad friend, but I've been noticing lately that whenever Stevie has one of her "brilliant" ideas, Carole and I seem to end up doing an awful lot of the work to make it happen. And it's definitely happening again.

Monday morning—was that really only yesterday???—I gave Carole and Stevie their copies of my list. I'd decided that the best way to handle the enormous list of chores was to spread out the huge ones, like sorting the riding clothes, over the whole week. That way we could get a little done each day, and also do some of the smaller chores each day.

Stevie gasped when she saw the list. "Does anyone ever get time off for good behavior?"

"Of course." Carole looked a bit peeved. "That's what's going to happen Friday night. That's what we're working for here, and I don't think you should joke about it."

"I'm not joking," Stevie said. "There's nothing funny about all the work Max expects us to do."

"Are you complaining?" I asked. I was a little suspicious—I had already noticed that I'd been doing a lot of work that was really Stevie's responsibility lately. Judging from the expression on Carole's face, I'd guess she was thinking the same thing. It really is a big list of jobs—we're *all* going to have to work hard if we expect to finish by Friday.

But Stevie surprised us. "Oh, no," she said. "Really I'm not. I just meant that there's so much work here that I hate to think how much more work Max must have to do himself!"

I hadn't thought about it that way, but Stevie did have a point. Sometimes it's easy to take what Max does for granted. But running a big, busy stable like Pine Hollow can't be easy.

"You're right," Carole told Stevie. "I guess I was only thinking about us—not about Max. Poor guy."

"Yeah," I agreed. "But what are we going to do about it?"

Stevie looked thoughtful. "We're going to do everything he asked us—plus something."

"What something?" I asked.

"I don't know yet," Stevie said. "The idea, though, is that he needs our help and he's going to thank us by taking us to the horse show. We need to find a way to thank him for that. Something fun."

In the meantime, we got to work. We each tackled one or two of the smaller chores from the list. When those were finished, we met up again at Max's house to start sorting through the fancy riding clothes in his attic. It was interesting. The place is absolutely stuffed with all sorts of specialized costumes, like formal outfits for saddle-seat equitation, sidesaddle skirts (actually, they're pants made to look like skirts), and shadbelly jackets. We had a great time digging through boxes and trying on all the clothes.

One of the outfits Carole tried on was the inspiration for Stevie's new idea. It was a pearl gray formal outfit with one of those sidesaddle skirts. Stevie topped it off with a piece of white mosquito netting she found, which made Carole look like a bride who was ready to ride down the aisle.

As we all exclaimed over the outfit, a certain look came into Stevie's eyes. "We can have a wedding!" she declared.

"We're only missing two things," I pointed out. "A bride and a groom."

"No, we've got them already. The new stallion is the groom and Delilah is the bride!" Stevie was doing that thing where she's thinking so fast, and talking so fast to keep up, that her words were tumbling over each other to escape from her mouth. "It's going to be great. We can do it on Saturday after the horse show. You can ride Delilah, wearing that outfit—you might want to consider adding a string of pearls somewhere—and then one of us can wear the outfit I had on before—you know, the Southern-gentleman thing—and that person can lead the stallion, and then the other one can be the justice of the peace."

"Just where is this going to take place?" Carole asked.

"In the paddock," Stevie said quickly. "Or maybe we'll think of someplace more romantic. Anyway, we can ask all the members of Horse Wise to bring food. We can make it a surprise for them, too . . ."

And she was off. I don't even remember all the plans she was thinking up right on the spot. I was too busy wondering how on earth she expected us to plan an entire wedding—even a horse wedding—in four days when we already had so much other work to do. But there's no stopping her when she's on a roll like that.

Part of the reason she's so excited is that Saturday is April Fools' Day, a holiday that must have been created with Stevie in mind. Apparently she and Carole had just been talking about it, and Carole was begging her not to pull her usual troublesome pranks this year. Stevie thought this was the perfect solution—it was a fun joke that everybody could enjoy. I guess she's right about that, but as she chattered on and on about her plans, it sounded like more and more work to me.

As I said, though, there's no stopping her. Today before riding class, she managed to convince everyone to bring refreshments to Saturday's Horse Wise meeting without actually telling them why they were doing it. I think she told most people it's Max's birthday on Saturday. She even convinced Adam Levine to bring the bunch of folding chairs that his parents have in their basement.

Of course, while she was running around doing all that, the clock was ticking. Class was only five minutes away when she finally got around to tacking up Topside. Carole and I knew there was no way she would make it without our help. So we pitched in. As usual.

But that's what The Saddle Club is about, right? Helping each other.

In class, Max announced the news about the stallion. He's definitely coming to Pine Hollow this weekend, and his name is Geronimo. Everyone in class was excited, and nobody minded a bit when Max asked us all to pitch in and help smooth out the ground in the paddock where Geronimo will be spending most of his time.

Well, nobody except me and Carole, that is—at least a little. We had a lot of chores to do from our list that day. But Max seemed to expect us to join in, so we did.

Stevie was another story. She told Max she couldn't stay because she had to go to a dentist's appointment. When she said that, Carole and I just looked at each other in disbelief. We knew it wasn't true.

"I've got to go to the shopping center and pick up some things for Saturday," Stevie whispered to us on her way out.

Carole and I did our best to look on the bright side as we set to work in the paddock with the others. Even though it seemed a little unfair that Stevie got to do something sort of fun, like shopping, while we were stuck spreading dirt around a lumpy paddock, we had to admit that she was probably the best one to go. The wedding was her idea, and she's great at finding interesting stuff to buy.

While we worked, Carole and I talked about the

show. I had no idea what Nigel's Gambler's Choice event was all about when Max first mentioned it, but Carole explained it to me. She said each rider in the event has a certain amount of time, maybe ninety seconds, to run the course. There are lots of different jumps out there, and they can choose which ones to go over. The easy ones are worth less, maybe ten or twenty points, and the harder ones are worth more, like forty or fifty points. That means riders can just go over the easy jumps again and again if they want. But if they want to win, they have to take chances—gamble. That's how the event gets its name. Then, at the end, there's a really huge jump called The Joker, which is worth tons of points. But if a rider attempts it and doesn't make it, that many points are deducted from the score. It sounds really exciting—I can't wait to see it in person! I only hope we finish all our chores in time to go . . .

Thornbury Hall
London, England

Dear Lisa,

Hi, sis! Your last letter was really interesting. It sounds like Carole had a close call with that riptide. And it sounds like you and Stevie learned a lot from Alice Jackson, even if it wasn't the easiest lesson.

I have some good news of my own. I had a few days off from my classes recently, and I got some work done on my screenplay. Actually, it's not really the screenplay itself. It's just some brief sketches of my three main characters. I thought you might like to see, so I've enclosed them with this letter. Let me know what you think of them!

Love,
Peter

Three Character Sketches
by Peter Atwood

L is a girl, thirteen or fourteen years old. She is slender and attractive, with shoulder-length light brown hair and a sprinkling of freckles across her nose. L is mature for her age, sensible and smart. She is logical and determined and knows exactly what she wants out of life. A straight-A student, she is very organized and resourceful. Her favorite after-school activity might be editing the yearbook or running the student council. She is the least likely of the three girls to stumble into trouble because she is so careful, though her courage, honesty, and loyalty to her friends would make her take any risk to help them. She would face down any danger to help a friend.

S is around the same age as L or a little younger. She is a rambunctious girl with dark blond hair and a quick laugh. S doesn't always look before she leaps. She likes to live life on the edge. Her favorite thing to do on the weekend might be cooking up wild pranks to play on people. Sometimes S gets into hot water because she isn't afraid of anything—even things she should be afraid of. She loves riding fast, playing hard, meeting new people, and most of all, having fun. She would face danger to prove she isn't afraid.

C is the same age as S. She's a slender African American girl with wavy long hair. She is an accomplished horseback rider and takes riding very seriously. She can be careless about other matters, and her friends sometimes tease her for being scatterbrained. She is the most likely of the three girls to wander into trouble, because she doesn't always pay attention. Her favorite daydream would be riding off into the sunset on the world's most perfect horse. She is so gentle and kind that she could be more easily duped than her friends. But she would face any danger to save a horse.

Dear Diary,

Wow, I can't believe it's Sunday already! I've been so busy that the time since my last diary entry has felt like one very long, very busy day. Of course, it's been a very fun day, too—at least for the most part.

But now that I've had a little time to rest, I'm ready to write it all down here. This past week definitely falls into the category of times I want to remember!

Wednesday after school, the three of us met at Pine Hollow as planned. Stevie wanted to hold a rehearsal for her horse wedding, so Carole and I spent far too much valuable time posing and smiling for the "photographer" (if you can use that word to describe Stevie squinting through her hands and wiggling her finger to pretend she was snapping rolls of film).

The good part was that this all took place during a

trail ride. Stevie had somehow managed to convince us that we needed to relax a little before getting down to work. I was riding Delilah, and I was discovering that she was just as sweet and wonderful as I'd always assumed. It was no wonder that Judge Gavin had been so grateful to Carole for matching him up with her.

But that was about the only good part of that afternoon. Stevie was being just about impossible, as only Stevie can be. Most of the time her impossible side is offset by her mischievous, fun-loving side. But that day her impossible side was coming out more than usual, and she was being downright bossy. Anytime Carole and I tried to have a conversation, Stevie broke in to return the topic to the wedding.

Finally we'd had enough. While Stevie started thinking out loud about the aisle the horses would walk down for the wedding, Carole and I exchanged glances. Without speaking, we both nudged our horses and trotted away down the trail. Stevie didn't even notice until we were already halfway across a nearby field. She called after us, but we ignored her, letting our horses drift to a halt in the middle of a patch of wildflowers. Delilah stretched her neck down to take a bite of grass, which also included a few yellow blossoms.

"She's always loved flowers," Carole observed. "They must taste good."

I nodded. "She reminds me of Ferdinand, the bull who likes to smell the flowers."

"That gives me an idea," Carole said. "I think I

know how we can make our point to Stevie." She dismounted, secured Starlight to a fence a few yards away, and then returned to the flower patch. "Let's be Ferdinand ourselves."

I understood right away. After tying Delilah up beside Starlight, I joined Carole in the middle of the flower patch. We plucked a few blossoms and smelled them. Then I started twining mine together to make a daisy chain. Carole wanted to know how to do it, so I showed her. When my chain was about a foot long, I wove the ends together to make a circle and then put it on top of my riding hat.

A moment later, I heard approaching hooves. I didn't look up. I was sure Stevie was going to be mad. I wasn't looking forward to facing her famous temper.

But when Stevie spoke, her voice sounded perfectly friendly. In fact, it sounded downright excited. "Nice!" she exclaimed. "I like it! I thought you two were giving up on me, but look at you! You've figured out how to get flowers into our wedding. Great!"

Carole and I looked at each other. We couldn't help laughing. Stevie really is one of a kind, even when she's being a tiny bit annoying. It just seemed a lot easier to go along with her than to try to rebel any further. We remounted and let ourselves be bossed around for the next hour or so before returning to Pine Hollow and getting to work on more of the chores on the list. Or rather, Carole and I got to work on the chores. Stevie insisted on racing back to her house to stow the flowers we'd picked in her refrigerator, and it took her a while to return. When she did, she suddenly remembered that she had to make some phone calls to make sure that everybody knew what to bring on Saturday.

That was pretty much how Thursday went, too. Carole and I worked our fingers to the bone while Stevie strained her brain with plans for the wedding. By the time Friday arrived, we weren't sure we'd ever finish everything Max had asked us to do. Still, most of it was done—enough to hope that Max would let us go to the horse show that evening.

The only other problem was Stevie. She was so gung ho about her wedding plans that she actually made us meet her at Pine Hollow *before* school for another wedding rehearsal. Then, right after school, we all returned for a couple of hours of hard work.

It was all worth it, though. Max came through with the tickets, and we headed for the show right after dinner. The minute we entered the arena, we could feel the excitement of the horse show. We were even more excited ourselves when we saw how great our seats were. We were practically *in* the ring!

Dorothy DeSoto found us shortly after we'd taken our seats. She had big hugs for Max and Mrs. Reg and for all of us.

"I'm so glad you could all come tonight!" she exclaimed. "This is one of my favorite nights of the show. It's going to be great."

We had to agree with that—especially when Dorothy invited us backstage to see what was going on behind the scenes. She also promised to introduce us to Nigel.

When we met him, he was not only incredibly handsome, but as nice as can be, too. "Nigel, here they are," Dorothy told him. "This is Carole, Stevie, and Lisa—better known as The Saddle Club."

"Ah, the American girls who ride at Max's stable," Nigel said with a smile.

I was a little awed by Nigel at first, actually. He's one of the most impressive people I've ever met. He was very tall and slender, with strong features, wide-set dark brown eyes, and impeccably combed hair. I might have been downright scared of him if it weren't for his wonderful, warm smile.

"I suppose it wasn't really me you wanted to meet, though, was it?" Nigel joked. "It was my horse, right?"

"Well, we do love horses," Stevie admitted with a grin.

"Then come right this way."

Dorothy excused herself, saying she'd meet us all back at our seats. We followed Nigel to the area where the British Equestrian Team was set up. There were four members of the team at the horse show, and they were competing in a variety of events, including the Gambler's Choice later that evening. Nigel introduced us to two of his teammates, Camilla Wentworth and Alastair Brown. Then we met the horses, who were positively wonderful, although Camilla was a bit worried about her horse, Elementary.

"He's been acting up, very frisky," she told Nigel with a little frown.

"Isn't that good?" Carole asked.

I was wondering the same thing. I'd always thought it was good to have a lively, fresh horse just before a performance.

"Not necessarily," Nigel said. "And not in this horse. Elementary is a very staid and steady performer. What's significant here is that his behavior is *different*."

That made sense. We watched while Nigel and Camilla checked over the horse carefully. They couldn't find any problems, so they decided it was probably nothing—though Camilla still looked kind of worried as she took the horse out of his stall for a warm-up walk.

After saying hello to Nigel's horse, Majesty, we left the riders to their preparations and returned to our seats. Before long, the show began. The whole evening was fun, but the later it got, the more I was looking forward to the final event of the evening, the Gambler's Choice.

Finally it came. After all the jumps were set up, the riders came out to walk the course.

As we watched, Max told us about the rules. "Unlike most jump courses, this one doesn't have a specified order that the riders have to follow," he explained.

"Instead, each jump has a point value, and the riders can choose whatever jumps they like. They can go over any jump up to two times during the first fifty seconds. Then, when the buzzer rings, they have fifteen seconds in which to decide whether they want to try The Joker."

Mrs. Reg nodded. "If they try and miss, they lose. If they make it, they get seventy points."

"If they don't attempt The Joker, they aren't penalized," Max continued. "But they aren't likely to have enough points to win, either."

"Look, there's Nigel!" I said a moment later, pointing. Nigel had spotted us, too. He came over to say hello and tell us that he would ride seventeenth.

A couple of minutes later, just as the riders were leaving the ring, Dorothy came to join us at our seats and tell us the same thing. "He'll be the first member of his team to go," she added. "They all drew high numbers."

Soon the event began. It took a few of the riders going through the course for me and my friends to get used to how it worked. We'd all seen plenty of jumping before, but never that daring and never that fast. And never that good, either.

They had to be good. Each rider was pressed for time, trying to make as many high-valued jumps as possible in the first fifty seconds. In most jumping events, if a horse knocks down a rail on a fence, there are penalty deductions. In the Gambler's Choice event, it just means that the rider and horse don't receive any points for the fence, and that's bad enough. Most of the riders concentrated on the twenty-five- and thirty-point jumps, since a lot of them seemed to have trouble with the one forty-pointer. There was also one ten-point jump that was right on the way to a thirty-pointer, so most of the riders went over that one, too.

Each time the buzzer announced the end of the first fifty seconds, there was a breathless silence in the arena as we all waited to see whether the rider would try The Joker. It loomed far higher than any of the other jumps—over six feet tall. Because the riders didn't stand a chance if they didn't try it, most did. But not more than half who tried made it over.

Finally it was Nigel's turn. I don't think Dorothy took a breath the entire time he was in the ring. Nigel chose a daring course, taking all the hardest jumps. His horse, Majesty, seemed to fly over every obstacle. He was wonderful. He was even more wonderful as he soared over The Joker without so much as nicking the top rail!

We all stood and applauded when he had finished. Nigel had scored very well and was certainly in the running for a ribbon.

After another couple of riders had gone, it was Camilla Wentworth's turn. She entered the ring on Elementary, still looking a bit worried as he pranced and tossed his head friskily. Most of the audience probably had no idea that there was anything wrong with the horse. He looked perfectly fine—no more lively than many of the other horses. But there was something wrong, and it soon became obvious. Elementary fought Camilla at one jump and stopped dead in his tracks, refusing the next. Camilla turned the horse around and retreated about fifteen feet before trying again. This time, instead of just stopping, Elementary bucked and then reared. He yanked his head to one side.

Camilla did everything she could to stay in the saddle, and in the end she managed to do that. But the violent yanking of the horse's head had pulled very hard at her left arm. Her right hand kept a firm grip on the reins, but the left one dropped limply to her side and hung there.

I guess Camilla was lucky she wasn't hurt more seriously. But I was sure she was disappointed as she left the arena, unable to complete her round.

"Is she going to be okay?" Stevie asked worriedly.

"I'm sure she is," Dorothy replied reassuringly. "Looks like she dislocated her arm. It hurts like crazy when that happens, but she'll be as good as new and back in the saddle in a couple of weeks or a . . ."

Her voice trailed off and a look of alarm crossed her face.

"Oh no!" she exclaimed. "I've got to go see Nigel!" Without another word, she stood and raced away.

The rest of us looked at each other in confusion.

"I guess that's what it's like when you're engaged," Stevie said philosophically. "When you've got to see the man you love, there's just no stopping you."

We returned our attention to the ring as the next rider entered. In the end, Nigel took third place. That meant he'd won a nice cash prize that we figured would help to pay for his upcoming honeymoon.

We were a little disappointed that we didn't get to see Nigel and Dorothy again before we left. "You'll see them tomorrow," Max reminded us. "When they bring Geronimo to his new home."

We didn't get much sleep that night. Stevie kept us up late—or maybe I should say early, since it was the wee hours of the morning before she let us go to bed. When she woke me up at six the next morning, I wasn't sure I'd actually been to sleep at all.

Stevie put us to work as soon as we arrived at Pine Hollow at six-thirty. We worked on the flowers first, turning the grape arbor near the stallion's paddock into a beautiful floral bower. I had to admit, it looked fantastic when we got it done.

Meanwhile, we were still sneaking around to keep anyone from guessing what we were really up to. We kept a close watch for Mrs. Reg, who arrived at seven-thirty—with Dorothy.

"She's probably here to sign the papers to sell

Geronimo," Carole whispered, peeking into the office from the tack room, where we were still working on our flower chains.

That seemed logical, until we heard the distinct sound of crying coming from the office. We doubted that Dorothy was crying because she was going to miss Geronimo, but we couldn't think of any other possible reason. So we cocked our ears and strained to hear what was going on.

That wasn't good enough for Stevie, though. After a few minutes she ran out of patience and marched into the office. "What happened?" she asked. Carole and I followed her into the office a bit more tentatively. I was afraid that Dorothy might not want us barging in, but she hardly seemed to notice.

"It's Camilla," she began before bursting into fresh tears.

"I thought she was going to be all right," I said. "It's just a dislocated shoulder, isn't it?"

"Did something happen to Elementary?" Carole added.

It took a while, but Dorothy finally collected herself enough to explain the situation. "They're both okay. Elementary is just fine, and Camilla will be fine in six weeks. The problem is that Camilla won't be able to ride and the team is competing in some very important shows during those weeks. They just can't be a person short. That means they have to use the alternates, but there are only two qualified alternates at the moment, and one of them is eight months pregnant and can't ride at all."

"So, what about the other one?" I asked.

Dorothy's eyes started to tear up again. "The other one was to replace Nigel while we got married and went on our h-h-honeymoon."

Finally we understood. Because Camilla could no longer ride, Nigel had to. That also meant he would have to fly off to Italy in a few days—and the wedding wasn't scheduled until the following weekend.

Carole spoke up tentatively. "Why can't you get married before next weekend?"

Dorothy blew her nose. "We can, of course, but it was going to be such a beautiful wedding. It wasn't going to be big, but it was going to be at my stable, and it was going to be so nice. I think that's what bothers me the most. We can reschedule our honeymoon."

"It's the wedding part," Stevie said sympathetically. "I know how it is. A girl dreams about her wedding for years. She plans it from earliest girlhood—the most important day of her life—and you can't stand the idea that all your dreams of a perfect wedding have been dashed against the rocks of misfortune."

Carole and I turned to stare at Stevie. When she started talking that way, it usually meant she was up to something. I saw Carole glance at the flowers she still held in her hand, and all of a sudden I had the funniest feeling that she and I had both just guessed what was in Stevie's mind.

194

Meanwhile, Stevie was still talking. "Some girls want to have big church weddings with thousands of guests," she said. "Others like the idea of a small chapel, maybe outdoors, with a few close friends. Others, like you, want to be surrounded by the people and the creatures they love best . . ."

Dorothy was nodding. "Yes, I really wanted to get married at my stable."

"How about Max's instead?" Stevie asked.

"Here?"

"And now," Stevie said.

"Now?" Dorothy looked confused. So did Mrs. Reg. Stevie glanced at her watch. "Well, maybe around ten o'clock when the chairs will be set up and the food will have arrived. You do like apple slices and sugar lumps, don't you?"

"What are you talking about?" Mrs. Reg asked.

I grinned, liking Stevie's new idea a lot. A whole lot. "Can't you tell?" I told Mrs. Reg, doing my best to keep from bursting into excited laughter. "We're planning a wedding!"

It took some explaining, but once Mrs. Reg remembered that it was April Fools' Day, she suddenly seemed a lot more willing to believe us. Dorothy was another matter. She didn't seem to understand that we were serious about having her wedding right then and there. When Nigel arrived, we had to explain the whole thing again to him.

And when Judge Gavin arrived, suddenly the whole

thing fell into place. You see, the one thing missing from Stevie's new scheme was someone to perform the ceremony. But the judge was perfectly qualified—and perfectly willing to preside at an impromptu wedding.

Finally, Dorothy and Nigel were convinced that it could actually work. And that's how we ended up having a real, honest-to-goodness, no-April-fooling wedding at Pine Hollow yesterday!

It was wonderful. Stevie, Carole, and I got to be the last-minute bridesmaids. Max was the spur-of-the-moment best man. And best of all, we were all on horseback. Nigel rode Comanche. Dorothy was aboard Pepper, who came out of retirement for the occasion. Even Judge Gavin was in the saddle, on Delilah. One of the best things of all was that Geronimo, the new stallion, came to the corner of his paddock to see what was going on. So it was almost as if he and Delilah were also getting married!

And in the end, thanks to Stevie's attention to detail, we all threw oats at the happy couple—instead of the more traditional rice. It was the perfect ending to a perfect wedding.

I guess Dorothy and Nigel thought it was pretty perfect, too. Because they left a note for us with Max. He gave it to us when we went over there this morning for a quick trail ride. I begged my friends to let me keep it and paste it in here, and they agreed. Here it is . . .

Dear brilliant and creative Saddle Club girls,

Thank you, thank you, a million times thank you for our marvelous wedding! It wasn't exactly the way we expected to tie the knot, but that made it even more magical. Just when we were sure that all hope was lost, you three came along and solved all our problems. And you made it all so much fun! I don't know how we'll ever manage to thank you properly, but you've really made a difference in our new life together. We'll never forget our magical wedding day—or the quick-thinking girls who made it all possible!

Lots of love,
Nigel and Dorothy (Mr. and Mrs.)

LOCAL JUDGE PRESIDES AT HORSEBACK WEDDING

by E. J. Smith, special to The Willow Creek Gazette

Some people dream of a wedding on a tropical island, others of tying the knot on a mountaintop or in a field of wildflowers or . . . on horseback? That last option is just what a visiting couple got at Pine Hollow Stables, a local riding establishment.

It seems that Dorothy DeSoto, a well-known trainer, and Nigel Hawthorne, a member of the British Equestrian Team, were in the area participating in the Washington Horse Show. The couple had planned their nuptials for next week at Ms. DeSoto's New York stable, but professional obligations required them to reschedule in a hurry. That's when

197

several local girls, students at Pine Hollow, stepped in to help.

Ms. Stephanie Lake, who attends Fenton Hall, was by all accounts the mastermind of the last-minute wedding plans. She was ably assisted by her friends Lisa Atwood and Carole Hanson, both students at Willow Creek Middle School. The trio provided flowers, music, food, and even guests for the wedding. They also provided horses on which both bride and groom trotted down the aisle (with permission from stable owner Maximillian Regnery III). The only thing the enterprising friends were missing was someone to perform the ceremony, and that's when well-known local judge Martin Gavin, who enjoys riding at Pine Hollow, stepped in and graciously volunteered to do the honors. Once the judge was on board, the entire wedding went off without a hitch . . . but *with* a hitching post for the equine attendees.

This reporter was unable to determine exactly how three young girls were able to make such extensive arrangements in such a short time. When asked, all Ms. Lake would say is "Love makes anything possible."

I'm sure we can all raise a wedding toast to that—and to the newly married couple.

Thornbury Hall
London, England

Dear Lisa,

I'm so glad you liked my character sketches! I was kind of nervous about what you'd say, since obviously they're based on you and your friends. I really wasn't sure whether I had captured the characters completely, if they sounded like real people your age. But your letter made me feel much better about that!

It sounds like you've been keeping busy lately, what with all that excitement during your winter break. I never realized you had such a busy life! It seems like all I did when I was your age was go to school and play a little baseball.

Luckily, my life is much more exciting these days. Actually, I have some pretty big news to share. I got a job!

I know, I know. You thought I already had a job. Well, I did. But the closer it came, the less I was looking forward to it. As I told you before, I really wasn't sure it was what I wanted to do with my life, even temporarily.

That's why I was so thrilled when this new opportunity came along. One of my professors liked the work I've done in his course, and he offered me a sort of work-study internship with a project he's planning during his sabbatical in Africa. The project has to do with sociology and family structures, and it will start just after the end of the school year and run for at least a year. He wants me to be his research assistant and also help him write articles for scholarly journals as the research progresses.

The last thing I expected to be doing this summer was flying off to another continent. I'm a little nervous about it, but mostly I'm just excited. It will be a lot of work—a lot more work than that real-estate job would have been—but it will mean that I'm using my brain and doing something important rather than just making a living. It will be a better, more interesting and useful way of earning a paycheck (even though that paycheck will be a whole lot smaller—don't think I'm not dreading telling Mom and Dad *that* part!). Plus I'm sure I'll still have enough free time to work on my screenplay on the side.

Speaking of which, I just finished mapping out the basic plotline. I hope to start the actual writing soon—I'll send you a scene or two as soon as I have something decent finished.

Love,
Peter

Dear Diary,

Why doesn't anyone ever listen to me?

Okay, I know that may be an exaggeration. But sometimes it seems that way, and right now is one of those times. Carole and Stevie are both asleep right now—we're having a sleepover at Carole's house. But I'm not sleepy yet. To be honest, I'm still kind of annoyed about something that happened today.

This morning when my friends and I got to the stable before Horse Wise, we decided to stop by and check on that mare that's due to foal soon. She seemed kind of edgy, not friendly and sweet like she usually is, and I couldn't help wondering if that meant something.

"It probably just means she's in a bad mood," Stevie said.

I wasn't sure that was all there was to it. "Couldn't it be a sign that the foal is coming soon?" I asked.

Carole shrugged. "Stevie could be right. Or the mare might be a little colicky. That's common in mares who are near term. She could also be about to foal. The vet will be here later. We can mention it to her."

"We *should* mention it to her, you mean," I said. I thought they were being awfully quick to dismiss my idea that the foal could be coming.

"Yes, right, we *should*," Carole agreed, which made me feel a little better—right then, at least. But I'll get back to that in a minute. First I want to write about what happened in our Horse Wise meeting.

It was time for it to start, so we hurried to Max's office and took our seats on the floor along with all the other members. There was a big stack of papers on Max's desk. As soon as the meeting began, he picked them up and began handing them out. At the top of the first page, it said "Know-Down."

"I don't want you looking at these now," he told us. "You have two weeks to look at them. So for now, just fold them and put them aside."

I did as he said, and so did my friends and the other Horse Wise members.

Then Max explained what the papers were for. "A Know-Down is a little bit like a spelling bee," he began. "You'll get the chance to test your knowledge of

201

horses by answering questions. Each of you will be able to choose the difficulty of your questions, from one to four points. A four-point question might have four points to the answer, like, for instance, 'Name the parts of a horse's back between the shoulder and the dock.' "

"Withers, back, loins, croup!" Stevie called out excitedly.

She was right, though Max scolded her for interrupting. Then he went on to explain that we'll be able to choose easier questions worth fewer points, but that if we want to win the Know-Down, we'll have to learn a lot of information.

"It's all there," he said. "Study hard. Two weeks from today at our next unmounted meeting, we'll have the Know-Down."

Out of the corner of my eye, I saw Carole and Stevie exchanging glances. I immediately guessed what they were thinking. A little earlier, they had reported that they'd invited Phil and Cam to come to our next unmounted Horse Wise meeting, and both boys had promised to be there. I guess I haven't written much about Carole and Cam in my diary lately, though I probably should have. They've been writing back and forth on e-mail pretty often, and they've talked on the phone a bunch of times since they met at the horse show a couple of months ago. But they haven't seen each other again in person, and even though Carole isn't talking much about it, I'm sure she's excited. Probably a little nervous, too.

Especially after she found out about the Know-Down. Carole isn't very confident around boys sometimes, and I know that when she first met Cam she was worried about which of them knew more about horses and that kind of thing. It's probably partly Stevie's fault—she's so hyper-competitive with Phil that the two of them don't exactly provide the best example for other couples to follow. Still, Carole isn't Stevie. Knowing her, she's just as worried that she'll do better than Cam at the Know-Down as she is that he'll do better than her.

Carole and Stevie whispered back and forth for a moment or two. I didn't bother to try to hear what they were talking about, since I was sure I already knew. Unfortunately, though, Max overheard their whispers.

"Ahem," he said, staring pointedly at Stevie. "Did you say something?"

Since Max had already yelled at Stevie just a couple of minutes earlier, I decided to jump in and save her. I had something I wanted to mention anyway. "No, it was me," I called. "Sorry, I should have raised my hand." I raised my hand, and when Max nodded, I continued. "We checked the mare before we came in here and she seems edgy. Doesn't that mean she's about to foal?"

"Maybe," Max said. "It could also mean nothing. Judy made her daily vet check yesterday and didn't seem concerned. She'll be back this afternoon and will check again."

"But I know that when a mare gets edgy, it's a sign that she's about to foal," I persisted, surprised that Max, too, seemed so careless about the pregnant mare's condition.

"It can be," Max agreed. "There are other signs, too. Does anybody know what they are?"

Hands went up all over the room, and the group began providing various answers. Soon we'd heard a whole list of possible symptoms that different mares might or might not have just before foaling.

"So," Max said at last, "it seems that the only way to be sure a mare is about to begin serious labor is when serious labor begins. It's just not a simple question."

When he said that, I felt almost as annoyed with him as I'd been with my friends earlier. Why wouldn't anyone pay attention to what I was saying? I'd seen that mare myself—her entire personality was different than it had been before. To me, that's a really strong indicator that she's going to foal soon. Maybe nobody is listening to me now, but the mare will prove me right soon enough. I just hope there's someone around to help her through foaling.

Anyway, one other thing happened right after the meeting. I was heading for the door when I heard Max call my name. He also called May Grover, one of the younger riders.

"I want you two to work together on something," he told us. "I'm going to start a Big Sister/Little Sister learning program, and you're my test case."

For a moment I forgot about the mare. That sounded interesting.

"One of the things we rarely have time for here," Max went on, pulling a small paperback off the office bookshelf, "is working with hitching horses and ponies to carts and wagons. It's just something we don't do much and that's too bad because it's fun. Lisa, I want you to take this book and learn how to do it yourself and teach May to do it. Then in ten days, after our Tuesday riding class, I'd like the two of you to do a demonstration for the rest of Horse Wise. Will you have time to work on this together? You can use Nickel and hitch him to the cart we use for pony rides sometimes. Then, if you'd like, you can take your classmates for rides."

I took the book from him. What could I say? May is a nice kid. She's smart, she works hard, and she's not afraid to speak her mind. And learning about hitching a horse to a cart did sound sort of interesting, I guess. Still, I wasn't crazy about Max's idea—at least not the timing of it. Preparing for the Know-Down is going to be a full-time job. Plus I was already planning on spending some extra time with the pregnant mare, since nobody else seemed very concerned about her.

But May seemed so excited . . . and Max seemed to expect an automatic yes from me . . . and the book isn't very long . . . I found myself nodding and saying "Sure."

So for the next half hour, I was stuck checking out

the pony cart with May. I didn't want to be there—I wanted to be at the mare's stall when Judy Barker arrived so I could hear her diagnosis for myself. But I had a responsibility to May now, and I didn't want to let her down. I did my best to stay focused on the little girl.

"Are you excited about the Know-Down?" I asked her as we headed for the shed where Max keeps the pony cart.

"Am I ever!" May declared. "The trouble is, I won't know which to work on harder—the Know-Down or our project."

"You'll find time for it all," I assured her. "All you have to do is study your sheets for the Know-Down."

"I know," May said. "I put them in my pocket so I wouldn't lose them . . ." Her voice trailed off, and she began patting one pocket, then the other. "Oh no!" she cried in dismay. "I've lost them already!"

"Don't worry," I said. "Max will give you another set. Just ask him when we get back."

"I don't want him to know I lost them," May said, her lower lip trembling slightly.

She looked terribly upset, and I understood how she felt. I hate losing things, too. "Here, take mine," I told her, pulling my own set out of my pocket. "I can borrow one of my friends' and copy them so Max will never know that either of us lost a set, okay?"

May was so happy about the idea that I was glad I'd made the offer. It even made the next few minutes seem to pass a little faster as we reached the shed and looked over the pony cart. May seemed fascinated by everything about the plain little wooden cart, but I didn't share the feeling. Our project might seem useful and worthwhile, but right now, I'm afraid it's just going to eat up too much of my valuable time.

I finally managed to drag May away from the shed, only to find out that Judy had already come and gone. I rushed to the mare's stall and found Carole and Stevie there.

"Where have you been?" Carole asked.

"I've been with May Grover—Oh, it's a long story." I didn't want to take the time to explain about the Big Sister/Little Sister project just then. "What did Judy say? Didn't she say that the mare's moodiness meant she's about to foal?"

Stevie shrugged. "Oh, I forgot to ask. Judy was only here for a minute."

I couldn't believe it. Weren't my friends paying attention at all? "But didn't she say the mare could foal at any time?"

"I don't think so," Carole said. "She just checked on her and nodded, like everything seems to be on schedule. She's not due to foal for another two weeks, you know."

I knew that. But I also knew that mares didn't always foal on schedule.

So why aren't my friends taking my ideas more seriously? Just because they've been riding longer than I have, does that mean they automatically think they know better than me about everything that has to do with horses? I don't think so. Maybe the Know-Down will be an opportunity to show them how much I've learned. Of course, having a brand-new foal toddling around Pine Hollow within the next few days—as I'm sure we will—will show them the same thing!

In any case, I'm not planning to let the mare out of my sight for long until she has her foal. I checked on her once more before we left this afternoon, and she still seemed cranky and skittish. I just hope she doesn't foal tonight. I don't want to miss it.

When we got back here to Carole's house, we fixed ourselves a snack. Colonel Hanson had to go to his office for a while because of some kind of minor emergency, and before he left, he warned us—well, actually Carole—not to touch anything on his desk. It was kind of a weird thing for him to say, but we soon figured out that it probably had to do with Carole's birthday, which is coming up in the not-too-distant future. (He also warned us not to eat all the peanut butter, which wasn't a weird thing for him to say at all—though it was a hard thing for us to do!)

After he left, we prepared to start studying for the Know-Down. That's when we realized that none of us had the study sheets Max had given us. I had given mine to May. Stevie and Carole had mailed theirs straight off to Cam and Phil, not wanting to have an unfair advantage over the visitors.

"What are we going to do?" Stevie asked.

I didn't know what to say. I knew it would be easy enough to ask Max for new sheets tomorrow, but we'd all been counting on getting a lot of studying done tonight.

"Dad," Carole said suddenly, her expression brightening. "He's a volunteer."

I had almost forgotten that Colonel Hanson is one of Horse Wise's parent volunteers. Of course he would have a copy of the sheets. But he might not be home for hours. After some debate, we decided to check on his desk. We figured it would be all right as long as Carole wasn't the one to do the checking and just as long as we didn't look too hard at anything other than the Know-Down sheets.

We were in luck. Stevie found the sheets right away. We hurried to a neighbor's house to make copies, and then, finally, we were able to get to work.

There were seven sheets, all of them chock-full of information about horses, starting with one-point questions and going up to four-pointers. We quizzed each other on everything—stable bandages, hand faults, conformation, and who knows what else. Finally, we called it quits and watched a movie. Carole and Stevie fell asleep right after that, and I think I'm finally about ready to follow their example.

I wonder if there really will be a brand-new foal waiting for us at the stable tomorrow? I can't wait to find out.

FROM: MayFlower
TO: LAtwood
SUBJECT: Big Sis/Little Sis
MESSAGE:

Hi, Lisa! It's me, May Grover. I hope you don't mind, but I looked up your e-mail address on the Horse Wise member list. I just wanted to write and say thanks again for promising to teach me all about hitching a pony to a cart. It's going to be fun—I can't wait! I even asked my mom to take me out and buy me a copy of that book Max gave you to read. It looked really interesting, and I bet it would help if we both read it, right?

Thanks again, Lisa. See you at the stable!

Dear Diary,

It's Monday night, and I'm feeling kind of guilty. Still, we didn't do anything wrong on purpose . . .

I'd better begin at the beginning. This afternoon at the stable, after checking on the mare—still no foal, surprisingly—I went in search of May. I'd accidentally left the book Max gave me at Carole's house on Saturday night, but luckily May had gone out and bought herself a copy on Sunday. She had also read it from cover to cover, which was a relief since I hadn't so much as skimmed it at the sleepover.

I was able to cover by asking May to explain what she'd learned. She was eager to figure things out for herself, so the session actually went pretty well. She'd read hard, studied hard, and learned, which meant that Max's project was working—though maybe not in quite the way he'd imagined. Still, as long as May learns what she's supposed to learn, I'm sure he'll be happy.

Anyway, I wasn't really concentrating very hard on May or our project. I was busy thinking about the mare and the Know-Down. I checked on the mare one more time before joining my friends for another study session. We decided to hold this one in Prancer's stall. It's a big box stall, and it's empty this week while Prancer is off getting some extra training. So it seemed like the perfect spot.

We settled down in the fresh, fragrant straw lining the stall floor and got started. It wasn't long before Veronica stuck her head over the wall and interrupted us. "What are you up to in there?" she demanded in her snottiest tone.

"We're studying," Stevie replied.

"What for?"

"The Know-Down, of course." Stevie rolled her eyes at Carole and me before glancing at Veronica. "Haven't you been studying? Or is that one of those things you get your butler to do for you?"

Veronica shot her a dirty look. "Certainly I've been studying," she said haughtily. "Very hard, in fact. Go ahead, test me."

Carole glanced down at the sheet she was holding and read the next question. "What's another word for *forging?*"

Veronica crinkled her forehead in thought. "Isn't that where a horse just eats whatever it comes across in the wild?"

I shook my head and glanced at my friends. Veronica was obviously confusing *foraging* with *forging*, which is another word for "overreaching." It happens when a horse's stride is too long and its hind toe hits its front heel.

Carole read the correct answer from the sheet to Veronica, who looked surprised and annoyed. "That's in there?" she demanded, glancing at the sheaf of papers Carole was holding.

"Uh-huh," Stevie replied. "As your butler no doubt knows."

Before Veronica could respond to Stevie's comment, there was a shriek from the far side of the stable. It sounded like May, and it sounded like she was in trouble.

We dropped everything and raced out of the stall and down the aisle. As soon as we reached the stable door, we saw that May had been working with Nickel and that the pony had escaped. We spent the next half hour recapturing the frisky pony and comforting May, who was pretty upset about the whole thing. By the time it was all over, it was time to leave the stable. That was when Carole discovered that her Know-

Down papers were gone. She found them soon enough, stacked neatly in the far corner of the empty stall where we'd been studying. The odd thing was, she didn't remember putting them there. But we didn't worry about it too much at the time.

As we were getting ready to leave, we ran into May again. She was still upset about what had happened with Nickel, but we managed to reassure her. Soon she was smiling again.

"There's something I'd like to know about," she said, pulling several papers out of her backpack. "It's this study sheet Max gave us. Can you help me with it?"

"No problem," Stevie said cheerfully. "Ask away."

May wanted us to explain the answer to a question about a horse's body temperature. But that's not the important part. The important thing is that when we looked at her papers, we realized they didn't look anything like the ones we'd been using to study for the past two days. May's sheets included lists of information, not questions and answers. They weren't divided by point value, either. They had some of the same information as ours, plus a lot more.

That's when we realized what had happened. Max had given the parent volunteers the actual questions and answers he was planning to use at the Know-Down. That was why Colonel Hanson had warned us against snooping on his desk. It hadn't had anything to do with Carole's birthday after all.

"You know what this means, don't you?" Stevie said once it had all sunk in.

"It means we're cheating," I replied, swallowing hard as I said it. I had never cheated on anything in my entire life. I'd never needed to. I'd never wanted to.

"That wasn't what I had in mind," Stevie said. "What it means is that we're just about guaranteed to do better on the Know-Down than anybody else."

"True," Carole said slowly. "We've been working very hard, too, and I know we're learning a lot."

I was starting to see their point. We really were studying awfully hard, no matter what sheets we were using. There was a lot of information in those questions and answers, and it wasn't going to be easy to remember it all, no matter what. "We're learning the things we're supposed to learn," I mused. "Also, I know from experience in taking tests that the teachers usually focus on the most important information when they make up the test. All the things they ask questions about are the things they really want you to know. The point is that Max must have put the most important information into the questions he plans to ask. That's what we *ought* to be focusing on. And since we've been studying exactly that, it *is* what we've been focusing on. We're learning what he wants us to learn."

We were all silent for a moment after that, each of us thinking our own thoughts. Finally, Carole spoke up. "Lisa's right, you know," she said.

214

That settled it. I wasn't completely confident about what I'd just said. But Carole is as honest as the day is long. If she doesn't think we're cheating, that's good enough for me. And for Stevie.

At least I think it is. We agreed to keep what happened between us, since we don't want Max to feel he has to go through all the work of coming up with new questions—new questions that probably won't be as good as the first set.

It all made perfect sense at the time. But when I got home, I found it hard to concentrate on other things. I tried to read that book about harnesses, but my mind kept wandering back to the Know-Down. Is what we're doing really all right? If the mix-up with the questions had happened at school, there would be no doubt—it would be wrong. But Pine Hollow isn't school, and the Know-Down isn't really a test. It's a game, and the idea is to show how much you've learned. And my friends and I have been working hard and learning a lot.

I just don't know what to think. It's been driving me crazy all evening. And reading boring information about harnesses hasn't been much of a distraction.

There is one other thing I've been thinking about a little, though. I've had the funniest feeling for the past few days that Carole and Stevie are feeling weird because they both have a boyfriend coming to the Know-Down and I don't. I'm not sure why I think that, but I do. It's something about the way they look at me—and at each other—whenever Phil's or Cam's name comes up.

The truth is, it doesn't bother me one bit. It's always fun to have Phil around, and Cam seems like a really nice guy. And a Horse Wise meeting isn't exactly the high-school prom or anything like that. I don't know why they think I'd mind not having a "date" for it, whether they do or not.

I'm not quite sure how to let them know that, though. They haven't said anything to me about it directly, and bringing it up seems kind of awkward. I mean, if I bring it up, that means I've been thinking about it. And if they think I've been thinking about it too much, they'll be more convinced than ever that I have some kind of problem with it. So I guess I'll just keep quiet, at least for now.

And I know one thing. Keeping quiet about that seems a lot easier just now than keeping quiet about those mixed-up Know-Down sheets.

Thornbury Hall
London, England

Dear Lisa,

Thanks for your nice letter and your congratulations. I'm really excited about my internship, and surprisingly, Mom and Dad seemed kind of impressed when I told them about it. Suddenly graduation doesn't seem quite so scary anymore!

Thanks, also, for telling me about the wedding you threw at your stable. It sounds like you had a lot of fun and really helped your friend Dorothy. Stevie sounds like a very creative person—kind of wacky, too! I wish I could meet her and Carole sometime. I doubt it will be anytime soon, though—it doesn't look like I'm going to make it back to the United States before I have to leave for Africa. Oh well.

So, speaking of love and romance, is there anything I should know about my little sister's love life? Mom just sent me your new school picture, and it's hard for me to believe that the gorgeous young lady in the picture is my little sister. I'm guessing that you're fighting the boys off with a stick these days. Don't be afraid to share all the details! Remember, I need all the info I can get if I want my screenplay to ring true. (And I promise not to tell your friends if you're afraid they'll be jealous!)

But seriously—I hope you know that you really can tell me anything you want and have it be just between us. A secret brother-sister thing. (Remember how I taught you to drive? I never did tell Mom and Dad about that—did you?) I never really noticed how much I missed you until I got to know you again through your letters. Keep them coming—please. The mail in Africa is bound to be a little slower, but that will just give me longer to look forward to hearing from you!

Love, Your brother,
Peter

P.S. I haven't forgotten that I promised to send you part of my screenplay soon. I'm working away on it, and I think I'll have some scenes ready to send off before long.

Dear Diary,

Okay, today definitely *wasn't* one of my best days ever. Actually, I'm sort of ashamed even to write down what happened. But I figure it's the kind of lesson I really don't want to forget, so I can make sure it doesn't happen again.

I won't go into detail—I don't want to remember *that* much—but suffice it to say that I learned even more from Max's Big Sis/Little Sis project than May did. You see, at today's riding lessons it was time for us to give our presentation. Tuesday isn't an official Pony Club day, but most of the kids in Horse Wise take lessons then, so they were all there to watch me and May hitch Nickel to the pony cart. Or rather, they were there to watch May do it. I mostly just stood there and looked like a dope. You see, I never did quite get around to reading that book. And I guess I didn't pay much attention when I was watching May practice what she was learning.

That's why I had no idea what to do when May asked for some help. She wanted me to do something with some piece of the harness—the crupper, I think she called it, though I wouldn't swear to it. It was one of the most embarrassing moments in my life, sort of like that dream I have sometimes that I have to take a big exam that I haven't studied for at all.

As usual, my friends stepped in to help. Stevie even managed to cover my ignorance, mostly. But I knew the truth, and so did she, and so did Carole. And so did Max, of course. He didn't say much about it, but I had the funniest feeling he knew exactly what had happened and why. I guess he figured I'd learned my lesson, so he didn't give me a hard time. I still feel terrible about the whole thing, though. Maybe May didn't end up needing my help—she learned everything she needed to know just fine on her own—but I really let Max down. I don't plan to let that happen again.

That's not the only important thing that happened today. We decided to tell Max the truth about the Know-Down study sheets.

I'm not exactly sure how it happened. I mean, I know how it happened for me. With each passing day, what we were doing seemed more and more like cheating. Each morning when I woke up, I was a little less happy about keeping our secret. I guess the same sort of thing was happening in my friends' heads, too. The Saddle Club seems to work that way sometimes.

After a quick Saddle Club meeting after our lesson, the decision was made. We went to talk to Max. Colonel Hanson and the other parent volunteers were in his office, which made what we had to do seem even harder. But we weren't about to back down.

"Max, there's something we have to tell you," I said. I went on to describe exactly what had happened, from the way we all gave away our study sheets to our theory about Carole's birthday to the discovery after Nickel's escape. "We're sorry, Max," I finished at last. "We really are. We didn't mean to do this. For a little while after we discovered it, it seemed like a great thing, but in the end we know it's just not right. We need to learn everything there is to know about horses, not just what we're going to be tested on."

Nobody said a thing for a few minutes. Max blew out a chestful of air and sat back in his chair, looking thoughtful. The other adults kept silent and still.

"You know what this means, don't you?" Max said at last. His voice was calm.

"Disqualified?" Carole asked anxiously. "Are we out?"

"No, I don't think so." Max gazed at us each in turn. "I suspect you three have been working very hard. No, what it means is that I'm going to have to make up new questions."

"It's going to be a lot more work and we're really sorry," Stevie said.

"I don't mind the work," Max said. "What I mind is that I thought I'd made the meanest, sneakiest, and toughest questions possible out of that material on the study sheets. Now I have to be meaner, sneakier, and tougher—all because of you."

"You're very good at it," Stevie told him sincerely. I

guess she realized then that what she'd said might not sound exactly like a compliment. "I mean, it takes one to know one," she added hastily.

Max smiled weakly. Then he stood up. "Back to the drawing board," he said. "Now get out of here. I've got a lot of work to do. And so do you."

We've been feeling kind of bad since we left the office, because we know we let Max down. We're also worried because we have a lot more studying to do if we want to be prepared for the Know-Down. But most of all, we're relieved. It's finally all out in the open. We did the right thing, and we're glad.

FROM:	Steviethegreat
TO:	LAtwood
TO:	HorseGal
SUBJECT:	HELP!
MESSAGE:	

What are the five major internal parasites? AARGH! I CAN'T BELIEVE WE ACTUALLY HAVE TO KNOW THIS STUFF!

Oh well. Maybe I can use the info to gross out my brothers sometime. If I ever remember the right answer.

HELP! MAYDAY! SOS!

Botflies, bloodworms, pinworms, intestinal worms, and stomach worms.

From now on, remind me not to answer my e-mail while I'm eating leftover spaghetti as an after-school snack. Ugh!

Dear Diary,

I just got back from visiting Promise at the stable. She's such a cute little filly! It's amazing that after being in the world for only a couple of days, she's already frolicking and running around like an old pro on her long, skinny little legs. Things seem to happen so fast sometimes . . . though some things don't happen quite as fast as I expect them to . . .

I still can't believe how worked up I was back when I thought her mother was going to give birth a week or two early. I was so sure I was right, that I knew what was going to happen. . . . I guess there's been a lot of that going around lately. I mean, just look at what happened with May and the pony cart project. I thought I was just there to help her, because I'm older, and she ended up teaching me a whole lot (even if she didn't know it). And now that I think about it, I guess Carole and Stevie's worries that I'd feel left out when their boyfriends came to Horse Wise fit into that, too. They thought they knew how I would feel about it, and once they made up their minds, they didn't even notice that they were totally wrong.

Actually, it turned out to be a lot of fun having the two boys at the Know-Down. I think they enjoyed it, too. And I know Carole and Stevie were glad to have them there. We were all a little nervous before the Know-Down started, but that didn't last too long. Max divided us into teams, with four members on each one. May and I ended up on the same team. I'm pretty sure Max did that on purpose just to make sure I hadn't forgotten what I'd learned from the Big Sis/Little Sis project, though naturally he would never admit such a thing. Carole was on a team with Cam, and Stevie and Phil were teammates, too.

For the first round, most people wanted to start with pretty easy questions. When it was Stevie's turn, she was daring and asked for a three-pointer.

"Where is the Spanish Riding School?" Max asked.

I almost laughed because I knew the answer to that right away, thanks to the first letter from Peter last summer. I crossed my fingers on Stevie's behalf, hoping she would remember, too. I'd mentioned Peter's visit to the Spanish Riding School when we'd first come across a reference to it on our study sheets. But as I recalled, around that same time Stevie had been distracted because her brothers kept poking their heads into her room, where we were studying at the time, and neighing like horses.

Stevie scrunched up her eyebrows as she thought. Suddenly her face lit up. "Austria," she said. "It's in Austria!"

"Yes," said Max.

"Nice," Phil commented, clapping Stevie on the back.

Stevie blushed, then shot me a quick, meaningful look. I smiled, then glanced around to see if anyone else had noticed. Nobody else seemed to, but one person did have a strange look on her face. Veronica. She looked confused and slightly annoyed, and I wondered why. As the game continued, I couldn't help noticing that she was missing a lot of pretty easy questions. That seemed odd, since we'd all seen her studying from her sheets all week.

It was Carole who first figured out what must have happened. When Nickel got loose that day, she'd left her study sheets—the old sheets, the question-and-answer ones—lying in Prancer's stall. Veronica must have suspected that our sheets were different from hers and had snitched them and made a copy before Carole returned to retrieve them. That was why she did poorly. She'd studied only the questions she thought Max was going to ask, not realizing that he had changed almost all his questions after we'd told him the truth about our study sheets. Therefore, she'd ended up not knowing any of the answers and looking like a real dummy. We figure it served her right!

Thornbury Hall
London, England

Dear Lisa,

Well, here it is. The moment you've been waiting for. My screenplay! Ta-da!!!!

Ha ha. Actually, what's here is just a sketchy idea of how one of the scenes might play out. I'm trying hard to nail down the proper atmosphere (not to mention the characters), and this scene is my best attempt so far. I'm not sure it will actually appear in the final version of the screenplay, but I still want your honest opinion about it so I can get an idea of whether I'm on the right track. I'll send more when it's ready, but in the meantime . . .

FADE IN:
INTERIOR an aisle in a well-kept stable. Three girls, S, L, and C, are carrying some tack down the aisle. The three girls are around thirteen years old, dressed in cutoff shorts, sneakers, and tank tops. It's nighttime, and moonlight pours through the stable windows.
CUT TO
CLOSE UP on L, an attractive girl with light brown hair.

225

L

This moonlit trail ride should be fun. I'm glad you
thought of it, S.

PAN TO shot of all three girls as they pause in front of a
stall with a tall white horse inside.

S

Me too. Just remember—we can't tell Mr. Renney when
he gets back from his vacation. You know he doesn't
think it's safe for young girls like us to ride at night.

C
(nervously)

I know. Are you sure this is a good idea? I mean, nobody
even knows where we are.

S opens the stall door and pats the white horse. Then she
begins putting the bridle and saddle on the horse while her
friends watch.

S
(confidently)

We know. Besides, what could happen? The three of us
can look out for each other. We're best friends.

C

Okay. Well, I'd better go tack up Starshine while you
finish with Moonglow.

226

The camera follows C and L as they move down the aisle. L stops in front of another stall.

L

Here I am at Dancer's stall. I'll meet you guys outside, okay?

As C nods and moves on, L enters the stall, where a beautiful bay Thoroughbred is waiting for her. L pulls a handful of sugar lumps out of her shorts pocket and begins feeding them to the horse.

L

Hi there, girl. Are you ready for a nice long ride?

The horse whinnies in response and licks L's hand as the girl begins to buckle on her bridle.

That's all I have so far. Be brutally honest when you write back. What do you think? Do I have the atmosphere right?

Love,
Peter

FROM: HorseGal

TO: LAtwood

SUBJECT: Your brother's screenplay

MESSAGE:

I just read the scene you gave us today. Parts of it are pretty good. The characters are interesting and I think showing them tacking up is a really good idea. It will give moviegoers a feel for stable life. But I do have a few comments about some of the specific details. First of all, obviously, the characters shouldn't be wearing shorts and sneakers to ride in. For another thing, they shouldn't be riding at night, especially if nobody knows where they are. It's not safe for them or for the horses. (And I can't help wondering if this is happening too soon after the horses have eaten their dinner, and if the characters have considered this.) Also, the way this is written makes it sound like the characters put on the horses' bridles before their saddles instead of the other way around. And if this Mr. Renney is supposed to be the stable owner or manager, it's not very realistic that he would be away on vacation. Can you remember the last time Max took a vacation? I can't. Also, he calls one of the horses "white" when it should probably really be "gray" or "light gray." Only albino horses are truly white; the rest are just darker or lighter shades of gray, even if they look white. And I would suggest changing the sugar lumps L feeds her horse to carrots or apples or something.

Too much sugar isn't good for a horse. And at the very end, he says that Dancer licks L's hand. Dancer is a horse, not a dog, so she wouldn't lick Lisa unless she was trying to lick the last few bits of sugar off her hand or something like that. More likely, she would snort or shake her head, and maybe nudge at L with her nose like Starlight usually does after I feed him a treat.

Those are the most important comments. In addition, it would be even better if Peter described things in a little more detail. What kind of stable is it? How many stalls? Do the doors open to an outdoor aisle or an interior one? What size are the stalls, and what bedding is used inside? Are the girls carrying English tack or Western? What do the horses look like? Are they all Thoroughbreds or just Dancer? How big are the horses? How old are they? What are their personalities like? Are they calm or skittish or friendly or sleepy?

Aside from that, it's really good.

FROM: Steviethegreat
TO: LAtwood
SUBJECT: Movie review
MESSAGE:

Okay, so Peter's little scene was pretty good. A worthy attempt, aside from a few little mistakes like having the girls ride in sneakers. But I don't think he's quite captured the

true essence of The Saddle Club. Not that I blame him—
it's a very complex and subtle thing. So rather than trying
to explain, I thought I'd provide an example you can send
to him. Tell him this kind of scene would be much more
typical of our daily life.

DRAMA ON THE TRAIL

a screenplay scene by S. Lake

FADE IN:
INTERIOR a stall at a stable.
CLOSE UP on S, a lovely middle-school girl with a great
smile and intelligent eyes. S is just finishing tacking up her
horse, CHAMPION, a tall bay Thoroughbred.

S

Ready for our trail ride, Champ?

PAN TO the door of the stall as C and L appear outside.
They are each leading a tacked-up horse.

L

Ready to go, S?

S

(as she finishes latching Champion's bridle)
Ready! Let's go!

CUT TO

EXTERIOR, a field behind the stable. The three girls are trotting along side by side on their horses.

C

Should we ride on the Winding Trail today, girls?

S

(looks worried)

I'm not sure about that. Our riding instructor, Matt, told us never to ride there. It's dangerous.

L

(laughs)

Don't be silly. We're all good riders. Especially you, S. Matt says you could ride in the Olympics someday— unless you decide to follow your headmistress's advice and run for president or become a Supreme Court justice. I'm sure someone as multitalented as you can handle the Winding Trail, and you can help us if we have trouble. Okay? Let's try it.

C

Yes! Come on, S. We're going whether you like it or not.

S

(still looks doubtful)

Well, if you insist. I guess I have to come along to make sure you're all right. I hope nothing bad happens.

FADE OUT
FADE IN on the three girls a few minutes later. They are
making their way along a spectacular mountain ridge. The
trail is wide and smooth, and the horses are trotting slowly.
The scenery is amazing, and C and L are gasping and ex-
claiming as they look out over an endless prairie of tall,
waving grass.

S glances around from side to side, still looking worried.

S

Maybe we should head back now. My sixth sense is telling
me something bad could happen soon.

C
(carelessly)
What could happen?

L
(glancing at S)
I don't know, C. You know S's sixth sense is never
wrong. It's probably the most reliable of all her
supernatural powers—even more reliable than her
ability to control the weather. Didn't she predict that
earthquake last month? And remember when she
saved the President from alien terrorists when he
visited our town? Then there was the time she foresaw the
breakup of that Hollywood marriage that everyone else
said—

232

L stops with a gasp.

L
(eyes widening)
D-Did you guys hear that?

C
Hear what?

From offscreen, there is the unmistakable sound of a
GROWL.

C
(suddenly looking frightened)
That sounds like—

CUT TO a stand of underbrush nearby, just as a huge
GRIZZLY BEAR bursts out of it with a CRASH and another series of GROWLS. C and L scream in terror, and all
three horses start rearing and trying to race off.

S
(shouting)
Keep your horses under control! It's our only chance to
escape!

L
I—I can't! *Aaaaaaaaaaah!*

Her horse, THUNDER, whirls and lets out a shriek of terror as the bear comes toward him. Thunder starts to run, heading straight for the edge of the cliff—a dropoff of hundreds of feet at least. L screams again and again as the reins slip out of her hands.

S
(bravely)
Hold on, L! I'll save you!

S rides toward L. Just as Thunder is about to leap over the cliff, S leans over from Champion's saddle and grabs the panicky horse's bridle, stopping him just in time.

L
(breathlessly)
Thank you, S! You saved my life! Again!

From nearby, there is a SHRIEK and another GROWL.

S
Uh-oh.

PAN TO follow her gaze as she looks and sees that C has fallen off her horse and is lying helplessly just beneath the grizzly's sharp claws. The bear raises one paw and prepares to swipe as C screams again.

Hold on, C! I'm coming . . .

Okay, I'm not sure what happens next, but I could come up with something if Peter wants me to.

Let me know what he thinks of my scene, okay? See you tomorrow at Pine Hollow!

Dear Diary,

I can't believe the school year ends in less than two weeks! It seems like we just started a few days ago . . . Oh well. Actually, I haven't been thinking about school too much. I've been too busy wondering what's going on with my parents. They've been acting really weird lately, and I have no idea why. They've been tiptoeing around the house and whispering to each other whenever they think I won't notice. But I have noticed. And it's starting to get really aggravating. I can't help thinking something bad is going on—maybe even something really bad, like Alice Jackson's parents . . . Well, I guess it won't do me much good to wonder and worry any more than I have to. I just hope they decide to let me in on the secret soon—even though I'm afraid I'm not going to like it, whatever it is.

Okay, I'm really going to try to stop worrying about it. At least until I get my creative writing assignment out of the way. It's our final assignment of the year.

We're supposed to write something that sums up how we feel about the school year that's just ending. It can be any format we like. In a way, that makes it harder to figure out what to do. I'd like my assignment to be something good and creative, not only for the grade, but also to sort of show Ms. Shields how much I've learned from her this year. I mean, I never knew how many ways there are to communicate something. If I were Stevie, I'd probably try something crazy like turning in a combination poem-story-essay-play-letter to show that. No, scratch that. If I were Stevie I probably wouldn't want to spend that much time on mere homework with summer so close. Ha ha!

Actually, though, maybe I will ask Stevie for suggestions when I see her at the stable tomorrow afternoon. After all, this is a *creative* writing assignment. And Stevie is nothing if not creative . . .

Summer's Approach
a haiku by Lisa Atwood

School—and life—move on;
lessons learned, so much remains.
That's what makes us real . . .

236

Dear Diary,

The haiku I just copied above this entry is the one I wrote for my final creative writing assignment. It was Stevie's idea to do a haiku—she thought it would be the shortest and easiest way to get the assignment done.

That's not why I did it, though. When she was talking about how nice and short a haiku is—*has* to be—I was thinking about something Ms. Shields told us once. She said it's sometimes harder to say or write a short, important thing than a long, ordinary one. I remember, because when she said it, it made me think about my letters to Peter. The parts of his letters where he says what he really feels about stuff are more meaningful than any of the other, longer stuff he writes about less important things. Also, I've found out how hard it is to condense everything that happens in my life into a diary or a letter or any other limited space. If I wrote about everything that happened to me (the way I thought those diary writers in that article did), I would never have time to do anything but write. So I have to decide what's important enough to mention and what I have to skip. That makes me think a little more about everything I do.

I bet Peter is discovering the same sort of thing as he works on his screenplay. I'm sure it will be a huge challenge for him to sum up the adventures of The Saddle Club in just one movie (even though I've already sort of narrowed it down for him in my letters). It makes me happier than ever that I decided not to send him Stevie's screenplay scene a few weeks back. If he really thought we ran into grizzly bears and earthquakes and the rest of it, he might just give up on writing about us entirely!

Oops, I'm getting a little off the topic, which is my haiku assignment. I turned it in yesterday, and I haven't been able to stop worrying about it since (except when I've been distracted by worrying about my parents' weird behavior, which is more mysterious than ever). I hope Ms. Shields understands why I decided to write a haiku instead of something longer. I guess there's no way for her to know that it probably took me just as long to get it right as it would have taken me to write an essay or something. I just hope she realizes why I chose to do it and doesn't think it's because of more, well, *Stevian* reasoning.

I guess it's too late to worry about that now, though. I'll just have to wait and see what Ms. Shields says. In the meantime, I'm starting to wonder if I should ask Mom and Dad if I can call Peter on the phone. I haven't heard from him since I sent my comments about his screenplay scene, and I think he finishes school soon, too. I hope I wasn't too harsh. I just told him it was mostly good and then passed on a few of the more important mistakes that Carole pointed out. She'd probably be annoyed if she knew I didn't bother to explain to him the difference between saying "white" and "gray." It's not like those Hollywood studios don't have fact checkers for that kind of stuff, right? At least I assume they do. Anyway, as I said, I didn't send him Stevie's screenplay sample at all. I told her it was because he might get confused, since there are no huge mountains *or* grizzly bears in Willow Creek. She was a little insulted, I think, but luckily Veronica happened along as I was breaking the news. She said something obnoxious, which made Stevie forget all about Peter and the screenplay and everything else. I guess Veronica does have her uses after all!

Dear Diary,

I'm stunned. That's the only word for it. Stunned. Stunned. Stunned.

I got a nice fat letter from Peter yesterday. The top sheet was a little note saying how grateful he was for my comments on the scene he sent before. He said he got so inspired that he wrote several partial scenes, which he was enclosing.

I set aside the top sheet and started reading. I finished a few minutes ago, and I still don't even know what to say about it. So for now, I'm just going to paste it in and let it speak for itself.

RIDING FOR YOUR LIFE

a screenplay by Peter Atwood

FADE IN:

INTERIOR a stable, twilight. Outside the high, narrow windows, the sky is red and ominous. Thunder rumbles in the distance.

PAN TO three teenage girls standing outside a stall. LILA, a lovely brunette dressed in riding breeches, is leaning against the wall. CARLA, an African American with big brown eyes, is looking into the stall. STELLA, a vivacious, fun-loving blonde in cutoff jeans, stands nearby. Inside the stall is a horse.

STELLA

Hurry up, Carla. Finish grooming Diablo so we can start the party.

LILA

(nervously)

I don't know. What if Mr. Renney finds out? He'll be really mad if he hears we held a party in his stable when he was out of town.

STELLA

Don't be such a worrier, Lila. How's he going to find out?

(giggles)

Those hot guys we met at the diner this afternoon aren't going to tell him, that's for sure.

CARLA

I kind of wish you hadn't invited those guys, Stella. We don't know anything about them. And they looked kind of unsavory, if you ask me.

CRASH OF THUNDER, closer now. The light outside has faded while they were talking, and the stable is now dimly lit by only a couple of bare bulbs hanging from the ceiling. As lightning flashes, the lights flicker, then resume their yellowish glow. A gust of wind blows down the stable aisle, setting the bulbs swinging, causing grotesque shadows to dance on the walls.

CARLA

(shudders and glances around)
It's kind of a spooky night, isn't it?

STELLA

(grins)
That's why we need those big strong guys to protect us.
(break—remainder of scene to come)
(new scene—later in film)

CUT TO Carla, huddled in the corner of a stall. She is barely visible in the dark of the stable. A large stallion stamps his feet nervously just in front of her. Both girl and horse are staring at the darkened stable doorway. The SOUND of something large being dragged down the aisle is audible over the howl of the storm.

CARLA
(speaks to horse in a nervous whisper)
Don't give me away, boy. They can't find me here.

The horse SNORTS loudly.
JAKE's head appears in the stable doorway. Even in the dim light of the pocket flashlight he is holding, his scar gleams on his forehead and his snake tattoo is visible on his neck.

JAKE
(nastily)
What's all the racket in here, you big stupid animal?

PAN TO Carla, still huddled in the corner, looking terrified. Jake's eyes gleam eagerly as he spots her.
CUT TO full scene as Jake steps forward.

JAKE
(even more nastily)
Aha! What have we here?

He opens the stall door. The stallion backs away, and nothing stands between Jake and Carla but some straw.
CLOSE UP on Carla's terrified face.

CARLA
(whimpers)
Please . . . don't . . .

CUT TO three-quarter head-on view of Jake. The stable aisle behind him is completely dark; only his small flashlight illuminates his face.

JAKE
Heh heh heh. Time to have some fun.

There is a sudden CRASH of thunder, which sounds like it's right on top of them. The accompanying LIGHTNING lights up the stable aisle behind Jake, and for a split second it is as bright as day. In that split second, a HOODED FIGURE dressed all in black is visible looming over Jake, holding a long set of leather reins in its gloved hands. Its face is hidden beneath the folds of its dark hood.
Carla SCREAMS at the top of her lungs.

Jake is unaware of what stands behind him. The hooded figure takes a slow step forward until it is standing just behind Jake, a shadowy presence at the edge of the flashlight beam.

JAKE
(a little startled by the thunder and surprised by Carla's scream)
Aw, come on. I only want to . . . AAARGH!

The rest of his comment is lost as the hooded figure swiftly loops the reins around the thug's neck and pulls them tight. Jake's eyes bulge out and his hands fly to his throat as he struggles to breathe, to escape.

CUT TO
CLOSE UP on Carla's horrified face. She is paralyzed with fear as she watches what is going on, too terrified to scream again. Offscreen, the sounds of GURGLES and GASPS as Jake chokes. After a moment, lit by another flash of lightning, Carla hides her face in her hands.
PULL OUT slightly to show all of Carla. There is a final THUD, and a second later Jake's lifeless hand flops, palm up, onto Carla's riding boot.
There is the sound of slow, heavy FOOTSTEPS moving away in the aisle outside as Carla shudders helplessly in the stall.

A moment later, the sound of Lila's voice from somewhere outside the stall window.

LILA
(offscreen, faraway; sounds nervous)
Carla! Stella! Where are you? Guys? This isn't funny . . .
(scene to be continued)

Dear Diary,

Okay, it's been a whole day since Peter's screenplay arrived, and I still can't believe it. I can't believe this is what he got from my life story. More importantly, I can't believe how awful it is. How could my brother write something so bad, so stupid? I don't want myself and my friends portrayed that way, even if he didn't use our real names. Not that anyone in Hollywood would ever be interested in such a lame screenplay anyway . . . or would they? I don't know. I've seen actual movies that weren't any better than this. Well, not *much* better, anyway.

But how can I tell him what I really think? He's been working on this thing for almost a year. It's something he really wants to do—not just for fun, but for a living. How can I tell him what I really think without hurting his feelings and totally discouraging him? And what if I do tell him the truth and he doesn't want to write to me anymore? I don't think I could stand that.

I really have no idea what to do . . .

Dear Diary,

Great news! Actually, make that great news times three. First of all, I got an A on my haiku. Ms. Shields totally got why I did it—she didn't think I was being lazy at all. In fact, she took me aside after class on the last day of school to tell me I ought to keep writing as much as I can. I'm definitely going to try to follow her advice, starting with this diary.

The second piece of great news isn't quite that great, because I'm still not sure I did the right thing. But it's great that it's over with, anyway. I finally wrote back to Peter a couple of days ago. I didn't really say that much about his screenplay—I just sort of praised the characterizations and the dramatic settings and a few other things, and corrected one or two minor things, like how he still has Stella wearing shorts around the stable, which she probably wouldn't. I didn't know what else to do. How do I even know the screenplay is even really that bad? Some people might actually like it, I guess.

On to my third piece of news, which is truly fantastic. You see, this morning when Carole arrived at Pine Hollow, she announced that she had a secret. At first I wasn't exactly thrilled about that, mostly because my parents' secret has been on my mind more than ever since the school year ended. But Carole's secret turned out to be the good kind. It was a letter from Kate

Devine. Carole gave it to me to keep after she read it, so here it is:

Bar None Ranch
17 Sidewinder Drive

Hello, Saddle Club! (c/o Carole)

How are things way over there on the East Coast? Out West, things have been very interesting. Do you three remember Eli Grimes, who used to be the head wrangler here at the Bar None? If so, I'm sure you also remember Jeannie Sanders, who also worked here for a while, and how we helped set them up with each other that time when you were out here visiting . . . well, I guess I probably don't have to remind you too much about that. But anyway, Jeannie ended up following Eli when he went back to college, and they finally got married this year. Don't bother to wonder why you didn't receive invitations to the wedding—my family didn't, either. That's because Jeannie and Eli eloped! Isn't that romantic? They just decided, spur of the moment (spur—get it? Ha ha!) during a vacation they took together, that it was time to get hitched (get it?), and so they went ahead and did it.

Anyway, that's only one of the reasons I'm writing to you now. I mean, I thought you'd be interested in hearing about their last-minute wedding, especially after what Carole told me when we talked on the phone last month—you know, about the wedding you guys threw for your friends and their horses. But I also have

247

some other news that also happens to involve Eli and Jeannie. I think you're going to like it. No, scratch that. I'm sure you're going to love it!

Eli and Jeannie have rented a ranch in Wyoming for the summer and they want to run a summer camp for kids there. Most of the kids who have signed up are younger than we are. Eli called Dad last week and asked him if he knew any riders who might like to come. He said he was hoping to find some really good riders who would both be able to have fun and to help the younger kids. He said he's going to need a lot of help and that it will be work so he's got to have good, reliable riders. He kept saying things like he hoped to find people with different kinds of riding skills—even English. Of course, he was just fishing. He meant me and you three. So? What do you think? It's for three weeks. It would be pretty hard work because it's not just a ranch, it's a farm, too, so we'd be kind of living off the land. Dad says I can go. He says we can even pick you guys up in the plane—and bring you home again. We'll come get you. Just give the word!

Your excited friend,
Kate

Dear Diary,

I've spent the past hour since I pasted Kate's letter in here trying to figure out the best way to ask my parents about the trip to Wyoming. They'll both be home from work soon, and I'm so nervous I can hardly stand it. They have to say yes! Kate sent a brochure from Eli and Jeannie's ranch, which is called High Meadow, and it looks absolutely fantastic. There were photos of breathtakingly beautiful scenery on the edge of the Rocky Mountains. It looks like the ranch itself is nestled in a gorgeous valley. I wish I could paste the brochure in here, but unfortunately Stevie managed to drop it in the manure pile while she was mucking out Topside's stall, so we didn't have much choice but to throw it away. We didn't really mind all that much, though, since we'll get to see the real thing in person soon. At least I hope we will . . . Mom and Dad have to let me go! I think I know just the way to approach the whole question. I'll wait until dinner starts, after they've each started to relax. The strongest point I'll need to make is that Eli is expecting us to work. It will really be more of a summer job than a summer vacation—he'll be counting on our expertise around the barn and our riding skills, and he'll want us to help a lot with the younger kids as well as with the general work. Maybe I'll even comment how great a job like that will look on my college applications someday. Mom and Dad should love that. I'm sure they—

Oops! I just heard a car pull in. I'd better go start setting the table!

FROM:	HorseGal
TO:	Steviethegreat
TO:	LAtwood
SUBJECT:	Good news!
MESSAGE:	

Guess what? Dad says I can go to High Meadow! It turns out he knew all about the trip before I even got a chance to ask him—Frank Devine called him at the office this afternoon, so it was probably all settled even before I showed you that letter. Isn't that cool?

Anyway, I didn't want to call and interrupt in case you two are in the middle of begging your parents to say yes or something like that. But I just couldn't wait to tell you! It's going to be so great! I can't wait to get there!!!!!!!!!!!!!!!!!!

FROM:	Steviethegreat
TO:	HorseGal
TO:	LAtwood
SUBJECT:	Good news! (2)
MESSAGE:	

Ditto, ditto, ditto!
Well, okay, not really ditto in the strictest sense of the

word. I mean, neither of my parents talked to Frank Devine this afternoon. And actually it was looking kind of dicey for a while, since my jerky brothers kept interrupting while I was trying to explain the whole thing to Mom and Dad at the dinner table. But that doesn't matter now. I definitely won't be thinking about my brothers when I'm riding the range at High Meadow in just a few short days . . .

I can't believe we're really going!!!!!!!!!!!!!!!!!!!!!!!!!!!!!!!!

Dear Diary,

This started out as one of the most exciting days of my life, and it ended up as one of the most horrible. I still can't believe what happened at dinner. I mean, there I was, getting ready to present my case for going to High Meadow with my friends. And then Mom and Dad drop their bombshell.

"Lisa, we've got some wonderful news for you," Mom said as she started eating her dinner.

"We sure do!" Dad added, picking up his fork.

"You tell," Mom told him.

"No, *you* do it," Dad replied with a kind of goofy smile.

I had no idea what they were talking about. All I was thinking about was High Meadow.

But then they told me. "Lisa, honey," Mom said, "we're going to Europe. We're leaving in just a few days. And we're staying for a whole month!"

"You are?" I said, confused.

251

"No, *we* are," Dad replied, reaching across the table to pat my hand. "All three of us."

Things went kind of blank for me for a few minutes after that sank in. I was vaguely aware that my parents were excitedly explaining the whole situation. They'd started planning this trip right after Christmas. We would be visiting England, France, and Italy. They had kept it secret as a special end-of-school surprise for me.

I was too stunned to respond at first. I've been dreaming of seeing Europe all my life—but I don't want to go now. Not when I'm supposed to leave for High Meadow next week with Carole and Stevie, to be a real hand on a real working ranch, helping Eli and teaching little kids.

"Isn't it exciting?" Mom's face was positively glowing with excitement. It was all I could do to nod numbly. Luckily I didn't have to say anything, since Dad launched into some long story about how hard they'd had to work to keep me from suspecting a thing.

I barely heard what he said, though. All that had really sunk in at that point were the words *Europe* and *four weeks*. I would be gone even before my friends left for High Meadow. I would be in places where they didn't have horses, where I couldn't ride every day, where they didn't even speak English.

I guess Mom and Dad took the blank look on my face for surprise and excitement. I was kind of glad about that. I didn't want to disappoint them, especially when they'd gone to so much trouble on my account.

Still, I knew I had to at least try to explain. I took a deep breath and interrupted their description of the Sistine Chapel. Or maybe it was the Eiffel Tower, I don't remember. But I remember what I said.

"Kate Devine's invited us all to go to a Western riding camp that Eli's running this summer," I told them. "It's called High Meadow. We'd be working—"

"No work for you this summer. Just pleasure!" Mom interrupted.

I think that was the moment when I really knew it. When I realized that the ranch trip was dead, that there was no chance I would be going to High Meadow. I was—I *am*—going to Europe with my parents.

I don't know how I'm ever going to break the news to my friends when I don't even want to believe it myself.

Dear Diary,

Well, we just took off. All I can see out the window of the plane are some big, fluffy clouds. I'm not even sure if we're over land or water. Probably water, though, I guess—there's a lot of that between Virginia and Paris, our first stop in Europe.

I have to admit, now that it's started, I'm sort of excited about this trip. I'm still sad, of course—I really wish I could have gone to High Meadow with Carole and Stevie. I'm sure they're going to have a fantastic time. I'm a little nervous, too. I don't know what it will be like to be in a place where most people don't speak English. I sort of wish we were going to England first instead of France—at least there all I'd have to adjust to, language-wise, would be their accents! Oh well. This way I'll get to test out all that French I took in school last year and the year before. It should be a much better test than that embarrassing little episode with Mr. French last summer. Actually, on second thought, it will be worse than that in at least one big way—it won't take place on horseback! Seriously, though, I want to practice my French as much as I can while we're in Paris.

I'm also planning to keep up with this diary during my trip. That way I'll remember everything and be able to tell my friends all the details when I get home. I also plan to write them lots of letters and postcards. I only wish they could do the same, but they really can't since we'll be moving around so much. Instead, Carole offered to keep a diary while she was at High Meadow. She and I tried to convince Stevie to do the same—I even bought Stevie a little diary just in case. But she's usually not too good at stuff like that, so I'm not holding my breath.

Just thinking about my friends is making me feel sad again. I miss them already, even though I just saw them yesterday. Four weeks is a long time. I've never been apart from them for that long ever since we became best friends. Even Carole's trip to Florida was only a week long.

That reminds me that there's someone else I haven't seen in much, much longer than four weeks—Peter. I think Mom and Dad are really disappointed that we won't get to see him on this trip. They started planning it when we all thought he was going to be working in London this summer, and now he's all the way in Africa. He called home a couple of weeks ago, just before he left, and it was great to hear his voice. It would have been great to see him—it might even have made up, a little bit, for missing my friends—but I can't help feeling the tiniest bit relieved that we've missed him. I still feel kind of weird about that screenplay he sent, and I'm not sure I could have pretended to like it if I were face to face with him.

Anyway, over the past couple of days Mom has dropped a few little comments that make it clear that she thinks Peter should have stayed in London for an extra couple of weeks to meet us, even though he explained that the project can't be postponed because of him. If he wanted the job, he had to agree to leave for Africa when his professor left. I don't think Mom quite understood that, but I do. I think it's wonderful that Peter gets to do something this summer that he seems to care so much about. He'll get to write and help people and learn a lot.

I guess I'll get to write (in my diary) and learn a lot

(about the stuff we see) in Europe, too. Too bad I won't be helping people while I'm at it—Carole and Stevie and Kate will have to hold up that end of the Saddle Club creed this summer without me. They're probably busy packing for their trip just about now. They'll leave for the ranch tomorrow—and I'll already be in Paris by then, missing them terribly. Sigh.

Hôtel Grand Monde
Paris, France

Dear Stevie and Carole,

    <u>Bonjour.</u> That's what they say here a lot. It means "hello" or "good day." They also say <u>merci</u> and then they say a million other things that I don't have a chance of understanding. It's really difficult. I know I've been studying French at school, but what you need in school and what you need in Paris are two very different things.

    My parents are crazy about being here, but they are worse in the language than I am and sometimes it leads to trouble. For example, today Dad thought he was getting lamb for lunch, but he ended up with a tongue sandwich. Ugh. He won't make that mistake again. We've been to the Eiffel Tower and the Louvre and we've traveled everywhere on the <u>métro</u>, which is what they call the subway. In fact, we've done more traveling on the <u>métro</u> than we planned since Mom got confused about which train we were supposed to take. None of us likes being lost!

    We also went to a museum in something that used to be a

train station, the Musée d'Orsay. I really liked that place. They have a very pretty collection of Impressionist paintings there. I wouldn't mind going back. I didn't like the Louvre too much. It was crammed with people and Mom kept running up to guards to ask them where we could find the <u>Mona Lisa.</u> They all looked at her blankly. It turns out that the French call that painting <u>La Joconde.</u> See what I mean about confusing?

Actually, sometimes it's fun not knowing what to say. After we'd walked our feet off, Mom wanted to walk some more. I wanted to take a nap. They finally agreed to let me stay in the hotel room by myself for an hour. The place is overbooked, so I'm on a rollaway bed in my parents' room, which is okay except for the fact that when I took the bed out of the closet, I could tell it had a broken wheel and that meant it had this humungous bump in the center of it. No way could I sleep on it. I know I could have taken a nap on Mom's bed, but I decided to see if I could handle the problem myself.

I went down to the hotel desk and there was this cute bell-boy who didn't speak a word of English. I pulled out my phrase book, but there wasn't anything even close to "The wheel on my rollaway bed is broken."

I smiled nicely, took a deep breath, and did my best. I said, "<u>Le pneu sur mon lit est cassé.</u>" Roughly translated, it means, "The tire on top of my bed is broken." At first the guy just looked at me blankly. Then he burst into laughter. It sounds awful, but he wasn't laughing at me, really. He was just laughing because what I'd said was so funny. And then the most wonderful thing happened. He actually understood me. He said, "<u>Attendez,</u>" which I knew meant I was sup-

257

posed to wait, and he brought me a new bed with working wheels.

Maybe this place isn't so confusing after all. I just hope I don't order a tongue sandwich by mistake the way Dad did!

I've been thinking about you a lot because I haven't seen a horse since we got here. I wish I could talk to you or get letters from you. I can't wait to read your diaries and learn everything that's happening.

Send lots of love to Kate, Eli, and Jeannie. Tell all the campers everything you've ever taught me about riding and they'll do fine.

Love,
Lisa

Dear Diary,

Someday, years and years from now, I may actually forget why I had time to copy over my entire letter to Stevie and Carole here in my diary. So for the record, it was because Mom accidentally made tonight's dinner reservation for nine-thirty instead of six-thirty like she meant to, so we're all sitting around on a bench in a little park near the restaurant, starving and watching the people go by.

Luckily I brought my backpack with this diary and the letter, which I just finished earlier today. I hadn't put the letter in an envelope yet, and I thought it summed up the first few days of our trip pretty well. Still, there were a few things I didn't quite know how

258

to explain to my friends in the letter. It's true that I've been having a lot of trouble with the language here in France. I'm not used to being in a place where it's hard to say what I want or need. I tried to talk to my parents about it a couple of times, but it's as if they don't want to admit it's a problem. They seem too afraid that, maybe, they aren't having as good a time as they think they've paid for. I guess that's why Dad ate every bite of that tongue sandwich without grimacing once.

It makes me miss my friends more than ever. If they were here, they would understand. Still, I didn't want to tell them how much I miss them, or sound like I was complaining about my trip. For one thing, I really am having fun—most of the time, anyway. And I don't want them to worry about me. If they're worried, they won't be able to have as much fun where they are.

I wonder what they're doing right now? I've lost track of the time difference between Paris and Willow Creek (let alone between Paris and Wyoming), but in any case, they should be at High Meadow by now. If it's daytime, they're probably riding the range and showing those younger kids the time of their life. If it's evening, they'll be cooking dinner over a campfire. And Stevie is probably telling one of her famously spooky ghost stories. Maybe she and Carole and Kate will even tell the kids the legend of the white stallion, like John told it to us the last time we were out West.

Sigh. Thinking about this is making me sad that I'm not there. And that's just stupid. It's a gorgeous evening here in Paris, the air is warm, the people walking by are all very interesting, and my stomach is growling. Well, okay, scratch that last part—I'm trying not to complain here. But I'm going to put this diary away now and do some serious people watching while I wait for my dinner.

Dear Diary,

What happened to me today is so incredible—I feel almost like a celebrity or something! Actually, that gives me an idea. I don't want to forget everything I learned in Ms. Shields's class this year, so I'm going to write about what happened as if I were a reporter writing a celebrity column in the newspaper.

Windsor. When young American tourist Miss Lisa Atwood landed in merry old England with her family, she never would have guessed what was in store for her there!

Miss Atwood and her parents took a train from London to Windsor for a day's sightseeing, hoping to tour the castle. However, they discovered to their disappointment that all tours were off because the Queen was in residence. Trying to make the best of the situation, they wandered about the quaint little town, looking at the shops and the outside of the castle.

Eventually they went to see the nearest park, a lovely grassy area with gently sloping hills and neat flower beds. The Atwoods sat on a bench in the park and began discussing their options for lunch.

When suddenly, what to Miss Atwood's wondering ears did arise but the familiar clip-clip of hoofbeats. Miss Atwood, an avid rider in her native Virginia, was naturally eager to determine the source of this sound, and she looked around as the hoofbeats came closer with great rapidity.

Soon she spotted a sleek bay Thoroughbred on a hilltop nearby. The horse was fully tacked up. His rider, however, was nowhere in sight.

Miss Atwood knew just what to do. She had to find the rider and make sure he or she was okay. A rider could get badly hurt being thrown from a horse, and the park was big enough that it might be quite a while before anyone found the injured rider.

The young American approached the horse, who stood patiently while Miss Atwood took his reins and followed obediently when she began to lead him. After checking to be sure the horse was calm enough, she mounted and rode back to tell her parents where she was going.

Mrs. Atwood expressed her extreme doubts about the wisdom of her daughter's action. Miss Atwood, however, knew what she had to do. She did her best to reassure her mother, then rode off, following the horse's trail as best she could.

After riding back down the trail a little while, Miss Atwood spotted the thrown rider. It was a girl, about Miss Atwood's own age, dressed in elegant riding attire. The girl was standing at the edge of the bridle path, rubbing her elbow and looking annoyed.

Miss Atwood pulled up beside the girl. "I think I found something that belongs to you," she told her.

The girl looked very relieved. "Thank you so much!" she exclaimed in a crisp British accent. "I was just wondering where this fellow went." After Miss Atwood had politely introduced herself, the British girl did the same. "Lady Theresa," she said, shaking Miss Atwood's hand vigorously.

Miss Atwood was rather at a loss. Despite her mother's many lessons on proper manners, she had no idea how she was supposed to act toward a lady—especially one who was clearly no older than she was. She decided on a direct approach. "Lady Theresa? That's what people call you?"

Lady Theresa's answering smile was warm and kind. "Not at all," she replied. "My friends call me Tessa."

After that, the girls were fast friends. Lady Theresa climbed aboard the horse behind Miss Atwood, and the two of them rode toward the royal stables, which, to Miss Atwood's shock, was where the horse they were riding belonged. That was when Lady Theresa explained that, because her mother was a distant cousin to Her Majesty, she was occasionally invited to ride the royal horses.

Miss Atwood, rather awed by all this royal business, suddenly remembered that her parents must be wondering where she was. When she explained as much to Lady Theresa, the two of them agreed that they should ride back and tell them what was happening. They did so, and then returned to the royal stables, which were just as wonderful as any stable, anywhere.

Miss Atwood had a simply marvelous time touring the stables with her new friend Tessa, who introduced her to everyone they met as "the American who rounded up my horse and saved my life."

Finally it was time for Miss Atwood to return to her parents, who were waiting for her at a local restaurant that Lady Theresa had specially recommended. The girls gave each other hugs, and then the visit, the magical time, was over.

Except for one more thing. Miss Atwood was sitting in the restaurant with her parents, who clearly didn't quite believe their daughter had really befriended a member of the royal family and toured the Queen's stables. They thought she was playing make-believe.

Then the door to the restaurant flew open. In walked a tall man in a spotless uniform. "Is there a Miss Lisa Atwood here?" he asked the room at large.

Mr. and Mrs. Atwood looked alarmed. Miss Atwood raised her hand. "I'm here," she said tentatively.

"Oh, good," the man said, approaching their table. "Her Majesty wanted to give you her personal thanks for rescuing her cousin Lady Theresa today. Her Majesty hopes you will accept this as a small token of her appreciation."

The man held out a box. Miss Atwood accepted it and opened it while everyone in the restaurant looked on. Inside was a small crystal horse, nearly a perfect replica of one of the Thoroughbreds from Her Majesty's stables.

It was the perfect ending to an exciting day for the American visitors.

Dear Diary,

Okay, that newspaper-reporter stuff was fun for a while. But it was a little hard to work in two important things I really wanted to say. The first thing is how wonderful it was to be in the saddle again after not riding for so many days—especially on that gorgeous, well-trained Thoroughbred. The second, which is even more important, is that Tessa really was incredibly nice. She's the kind of person I felt was an instant friend—even though we only spent part of one day together, I know we'll keep in touch. Sometimes things just happen like that. I only wish that Stevie and Carole could have met her, too. I know they'd like her just as much as I did. And she would absolutely love them, too. She'd probably think that Stevie's sense of humor was simply "smashing," and she would be terribly impressed with Carole's horse sense as well as her sweet personality.

Oh well. Maybe someday they'll get to meet her. You never know . . .

Dear Carole, Kate, and Stevie, and Eli and Jeannie, too,

I'm getting to like traveling in Europe. In fact, it seems that the more I get to like it, the less my parents like it. That's pretty strange. Of course, that doesn't mean I don't wish I were with you guys. I do. I really do! Especially since you guys already know what you're doing. I'm learning something new every day.

I'm writing to you from Italy now. Today we drove through the area known as Tuscany. It's just beautiful here. Very hilly (though nothing compared to the Rockies, but you know what I mean). There are little towns tucked in the hillsides with old, old houses that have orange tile roofs. It's something.

We stopped in a small town to get some lunch and fill up our tank with gas. It's a good thing we don't do that much— gas is over six dollars a gallon, if I've done my math correctly. Mom and Dad kept looking at the menu and couldn't make any sense of it. Naturally, I had my phrase book handy. They told me what they wanted and I ordered it for them. They seemed pretty grateful. The waiter was really impressed. Honestly, so was I. I'm actually getting good at it—thumbing through the phrase book, I mean, not speaking Italian!

That's not what I really wanted to tell you about, though. The really fantastic thing happened later.

After lunch Dad went and found a telephone. He wanted to call the hotel to make sure our reservation was okay. Mom went with him and took the phrase book. While they were away from the table, I got into a conversation with a woman at the table next to us. I was wearing my Saddle Club pin and she noticed it. She spoke a little English; I spoke a little Italian. We made out okay.

What I realized as we started talking was that she was actually wearing riding clothes! It took two or three times around the vocabulary list for me to realize that she was asking me if my parents and I were attending the horse show in the next town. Can you believe it? There was actually a horse show going on and I didn't know it until she told me.

Well, of course, I just had to go. Mom had been talking about some ancient ruin, but what's an ancient ruin compared to a horse show? I didn't think I'd have too much trouble convincing Dad, because he'd had it up to here with ancient ruins. I was all ready to do my convincing talk when the looks on their faces told me there was trouble.

It turned out that the hotel at which we had a reservation was totally booked because of the horse show. My parents had gone all through the phrase book, looking for a way to threaten to sue. The best they could do was to get a promise that, if we showed up, they'd see what they could do to find us a place to stay.

Since it was my idea to go to the horse show anyway, I thought that was fine. We paid our bill and drove on over to the hotel. My parents were very upset. I guess I can't blame them, but I was pretty sure something would work out. It's always seemed to me that when there are horses around, everything else works out. Know what I mean?

So, while they went to try to sweet talk the hotel into finding a place for us to stay, I walked on over to the horse show. It was practically across the street.

I bought a ticket, got a program that I hardly understood, and just walked around. Everything was outdoors. There were about four rings with events going on all at the same time. I watched a dressage exhibition in the main ring and

266

watched a preliminary jumping event in a smaller ring. It was really fun. I missed you guys, though, because there wasn't anybody for me to talk to. Even if my parents had been there (and they were still at the hotel then), they wouldn't have understood what they were watching. Mom judges horses by their looks and their pedigrees, rather than by their performance, and Dad tends to want to know how much money they're going to win and who is betting on them—that is, if he's not preoccupied with where he's going to eat his next meal.

Anyway—this is the really interesting, nearly unbelievable, but absolutely true part. I wandered over to the area where the junior competitors were having their events. They were doing hunter jumping and they were pretty good. There was one boy who was far and away better than any of the rest of them. I was really impressed. He went through the first round with flying colors, and then when he brought his horse out for the conformation judging, I couldn't believe my eyes.

Enrico. It was actually _Enrico_. Remember him? One of the four Italian boys we met when they visited Pine Hollow last year?

I didn't want to upset him during the judging, but as soon as he brought his horse over to the side of the ring, I started yelling and waving. I only made a slight idiot of myself before he saw me. He told me to wait right there—until the ribbons were handed out. Of course, he got a blue. Then he came over and gave me this most gigantic hug. He asked me what I was doing there and how you guys are and what was going on and everything. I couldn't answer all his questions at once, but the minute I told him about the hotel, he got this wonderful look on his face.

"But you and your parents—you will stay with us!"

"You have room for all of us?" I asked. He told me that of course he did. Little did I know.

Right then my parents showed up. They were as mad as could be and Dad was on the verge of saying all sorts of things about Italian innkeepers. I introduced them to Enrico and told them we had a place to stay.

I won't bore you with all the details now—I'll have months and months to do that when I get home—but I will tell you that as I write this, I'm sitting at an antique Italian secretary (that's a fancy word for a small desk) in Enrico's family <u>mansion.</u> This isn't just a house. Oh, it also turns out that the horse show isn't being held in any funky old public park. It is being held on Enrico's family estate. I mean <u>estate</u>. It goes on for acres and acres and it's been in his family for generations. My parents and I are in our very own wing or something. I'm not sure exactly because the place is just too big for me to be completely oriented. I do know that when we want breakfast, we're supposed to ring for a servant who will either bring it to us or show us the way to the dining room. I'm telling you, you've never seen anything like this.

Now I think I'll take a bath. The bathtub is about the size of a small swimming pool. Of course, the one in my parents' bathroom is much larger . . .

Just kidding. Still, it's all pretty grand.

It's hard to believe this vacation is almost over. It's been so *interesting. When I think about it, before I left, I was scared to death about being in unfamiliar places with unfamiliar languages. I've realized that people are people, and if you try to be nice and try to speak to them in their own language, no matter how badly you mangle the phrases from the phrase book, they want to be helpful and welcoming. I've enjoyed the trip. I'm a little sorry it's almost over, but I can't wait to see you guys and hear everything about High Meadow. I get to read your diaries, right? Don't leave <u>anything</u> out.*

Love,
Lisa

Dear Diary,

Wow, I can't believe my trip to Europe is over and we're flying home already. Before we left home, four weeks seemed like forever. And a few times, like that night in Paris when we had to wait three hours for dinner, or the morning Mom insisted on pointing out every old rock in Windsor, or a few times when I was trapped in the car in Italy when Mom and Dad were arguing over directions, it really did feel like time was standing still!

But a lot of the time, the hours just flew by. Like when I was in the Musée d'Orsay. Or the afternoon I spent getting to know Tessa. Or the couple of days we spent at Enrico's home. Or the hour last night we spent on the phone with Peter.

It was so great to talk to him, even though Mom hogged the phone. I only got about five or ten minutes—and I think I only got that much because Peter asked for me specifically, which made me feel really good—but we managed to catch up on a lot in that short time. I told him about our trip, and what Stevie and Carole were doing while I was in Europe, and he told me about the work he's doing in Africa, which sounds pretty interesting. The only slightly awkward moment was when he mentioned his screenplay. I didn't say too much, and I guess he thought that meant I'd liked it as much as I said in my letter. I feel kind of weird about that. I still don't want to hurt his feelings, but I also don't want to lie . . . Oh well. I'll have to think about that more when I get home.

Anyway, I think Mom and Dad were really glad to hear Peter's voice. They seemed a lot more cheerful after they called. And their moods improved even more when they saw the restaurant where we were having dinner. Enrico's parents had suggested it the day before when we'd left their place. They said it was their favorite restaurant in Florence, and I can believe it. It was wonderful. Our table was on a huge stone balcony overlooking a busy city square. People bustled around below us as we sipped wine (Mom and Dad) and mineral water (me) and ate pounds and pounds of delicious Italian food. We had a perfect view of the sun as it set over the ancient-looking buildings, and as it grew dark, a little orchestra set up in the square and started a concert, so we got to hear and see that as we ate, too. It was positively perfect. I think Mom and Dad thought so, too, and I'm glad about that. I'm not sure they had as good a time in Europe as I did, although I think there were moments they enjoyed a lot. Mom loved staying at Enrico's mansion, and I think she really did like touring some of those dusty old ruins and fancy churches. Dad loved trying all the different food in the different countries—well, except maybe for that tongue sandwich back in Paris. But he now claims that gelato (that's Italian ice cream) is his new favorite food. And he even seemed to like the steak and kidney pie he had in England, though I thought it was awful.

So now here we are on another plane, heading back across the Atlantic. I'm sad to leave Europe behind—there's so much more that I didn't get to see. But even more, I'm happy to be going home. I miss my friends so much I can hardly stand it. I can't wait to hear all about their adventures at High Meadow. I hope they kept good diaries! (At least Carole . . .) I want to know about every second of their trip.

Because I'm definitely going to make them listen to me talk about every second of mine!

Stevie's High Meadow Diary

Okay, I know I didn't make any promises about this diary. In fact, I pretty much told you (Lisa, that is) not to count on me. But it's the night before we leave for

High Meadow, and I'm too excited to sleep, so I figured I'd jot down a few words. Who knows? Maybe I'll be inspired to keep it up through the whole trip. Maybe I'll even decide to start keeping a diary regularly, like forever! Wouldn't that be something? It would be like going to High Meadow had changed my whole entire life! My parents would practically die of shock, and Miss Fenton would probably think I'd been kidnapped by aliens and undergone an entire personality transplant. Hmmm. Maybe I'll tell her I'm keeping a diary, even if I decide not to. It might be worth it just to see the look on her face.

But anyway, back to the trip. Lisa, I really wish you were coming with us. I know I should be tactful here and say stuff about how it probably won't be any fun without you. And it's true that it won't be as *much* fun with you way over in Europe somewhere. But it's still going to be fun! I just hope you're having even more fun checking out the Eiffel Tower and everything, so Carole and I won't have any reason to feel guilty.

As I was saying, though, I think this trip will be really cool. Those little campers aren't going to know what hit them. By the time Carole gets through with them, they'll know everything there is to know about riding and then some. And by the time I get through with them—well, let's just say I'm not going to let all the fun pranks and silly songs and stories I've picked up at camp over the years go to waste. They're going to wonder how they had the good luck to end up with such a cool counselor! I can't wait.

I also can't wait to see Kate, of course, and Eli and Jeannie, too. We're all going to have such a blast! Now if only I could manage to fall asleep so morning would come sooner . . . Well, I guess I'd better go give it a try. I'll write more when we get there.

Carole's High Meadow Diary

Dear Diary (or really Lisa since that's who's going to read this eventually. I certainly don't plan on looking at it again!),

I can't believe the day we just had! Both Stevie and Kate are sleeping soundly, but I have a lot on my mind and I can't sleep.

The day started off wrong and it just never got any better. First of all, we were so tired that when the bell rang to wake us up, we fell right back to sleep again. All that traveling yesterday was more tiring than any of us had realized. So when the breakfast bell rang, we did the same thing. Eventually Jeannie came and woke us up. She was more or less nice about it, but we're here to help, not to cause trouble. We were causing trouble then because there was going to be a ride and nobody could go until we were ready.

It didn't get much better when we went for our ride. I guess Eli and Jeannie must have been talking about us to the campers, who have been here a couple of days already. They took one look at Stevie and me in our brand-new Western riding clothes and they started calling us dudes. Most of them are from out West and they don't have a very high opinion of English riding. They've got a lot to learn on that subject, but we didn't do much of a job teaching them today.

First of all, I was having trouble with my horse. He's a good horse (I don't think there's any such thing as a bad horse, just bad riders), but we aren't used to one another yet. I forgot for one little second that in Western riding you use neck reining. The horse didn't do what I wanted and three of the kids kept laughing about it. Little monsters. Remind me to tell you more about Lois, Larry, and Linc. Stevie dubbed them the Lions. It's just like her to come up with something like that. Anyway, these kids are really obnoxious, and I'm sure they're going to be our biggest problem.

Check that. I'm not sure they're going to be our biggest problem. I'm beginning to think that *we* are going to be our biggest problems. We don't seem to have any idea of what's going on. Every time the triangle rang, everybody else knew exactly what to do and Stevie, Kate, and I were left standing there, looking blankly at one another. The kids thought it was hysterical. Eli seemed a little perturbed, and Jeannie, who never quite recovered from having to dig us out of bed this morning, just looked peeved.

What's weird is that the three of us arrived here thinking of ourselves as Eli and Jeannie's saviors. We thought they had all these gigantic problems that we were going to solve, and now it looks like the three of us—Stevie and me particularly—are just causing more problems.

And I haven't even told you what happened when we tried to help in the garden this afternoon. Trust me, you don't want to know. I'll only say that it had to do with a worm that one of the L-ions dug up and everybody else thought it was a riot. It wasn't.

So, although Dad always tells me not to complain, here I am complaining. I can't help it. If we don't start being useful to Eli and Jeannie pretty soon, I'm sure they're going to want to put us on a plane and send us back home. I wouldn't blame them one bit, either.

But I'm not going to let that happen. Neither will Stevie or Kate. We came here to be helpful and we're going to be helpful. Whatever it is that Eli and Jeannie need us to do, we'll do. If we don't know what we're supposed to do, we'll ask, and we'll learn, really fast. At least I hope so.

Eli told us what our morning chores are for tomorrow. Stevie's going to work in the vegetable patch (no worms!) and I'm supposed to collect eggs from the henhouse. Kate is going to help with the kitchen crew.

So, when do we get to ride again? Oops, that

sounded like a complaint. I didn't mean it. I may even cross it out. No I won't. This is a diary and diaries are supposed to be honest. Grrr.

Good night.

Carole

Stevie's High Meadow Diary

Too tired to write now—remember to write more tomorrow about chicken biting Carole and stupid difference between stupid onions and stupid weeds.

Carole's High Meadow Diary

What a humiliating day! I can't believe I actually fell off my horse during our trail ride. Yes, Lisa, you read that right—I fell off my horse. It was just a stupid mistake, because I wasn't paying close enough attention, but Stevie and Kate and I seem to be making a lot of stupid mistakes today. For instance, this morning I made the mistake of thinking the hens in the henhouse wouldn't mind one bit if I took all their eggs. Well, one of them sure taught me different, and I have the scratch to prove it. Kate's big boo-boo of the day was herding all the horses into a field where they weren't supposed to be, so she basically had to do the same job twice.

Who ever said we were here to help Jeannie and

Eli? As far as I can tell, all we're doing is causing extra problems. Stevie says we just have to try harder. My only question is: How?

Stevie's High Meadow Diary

Today we had a stampede on our cattle drive, but it turned out okay in the end. Too tired to write more. Good night.

Carole's High Meadow Diary

It's been pretty peaceful here at camp for the past couple of days while the others are off on their cattle drive. They're supposed to get back tomorrow, I think. Actually, I think they were supposed to be here today, but Eli called Jeannie this morning and told her they would need an extra day. I don't know what that's all about. I just hope Stevie and Kate are doing better than I did here for the first day or two after they left. See, what happened was I separated the wrong horse from the herd. The horse that was supposed to be in a field by himself ended up with the rest of the horses. His name is Arthur, and he's a troublemaker—in the middle of the night, he ended up convincing all the others to follow him as he jumped the fence and took off for the hills. I ended up having to go out and round them up. Jeannie was happy that I was so successful at that—though I'm sure she would have been a lot happier if I hadn't made the mistake that caused the problem in the first place.

Since then, though, things have been a lot better. I think I'm finally starting to get the hang of the routine around here. It's a little lonely without Stevie and Kate, but like I said, they'll be back soon. I can't wait to hear all about the cattle drive!

Dear Diary,

From what they wrote in their diaries, it sounds like my friends had a terrible time at High Meadow! Well, they didn't. Not really. They told me all about it after I got back from Europe last week. It sounds like there were some problems, especially early on—they had trouble getting used to all the chores on a working ranch, like weeding the garden and collecting eggs, and some of the younger campers made fun of them and called them dudes because they knew more about English riding than Western. But they got the hang of it all eventually, and in the end they were as sad to leave the ranch and the campers as the campers were to leave them.

As Stevie put it, it was wonderful, it just didn't seem that way all the time. I guess that's sort of how my trip to Europe was, too. Looking back on it now, all I seem to remember most of the time are the wonderful parts. But at the time, I can't say that I had fun every second of every day.

Now that I think about it, I guess that's the whole point of this diary—or scrapbook or whatever I should call it. It's supposed to help me remember the wonderful times in my life. And if it helps me remember the not-so-wonderful ones at the same time, well, I guess that will just make the wonderful ones seem even better.

Speaking of this diary—I can hardly believe it. I just realized that there are only a few blank pages left. When I first got it, I was sure it would last for ages, but I've filled it up in just one year, even though I feel as though I didn't write nearly often enough. Still, I'm pretty happy with it overall. I think writing in here has helped me sort through things. I also think it's helped me "find my own voice," as Ms. Shields would put it. That means I think that the stuff I write in here is the truth as I see and describe it, and I don't try to write it for anyone else but myself. Or something like that, anyway.

I think writing all those letters to my brother helped with that, too. At first I was trying to impress him, but once I relaxed and wrote what I was really thinking and feeling, everything got a lot better.

Reading back over what I just wrote reminds me of the one thing I wrote to Peter that wasn't what I really thought or felt. I still feel weird about lying to him about what I thought of his screenplay. Should I have been more honest, even if it meant being hurtful? Should I have tried to come up with some more constructive criticism? Should I have just pretended the stupid thing got lost in the mail and never got here? I really don't know. I guess I'll have to think about that some more.

But not now. Mom's calling. A letter just came for me from Peter!

Dear Lisa,

It was so great to hear your voice on the phone the other day! I hope you and Mom and Dad enjoyed your last evening in Italy, and that you had a good flight home.

That's not really why I'm writing, though. I have some bad news. I hope you won't be too disappointed, but I've decided not to finish *Riding for Your Life*. I was reading it over the other day and I realized I wasn't writing because I really believed in the story—I was writing because I thought some people off in Hollywood might be interested in that kind of story. It really wasn't what *I* wanted to write at all. I don't care about escaped murderers or shadows and suspense. I don't even go to see that kind of movie—why should I waste my time trying to write one? I hope you're not too disappointed that you and your friends won't be appearing "at a theater near you" anytime soon, or that you'll never get to see how the story might have turned out. I know kids your age like that kind of movie. But I know now that I couldn't possibly finish a script I don't care about. I hope you can understand that. At this point, I don't quite know what I want to write about instead, but I'm sure I'll figure that out when the time is right. In the meantime, that old screenplay is going in the bottom of my suitcase. I was tempted to throw it out, but I figured I might need it someday to remind me what *not* to do.

In any case, my new job here in Africa is keeping me so busy I don't have as much time as I thought I would for writing. That's okay, though. I'm meeting some really interesting people in the villages we're visiting, and my professor—oops, I guess now I should say my boss—is becoming a good friend even though he's quite a bit older than me. I'm realizing more and more what a special time this is in my life. I really want to savor it and appreciate every moment. Maybe someday, when it's all over, I'll decide to write a screenplay about my experiences. Or maybe I'll write about something else. But it will definitely be something I know something about.

Anyway, Lisa, I really hope you're not offended or anything like that. I don't mean to imply that I quit that script because I don't care about you or think your life isn't interesting. You should know that that's not true. It's just that I sort of forgot what all my writing teachers told me throughout school: "Write what you know." I never thought that old saying was true; I figured if it was, nobody could ever write about visiting other planets or traveling to the past or the future. But I guess that's not really what they meant. They just meant that if you're trying to write a story you're pulling from somewhere outside of yourself, or for some reason other than because you really, really want to tell it, it will never work. It has to come from *inside*. Does that make sense to you? I hope so, because I think it's important. I also hope you'll keep writing to me about what you're doing even if it's not going to be in the movies. Because whatever else I've learned from that ridiculous screenplay, the most important thing I've learned is to appreciate my little sister again.

Love,
Peter

Dear Diary,

Well, I just pasted in Peter's letter and then went back and read through the entire diary. I sure did a lot this year! Fun things just always seem to happen whenever Carole, Stevie, and I get together. I guess that's the magic of The Saddle Club. Or maybe it's just the magic of friendship. Or maybe they're one and the same.

As things turned out, I'm glad I didn't tell Peter what I really thought of his screenplay. Maybe someday, when I can sit down and talk to him face to face, I'll explain that not everybody my age likes the same things. Some kids might have loved that silly horror movie he was trying to write. In fact, Stevie's twin brother, Alex, probably would have thought it was great—he has terrible taste in movies. But my friends and I will probably end up liking whatever Peter writes next a lot better, especially if it comes from his heart instead of his ideas about kids my age.

For now, though, I guess it's probably better that Peter decided on his own to give up on his movie. Some things you just have to figure out for yourself. Even if I had told him what I really thought, it might not have made a difference—sort of the way I didn't believe I could survive four weeks in Europe without my friends until I actually did it. Or the way Carole and Stevie thought they knew everything there was to know about ranch life until High Meadow proved them wrong. Or the way I was so sure that mare was going to foal despite what the vet said, or how I insisted on riding Prancer in that horse show when she wasn't ready, or how I thought I could get away with letting May do all the work in our Big Sister/Little Sister project. I didn't listen to anything anyone else tried to tell me any of those times—I had to learn the hard way. So did Kate, sort of, when she wanted to adopt that wild stallion with the nick in his ear. And it's the same kind of thing as how Nigel and Dorothy didn't believe we could really throw them a wedding until we proved it. Or how Stevie and I didn't believe Alice Jackson might have reasons for not wanting to jump until we absolutely couldn't avoid the fact anymore. Or how Stevie was so sure she had that feed order right that Pine Hollow almost ended up with a whole stable full of feed and hay it didn't need. And about a million other things we all did this year that didn't turn out the way we expected.

Maybe that's the best thing about this diary. If I hadn't just read about all those things, I might never have noticed how much I've learned and changed and grown just in the past year. I wasn't planning to let Carole and Stevie read it, but maybe I will after all. I don't want to hog all this learning to myself!

Dear Peter,

Wow, it seems weird to be writing to you in Africa. What's it like there? You didn't say that much about it in your last letter. I'd love to hear all about what you're doing and seeing.

By the way, I'm writing the rough draft of this letter in the last few pages of my diary. For one thing, I thought it would be a nice way to remind myself of our correspondence. Also, I wanted to get what I want to say next just right.

It's about your movie. Even though it would have been nice to see a movie all about The Saddle Club, I just want you to know that I'm not disappointed at all that you won't be finishing that particular screenplay. You see, I understood exactly what you were saying about writing from inside, because that's what I've been trying to do all year here in my diary. (Even if I didn't quite know that was what I was doing until just recently.) Keeping track of my life here—and in my letters to you—has made it easier to learn from my mistakes. It's also helped me remember all the fun and adventures I've had over the year. That's why I'm sending you a brand-new diary along with this letter. It's sort of an early birthday present, I guess. I thought it was important for you to have it now, in case you want to start writing down what you're doing there in Africa. It will help you remember your time there forever, and who knows?—maybe someday it will help you write a fantastic, award-winning screenplay about your experiences! But even if it doesn't, I think you'd get as much out of keeping a diary as I have. Now, and in the future, too.

284

When I went to the stationery store to buy you your diary, I picked up a new one for myself as well. Because like I said, this one is just about full. And when you're part of The Saddle Club, life is always full of adventure.

I want to be ready!

Love,
Lisa

ABOUT THE AUTHOR

Bonnie Bryant is the author of more than a hundred books about horses, including The Saddle Club series, Saddle Club Super Editions, and the Pony Tails series. She has also written novels and movie novelizations under her married name, B. B. Hiller.

Ms. Bryant began writing The Saddle Club in 1986. Although she had done some riding before that, she intensified her studies then and found herself learning right along with her characters Stevie, Carole, and Lisa. She claims that they are all much better riders than she is.

Ms. Bryant was born and raised in New York City. She still lives there, in Greenwich Village, with her two sons.

Don't miss the next exciting
Saddle Club adventure . . .

SIDESADDLE
Saddle Club #88

There's a new rider at Pine Hollow Stables, and her name is Tiffani. Carole Hanson and Lisa Atwood think Tiffani's a good rider, but Stevie Lake can't get over her riding gear—it's pink and covered in lace and frills. On top of that, Stevie just doesn't like Tiffani. It doesn't make sense, but she can't help it. When her boyfriend flirts with the new girl, Stevie stops seeing pink and starts seeing red. And when he praises Tiffani's riding skills, Stevie goes wild.

Suddenly she's in competition with Tiffani and she'll do anything to win—even if it means learning to jump fences while riding sidesaddle. Stevie's friends are convinced she's lost her mind. But Stevie's determined to "out-girl" Tiffani. She's even bought a fluffy pink sweater!

STEVIE: THE INSIDE STORY

Stevie Lake is in trouble. Big trouble. She's failing classes, and if she doesn't pull her grades up fast it means summer school and, worst of all, no riding. She has one last chance to redeem herself. She's got to write a report explaining why she hasn't done her homework or studied for the past few months—and the explanation had better be good. Stevie's determined. She's committed. And she's going to get this assignment done if it kills her.

Of course her best friends want to help—and give their side of the story. By the time they're finished with the encouraging e-mails, personal essays, screenplays, and phone calls, Stevie will have more than a simple homework assignment. She'll have a multimedia spectacular!

Covers events in The Saddle Club books 20 through 22.

PINE HOLLOW

New Series from Bonnie Bryant

Friends always come first . . . don't they?

A lot of new things are happening, but one thing remains the same: Stevie, Lisa, and Carole are still best friends.

Even so, growing up and taking on new responsibilities can be difficult. Now with **high school**, **driver's licenses**, **boyfriends**, and **jobs**, they hardly have time for themselves—not to mention each other and their horses!

Then an accident leaves a girl's life in the balance, and someone has to take the blame. Can even best friends survive this test?

Coming July 1998 from Bantam Books.